I0676547

HALWENDE'S RESURRECTION

HALWENDE'S LEGACY
BOOK 2

JOHN WEGENER

Halwende's Resurrection

Written by John Wegener.
Published by John Wegener.
Copyright © 2022 John Wegener.
Copyright © 2022Cover designed by Fiona Jayde Media.

All characters in this publication are fictitious, any resemblance to real persons, living or dead, is purely coincidental.
All rights reserved.

This book is licensed for your personal enjoyment only. This book may not be re-sold or given away to other people. If you would like to share this book with another person, please purchase an additional copy for each recipient. If you're reading this book and did not purchase it, or it was not purchased for your use only, then please return to your favorite book retailer and purchase your own copy. Thank you for respecting the hard work of this author.

John Wegener asserts his moral right to be identified as the author of this book.

1

LEAVING HELHEIM

I stare at Helheim, and the city of Heimstadt, disappearing below as our ship leaves with Balashi and Udama at the helm. My heart aches for Adala, the crowned Queen of Helheim, and the ever-increasing distance between us stretches my pain to breaking point. As I sigh away my longing, the planet dwindles to the size of a pinhead.

With no responsibilities, I wander the freighter to pass the time. The trip to Santori will take five days, and Balashi and Udama don't need my help. They don't want me to help them. This I understand. A trader's ship is personal to them. Someone else flying is a violation, so I leave them to their work. Once the ship is underway, they both join me in the galley aft of the helm.

"So, Halwende, you ready to sample the talent on Santori?" Udama asks me.

Taken aback, I wonder why he hasn't learned his lesson after his crass comments on Helheim received such a cold response. "I'll be just fine without venturing out for talent."

"But Balashi never wants to go with me, and it's unsafe sometimes without a wingman."

"That's your problem," Balashi pipes up. "Leave Halwende alone.

Why would he welcome trouble? I dare say he'd have some explaining to do if the news ever returned to his queen. Anyway, why would he when he has someone like her waiting for him?"

I smile wanly at them, not wishing to contribute to the conversation any further. I grab a coffee from the dispenser and return to the bench seat. "So, who are we seeing on Santori?"

"We have to unload our cargo at the warehouse for the Grabino's first," Balashi says. "We could arrange for you to meet them. They have an extensive choice of goods."

"Do they sell spaceships?"

"No, you need to talk to the planetary shipping authority for that. They register all ship purchases."

"I bought my ship a long time ago when things were different." They aren't to know I obtained my ship in a shady negotiation with an underground syndicate to keep the ship untraceable until I registered it under a new entity.

"Well, that's the law now." Balashi glances at me as if I should know that fact. I need to take more care of concealing my past life. "So, how did you crash into Helheim? It isn't on any astrogation chart. Did you fly into it in hyperspace or something?"

"Nothing like that. I hit an asteroid, and the planet was the nearest place I could land safely, although the drive almost exploded before I did."

"But why detour from the Santori route?"

The questions are becoming more like an interrogation, but I answer since it's the truth. "I wanted a faster trip. Now I know why it's not the recommended one."

"How did you get involved with Adala then?" Udama asks.

I bristle at his disrespect of her. "*Queen* Adala! I helped her in a war against a usurper."

"Rather reckless. You could have got yourself killed."

"I had nothing better to do. I wasn't hopeful of being rescued."

"It's strange your being there," Balashi comments.

"Is this an interrogation or something? I'm the queen's trade representative. That should be enough for you. You're getting a good sum to transport me."

"Just filling the time." Udama resents my reproach.

Both fall silent, and we sit for a time without exchanging a word. I leave them to make my way to the ship's bow, eager to check out the helm. Its setup is typical for a freighter — captain's chair and console, engineering, and astrogation. I frown as I catch sight of the astrogation console. *Why are we traveling away from Santori and toward Eridu?*

I hear Balashi behind me and turn with the question on my lips, "Why are we going to Eridu?" Then I see the nerve disruptor in his hand.

"It took us a while to recognize you," he says, "but we couldn't believe our luck when we realized you're the most wanted person on Eridu. The empire's been looking everywhere for you. Do you realize there's a nice bounty for your capture? And now we have you to ourselves on our ship. How good is that?"

"This trade stuff was a sham then?" I can't help but feel disappointed in Balashi, in particular.

"Oh, no. That's real. We're just going on a minor detour to drop you off first. We'll go back to Santori then."

"And what of trade with Helheim?"

"Hel-what? No one will ever know it exists."

"Until someone else stumbles on it."

"By then, you'll be in prison, and no one will remember us."

"Queen Adala will remember you, and Sentinel will scour the galaxy to find you."

"He can try."

I search for an avenue of escape or means of overpowering Balashi, but I have no options while he holds the nerve disruptor. "So, what happens now?"

"Now we put you somewhere nice and safe." He presses the trigger on the disruptor, and my mind goes blank.

When I awaken, I am lying on the floor with pins and needles attacking my entire body as the last remnant of the disruptor's effects dissipates. I'm in a room five meters by five. It looks like a storage space but contains little at present. A bottle filled with water stands next to me. My first attempt to sit fails, my arms refusing to respond to my will, so I gaze at the ceiling instead, wondering what I can do. The odds are two-to-one, but Udama's easy to manipulate. After ten minutes, I try sitting again and have better luck, making it to a sitting position with minimal effort. A side-effect of a disruptor shot is extreme thirst when you wake, and I experience it like anyone else. I'm thankful for the water and gulp a copious quantity before I'm sated.

After another ten minutes, I stand and shuffle around, exploring my prison, searching for items I can use as weapons. As the trip to Eridu will last at least seven days, they will feed me. I need a plan of attack for when they do. There's a bank of closets along one wall, their doors unlocked. Most are empty, but a few contain cans of lubricant. Could I create a small fire to distract them? Caution prevents me from adopting the idea because I would be at a greater risk than they. I keep looking. There's a bench in another corner. The top is bare, but it has doors underneath it. I smile when I open them. There are various tools packed inside, including screwdrivers, hammers, and spanners. The idiots didn't check the room's contents before they placed me in here. I rummage through the shelves and pick out a screwdriver, two hammers, and two large spanners and stash them behind a small, loose piece of the wall panel, safe from prying eyes until I'm ready to use them.

The door to the cabin rattles open, and Udama enters, carefully balancing a laser pistol and a tray of food. "No funny business," he warns. He sidles beside the door and squats, setting the tray on the floor as he concentrates on me.

I stare at him. "Wouldn't dream of it. I'll leave the funny business to you. You're good at it."

Udama gives a toothy smile. "Yeah, well. Here's some food for you."

"What if I need the toilet?"

"You'll have to attract our attention."

"How?"

"Use your imagination." He straightens and leaves, the door locking moments later, leaving me alone again.

The smell of steaming food interrupts my thoughts, and I stroll over to the tray. I'm impressed — beef steak and vegetables. They treat their prisoners well. Maybe they have to deliver me in good condition. With nothing better to do, I sit and scoff the food and follow it up with a flask of hot coffee that tastes like dishwater but is better than nothing. I move the tray further from the door as a possible escape idea develops in my mind.

The door is in the center of one wall and swings inward instead of sliding into the wall cavity — a very space-consuming and antiquated design. It surprises me as the ship looks new, but it gives me an idea. With plenty of tools still lying in the drawers, I grab a screwdriver and hammer, placing them behind the door where they will be hidden when it opens. I could wait, or I could pretend to need the toilet. I wait. The longer the delay, the laxer they will become.

With nothing to do, I consider other alternatives for overpowering my opponents. A smile spreads on my face as I complete my preparations. I sit back and wait, hoping it's Udama who returns. He will be easier to distract than Balashi. Several hours go by before the sound of the door unlocking alerts me.

Udama has come again, and I inwardly smile. Once again, he holds a laser pistol and a tray. I wonder if he realizes how vulnerable it makes him. He scans the room. "Where's the other tray?"

"On the bench."

"Bring it to me."

"You get it."

"You want something else to eat?"

I stare back at him but relent. It's what I want, anyway. Removing the tray from the counter, I begin to move toward him.

"Slowly."

I shrug and slow my pace, stopping two meters in front of him. I observe that he's lowered the pistol, which is now pointing at the floor. My mind bursts with disbelief at my good fortune when I see the safety's still on. Udama may look armed, but he might as well have nothing. The locked gun is only suitable as a hammer or cudgel. "Where do you want it?" I ask.

"Put it on the floor."

I bow, placing the tray on the deck, but when I go to straighten up, my arms shoot out and grab Udama's wrists, pulling him into the room with a violent jerk. Udama lets out a surprised yelp, which I silence with a quick jab of my elbow to the nape of his neck and a punch to his temple, rendering him unconscious. I close the door behind us and stand over him. *You should spend more time practicing your defensive skills and thinking less about the talent.* Once I relieve Udama of the pistol, I check it over. It's got a full charge, so I tuck the muzzle behind me. The bench has a roll of repair tape, perfect for tying him. I secure his hands behind his back, his legs together at the ankles, and then his arms to his legs, leaving him with no chance to escape when he awakens.

Still surprised at my good luck, I grab the pistol, unlock the safety, and crack open the door. No one's in the corridor. I dash out and close the door behind me. Balashi, being the pilot, would spend his time in the helm. So, I head that way, creeping forward. This style of ship only has one deck level, the rest taken up by cargo storage, which makes my job easier. Unless Balashi is below in the cargo space — most unlikely — he will be somewhere on this level.

I check any open areas as I move toward the helm's door and push the button to open it. It slides into the wall panel.

"About time you returned," Balashi says without glancing up from his console.

"He's busy," I say, with the pistol trained on him.

Balashi jerks his head around, his eyes wide with surprise and fear as he sees the pistol's muzzle, staring at it for a moment and then at me.

"You shouldn't ask an idiot to do a man's job." I step into the helm with my back to the wall, keeping my eyes on Balashi, noting his hand movements in particular, expecting him to keep me busy talking while he thinks of something to do.

"What are your intentions?"

"That depends on you. You can sit quietly in a nice warm room if you behave. Then I'll return your ship to you when we get to Santori. Otherwise, you might find a laser hole in you or enjoy the experience of the vacuum of space."

"The first option sounds promising."

"That's the one I'd choose."

"Where's Udama?"

"He's enjoying a nap." I notice Balashi's right hand creep toward a small cavity below his console. "I wouldn't do that."

"Do what?"

"Let your hand wander where I can't see it. I might have to shoot it off, and I'm an excellent shot." His hand stops moving in that direction and comes up into view. "Now, please be so kind to stand up while we find somewhere for you to spend the next few days."

Balashi shrugs. I move aside, letting him through the door and follow him with the pistol trained on his back. When we both enter the corridor, I make a swift move and knock him out, not wanting the bother of keeping guard over him. I drag him into the room with Udama, who is still unconscious. After emptying the space of weapons that they could use against me, including the tools hidden in the wall, I cut Udama loose and lock the door behind me, heading for the helm to change our destination.

2

SANTORI

The world of Santori looms increasingly larger as we thread our way through the primary star's solar system. Santori orbits the star Babylonius along with two other solid planets and three gas giants. The hazy, oxygen blue atmosphere glows as we near it and start our descent to the surface. I communicate with the planet's Space Control and change the ship's vectors to the approved route.

With the trajectory programmed, I sit in comfort in the pilot's seat and enjoy the view. The characteristic green, brown, and white continents and blue oceans I know well come into focus where cloud cover doesn't mask their details on the daytime side where my destination lies. The calm atmosphere today means there is little turbulence to consider as I descend.

The large number of other spaceships parked in designated bays of the spaceport suggests the planet's trade is healthy. Many freighters like Balashi's and Udama's are present. Larger cargo transports zip from them to the terminal warehouses as they unload the ships. My ship lands in its assigned location as I watch.

Balashi and Udama have given me no trouble along the way, though their sour faces will long be imprinted on my mind. I have time-locked their door, so they can escape their prison once I'm well away from them.

As I exit the ship's hatch, I order a passenger transit vehicle. It stops in front of me ten minutes later, and I hop in, transferring to a taxi at the terminal to speed off into the capital's central district. Skyscrapers litter the skyline, each one owned by corporations with too much money. How do I know this? Conversations on my previous visits informed me of the buildings' owners and their high occupancy vacancies. I direct the taxi to a luxury hotel — in line with my new position as Trade Minister of Helheim — check into my room and then call my contacts, including a potential spaceship supplier. After dialing the number, I wait for the video connection. "Shazza here."

"Hi, I'm Lord Heinrich, the Trade Minister of Helheim. I wish to discuss the purchase of a yacht for my queen."

Shazza's eyes narrow in suspicion. Or maybe he's assessing me to gauge my gullibility. "I have a gap in my schedule at 5 pm if that is suitable for you."

"That's perfect."

He gives me his details, and I prepare to make the trip to his offices, donning clothing suited to the eminence of a Trade Minister.

I walk into the building complex at the appointed time. Burnished brass covers every surface of the foyer. If they want to impress, it's working on me. The assistant directs me to Shazza's office when I inquire, and I'm in his presence two minutes later.

"Lord Heinrich. I'm pleased to meet you," he says as he rises from his seat and rounds the desk to greet me.

I shake his hand while assessing his demeanor. His tall, thin frame makes him appear fragile as if a puff of wind could break his back. But I'm not fooled. His eyes show cunning and a willingness to use unconventional methods to get his way — legal or illegal. "I'm glad you could see me at such short notice. I'm only visiting for a few days and intend purchasing a spaceship while I'm here."

"Please, take a seat over here." He points to a small conference table in one corner of the office. "You've come to the right place. Can I offer you refreshments?"

"A chilled beer would be welcome." I stroll to the table and sit.

"Certainly." Shazza returns to his desk and presses the intercom. "Cradula, two beers and make it snappy." I raise my brow at the abruptness of the request. He sees this and shrugs. "The girl's new. She dawdles if I don't command her."

A flustered woman bursts in on us a minute later, carrying a tray, the beers in danger of toppling. She is pretty, very young, and I wonder how she got the job in such a high-powered enterprise. She looks at Shazza as if waiting for further instructions.

"Well, get to it. One for Lord Heinrich here and one for me. Put them on the table over there. We will conduct our business there," he says as he points to the table, annoyed.

She gulps and does as she's told before leaving in a hurry. Shazza's eyes ogle her as she departs. He moves away from his desk and sits with me, raising his glass. I do likewise. "I hope we can come to a constructive arrangement," he says.

"As do I."

We both sip our beers.

"Now, what were you considering? We have a full range of vessels available from small runabouts to large freighters."

"The freighters may be of interest another time if we can negotiate a suitable arrangement today for a luxury spaceship," I say.

Shazza's eyes sparkle. "You've contacted the right establishment. We produce several models, but I would think the prestige model is most suited to your needs. It's such an appealing ship, and we can outfit it with any feature your queen desires."

"I see. Do you have any available for inspection?"

"You're in luck. Our manufacturing center completed one yesterday. They are just finishing the punch list before delivering it to our showroom docking display."

"That sounds interesting. Price?"

"Ten billion credits."

I frown. It's either an exceptional ship or the price is inflated to gauge my reaction. I give a fake smile to hide my thoughts and say, "Well, let's inspect it, and we can discuss the price afterward."

"Marvelous! Let me arrange transportation, and we'll be on our way."

He strides to his desk and uses his comm while I sip on my beer and consider my options. I need a ship to leave from here since my ride with Balashi and Udama won't be continuing. With credits stored away myself, I can complete the purchase without establishing a line of credit for Helheim, which wouldn't be easy to do since Helheim is unknown and has no creditworthiness rating. The kingdom has immense wealth, but no one knows that. It will be easier to pay the deposit myself and set up the line of credit later.

"Our transport is ready," Shazza says as he returns to me.

I nod, finish my beer in one gulp, and stand. "Lead the way."

We weave through to the building's basement and into a limousine shuttle able to reach low orbit. The craft takes off and ascends to an orbiting dockyard in forty minutes. As I peer out the window, I see a multitude of crafts sitting in dock around a space station's six spikes, which radiate from it like snowflakes. Each spike has docking arms extending from them — dandelions in seed. Spacecraft occupy most of them. Some are being built, others appear brand new, while several are in various stages of maintenance and repair.

Shazza reaches over to me and points out the viewing port. "That's the one."

I gaze in the direction and my brow rises, impressed by what I see. The ship is sparkling in the Babylonius sunlight. It's sleek with a flat base and elliptical cross-section, the front displaying a full-length viewing window across it, taking up the ship's top level. Six drives encircle the back of the ship, with a hyper-drive mounted at the center. "It looks like it might be adequate. What is the shielding arrangement?"

"There are independent front, rear, and side shields adjustable in strength and power, and transferable between them if you need more in one section than others, or if a shield power reactor is deactivated and you need power diverted from another one."

I nod. Just what I was hoping. It would withstand a sustained attack from any hostile force. I refrain from asking about weapons

capability, as I don't want to give the impression of being too interested in warfare.

As if reading my mind, Shazza adds, "There are two mazer
cannons on this ship, and you could install more if needed, including
four antimatter torpedo outlets."

Well, that answers that question. I glance at him. "Let's check
inside then."

"Let's." Our shuttle coasts to one of the smaller docking arms
used for passenger transfers and docks. Five minutes later, the seal
lights turn green, and the hatch opens for us to exit.

The space station corridors come into view as we step inside.
People are bustling along, intent on their own business, but overall,
our quadrant of the station is quiet. Shazza leads me to a runabout
used for quick travel within the base and we get on, scooting to our
destination moments later. People zip past us as we go. We hop off
and walk through an access tunnel and into the internals of a spaceship, the smell of newness surrounding me as I step through the
threshold. Everything I survey says luxury — just what a yacht for
Queen Adala should exude. Spacious corridors welcome me as
Shazza escorts me through the vessel.

"The VIP cabin," Shazza says as he shows me an immense set of
cabins that extends across the vessel on two levels, the only interruption being the corridor on the top level. The fittings shine of gold.
Plush carpets cover the floors throughout. Just looking at the rooms
suggests the price tag Shazza quoted is worth it. He may have even
put a discount on it to encourage future business.

We weave our way through the rest of the ship until we reach the
helm. I've stood in many helms, but this one takes my breath away —
top-quality equipment used throughout. I amble my way around and
linger by the captain's chair, looking at the consoles and screens. The
temptation is too great, so I sit and fiddle with the gadgets that won't
cause harm, but I notice Shazza is nervous as if I might break something. A separate weapons station abuts a sidewall of the helm. I
stand and wander over to it, looking over the controls and targeting
systems. Returning to the captain's console, I flick through the display

screens, locating an auxiliary weapons screen containing most functions available at the weapons station.

Shazza studies me as I inspect the ship, sizing me up, seeing where my weak spots might be to use in the ensuing negotiations. I glance over at him. "Your pricing is reasonable."

He gazes at me, a selling smile on his face and a pregnant silence in the air before he replies, "You mentioned the possibility of later purchases. Even though I never place exorbitant prices on my products, unlike my competitors, I have suggested a discount price for you to consider. I'll be honest, I'm hoping to make my profit on future sales."

I nod, appreciative of his honesty, if any salesperson is ever honest. There's a catch in there somewhere, but the ship is worth every credit of his asking price. Not being one to accept the first offer without bartering, I say, "If you'll accept nine billion, we'll have a deal."

Shazza gives me a Cheshire Cat grin. "I appreciate your willingness to negotiate, but even I have a floor I can't cross. I might consider nine-six."

It's my turn to grin. "Nine-five."

"You drive a hard bargain. My superiors will require a convincing explanation if I give it to you for that price."

I shrug and wait for an answer. When he doesn't respond, I say, "I could go elsewhere with my shopping list."

Shazza shakes his head and holds his hands up in surrender. "You win. Nine-five." He extends his hand, and I shake it to seal the contract.

"I wish to fly off once we complete the transfer."

"Once you transfer the funds, we can have everything completed within the hour."

"I'll get onto it immediately." My mind races, trying to work out a means of payment. I should just manage it.

"Let's return to the planet and you can organize your funding."

We retrace our steps, and within two hours I am walking out of his offices in Santori, heading back to the hotel.

I stop dead in my tracks as I disembark from the taxi. Three planetary security personnel stand in the foyer, one talking to the receptionist. It can't be a coincidence that they are here. I assume Balashi told planetary security of my presence, and they traced me to the place. I want my belongings but can leave without them as I carry my essential possessions on me. A park extends across the walkway, so I dawdle over to it and sit on a bench seat where I can survey the hotel's interior and wait. I worry they will trace my call to Shazza and go there, spoiling any chance of purchasing the spaceship.

With nothing else to do, I transfer funds from my emergency assets scattered throughout the empire to a temporary account for the acquisition. The security people are still there when I finish, so I call Shazza again and tell him I'm ready to finish the exchange. He sounds surprised that I received the finance so quickly but tells me to return to complete the ownership transfer. I walk to another hotel nearby and hail a taxi back to Shazza's office. I transfer the credits, he completes the paperwork, and I own a brand-new ship.

"Let's open a bottle of champagne to celebrate, shall we?" Shazza says.

I'm itching to gain distance between myself and planetary security, but out of politeness, I oblige. He gruffs the order to Cradula, who enters his office moments later with the bottle and glasses. She looks worn out and needing rest. She pours the champagne into the glasses and gives one to each of us.

"Why don't you stay and have one too, Cradula?" Shazza says.

Cradula stands in shock for a second, as if she's unsure she heard right. "Sure." She rushes out and comes back with another glass, fresh lipstick applied, and an enticing smile. I now know how she received the job. She pours a glass for herself and, with Shazza's encouragement, joins in the conversation, making sure she nestles up to me in a way that gives me an ample view of her cleavage. I stifle a laugh.

After conversing for what I consider a polite period, I drain my drink and stand up. "I must be off."

"May I arrange transfer to the ship for you as a courtesy?"

I accept the offer and step onto my brand-new vessel — which I've dubbed the *Queen Rosalind* in honor of Adala's mother — an hour later. With the urge to return to space quickly, I power up the drives and start undocking procedures, ready to disengage from the space station. It would have been easier with a crew, but I manage. I seal the ship within the hour, getting permission to undock soon afterward. A vibration resounds through the yacht as it separates and I power the drives, steering it away from the station and following a taxi lane until I'm free to set my course. I ramp the drives up to half power and speed away from Santori.

"*Queen Rosalind,* return to Santori at once!" I hear on the comm.

I smile and put full power into the drives.

3

LARSA

Once I gain a safe distance from Santori and enter hyperspace, I start to feel the pangs of hunger and regret that I forgot to load food for my trip. But, to my relief, I soon find they have equipped the VIP cabin with a meal dispenser. After selecting an energy drink, I sit at a table in the suite and sip it while thinking about what to do next. I wonder whether they will place an alert throughout the empire for the yacht. I can't do anything about that. I debate returning to Helheim, but I haven't finished my work yet. I want to chase up my contacts on Larsa first.

Time passes quickly, and I enter the Larsa system six days later. Larsa is also the primary planet, the second from its sun. Being 1.05 Earth masses, but 1.1 Earth diameter, its gravity is only eighty percent Earth standard. I've often asked why they base everything on this mythical Earth but have never got a satisfactory answer. It's unimportant in the scheme of things. With nothing to do and recalling that the ship should contain a small shuttlecraft to use while parking the main ship in orbit, I go exploring the ship's bowels until I find it. Now I can leave the *Queen Rosalind* and descend to Larsa in the shuttle. The shuttle can travel within a radius of five AU of a star (another measurement I've never found the source of), so I park my ship in orbit around the third planet and fly to Larsa's surface in the shuttle. Space control doesn't impede me or question my identity. As I maneuver to the descent trajectory they give me, my optimism improves regarding my anonymity.

Immigration is busy when I join the queue after parking the shuttle, and I'm ushered through without incident when my turn comes. Before checking into a hotel, I visit the retail district to replace the clothes and other possessions still on Sartori.

I know from frequenting Larsa during my travels that it is a pleasant place. I have my fellow traders to glean the current gossip circulating in the empire. After an afternoon nap, I get a bite to eat at the hotel and head off to a bar in downtown Larsa City called RJ's. It's a sports bar that attracts spacefarers like moths to light. Music drifts out to me as I approach the entrance, bringing a reminiscent smile to my face. The volume increases to a blaring din when I open the door and enter. Men and women, sitting or standing, pack the bar and chat loudly, shouting above the noise. Several holo-vision screens hang from the ceiling, displaying live sports events from across the empire. Any hope of hearing the commentator's words is futile. Human sweat lingers in the stagnant air as I weave through the crowd to the bar. I don't see anyone I know, but it's still early. A vacant stool materializes, so I sit at the bar and order a drink, realizing the music is coming from a live band, a novelty for the venue. That could explain the mob.

As I sip on my drink, a woman nuzzles up next to me and smiles when I glance over at her. She wants me to buy her a drink, hoping I will be interested in more later. Before Helheim, I might have been, but everything changed when I met Adala. I smile back at her and then ignore her. Moments later, she leaves me for more promising pastures.

After an hour, Bazi, a fellow trader, walks in casing the place. I wave, and his brow rises when he sees me. He waves and comes over to me.

"Where've you been?" he yells above the music as he buys a drink and sits next to me, pushing the occupant off to lay claim to the stool.

"Got trapped on a planet. Just returned to civilization."

"People were worried about you. We organized a search party when your customers started querying where their cargo was but couldn't find you."

"Oh. What happened?"

"Wiped you off, and the supplier sent another shipment."

"So, the supplier is after me?"

"Suppose so."

"What else is new?"

Bazi shrugs. "Not much. More taxes on shipments from the bastard running this mess. More protests, more arrests, and more violence. You get the sense something's going to happen soon. A stench in the air that reeks of trouble on its way."

I nod and take in the information. "You know who's doing big contracts now? I've got a client with money to burn and wants to set up business agreements."

"Depends on what merchandise you want."

"Tech products, gadgets, that sort of thing. The planet's starved of them and wishes to modernize."

"You can't go past Acropolis for that stuff these days. They're getting bigger by the second. They're cutting out the middleman, though. Just engage couriers to transport the goods for nothing. Hardly worth becoming involved with them. There's no profit in it."

Things have changed since I got stuck on Helheim. I shake my head, amazed at how quickly change happens these days. "What about bigger items?"

"You name it, they sell it." Bazi goes silent and thinks for a moment. "There's Persia Industries and Sumer. They have an excellent range with a good commission too. I'd investigate them."

"Great. I'll do that."

"Where've you been, anyway?"

"Hit an asteroid and crashed on a planet. Must be a year ago now. Just got rescued."

"Shit happens. How d'you manage to hit an asteroid? You fly pissed or something?"

"It came from nowhere," I say, chuckling.

We continue drinking and talking the night away, getting progressively inebriated but enjoying each other's company after a protracted absence. I stagger out at one in the morning and hail a taxi to return me to the hotel, falling face down on my bed and passing out.

The next morning, my head throbs like someone's hit it with a hammer. I remember what caused it and smile at having met Bazi again. We go back a long way. He knows I have a secret but has never probed. After rolling over, I sit and rub the sleep from my eyes, considering my day's activities. First, I drink an entire bottle of water from the room's bar. My frazzled head settles, and I shower and have breakfast.

Acropolis sounded interesting. So, I investigate them and find out it's easy for anyone to buy from them just by using online ordering. I try opening an account but come to a stumbling block when it asks for the planet. Helheim's not listed, and the vendor won't accept a manual entry. Adala will have to register Helheim with the Registrar of Planets. I realize that could be a problem as the emperor may notice a new planet and consider it fair game to conquer. I'll talk to Adala about it when I return. She'll have to do something, but that's her decision, not mine.

Once I've checked out Acropolis, I search for Persia Industries and Sumer and visit both of them. Persia Industries sells mobile equipment and heavy machinery, items lacking on Helheim, and I get excellent quotes from them for purchases. As Sumer is a provider of satellites and communications networks, again something lacking on Helheim, I can see potential in pursuing agreements with them to set up communication systems for Adala.

Feeling pleased with my progress, I call it quits and return to the hotel to relax by the pool and consider my next business needs before venturing out to another bar frequented by most traders when on the planet — Galaxia.

4

HALWENDE?

Galaxia is as bustling and full of action as I remember it. Scantily clad staff weave through the crowd, collecting orders and returning with drinks. The madame constantly scans the bar, vulture-like in her search for patrons to tempt with male or female company. She looks my way, stares, considers, and moves on to her next prey. My stance has alerted her to my lack of interest tonight. I've frequented the place and accepted her offers before, so she must smell a change in my temperament to discourage her. I have no complaints. Her radar is right. It's not long before other familiar traders drift in and congregate to compare business since they met last and share jokes and other matters from their ventures. I join them.

"Halwende," Zizi says as he makes room for me.

I respond, "How're things?" The others either raise their glasses in greeting or nod as they continue their discussions with the person next to them.

"So-so. Trading's getting tougher. I think the emperor wants to stifle business, the way he's increasing taxes on freight and licensing fees. You should know that."

"I've been out of circulation. Crashed on a planet and just

returned." The group's ears prick at the word 'crashed', and they grow silent as I relay the details without mentioning where the planet is or that I got involved in a war and everything else that happened in helping Adala regain her kingdom. We continue talking until I decide to leave, not wanting a repeat of last night. I say farewell and turn to go, bumping into a passing patron. "Sorry."

He looks at me, and we both freeze. After an eternity, the person speaks, "Halwende?"

I scan the bar, fear engulfing me as I search for anyone showing an interest in either of us. "Kalbum, what are you doing here?"

"Why are you alive?"

"Let's go somewhere less conspicuous."

Kalbum sculls his drink, and we leave, heading for a nearby coffee lounge where we locate a booth at the back away from probing eyes and ears.

"So," Kalbum continues once we settle, "I thought you were dead. We all did. How can you be alive and not contact us?"

Embarrassed, I stare at him. "I couldn't. I had to disappear after what happened on Eridu, for everyone's sake, including mine."

Kalbum looks at me, studying me for several seconds.

"I had to keep away. And then I crashed, was stranded on a planet for a year before traders rescued me. They recognized me and got greedy, wanting the reward for my capture."

"Yeah, the emperor's desperate for you. They couldn't find you, dead or alive." He paused and then said, "You're unaware of what it's like on Eridu now, aren't you?"

"What happened? How did we get things so wrong? One minute we're attacking and winning, and the next the imperial forces are annihilating us, knowing our positions and plans."

"Someone betrayed us."

"Who?"

"General Barak. He turned. He's Emperor Shulgi's top general now."

I sit back, staggered. Barak was my friend. At least I thought he was. He knew everything. No wonder the emperor overpowered us with ease. A wave of anger wells up from my stomach and rises as I remember the pain and suffering that he caused. I glare at Kalbum. "He arranged for Charlotte and Genevieve?"

He shrugs. "How better to distract you than kill your family?"

I can't speak for a time. There is nothing to say. Barak's treachery rips me apart, and tears threaten to escape. After wiping the moisture away, I ask, "What's happening, then?"

Kalbum scans our surroundings before replying, "You sure you want to continue now? Maybe you should absorb this information first."

"No, I need to hear."

"Things are ... tough. Eridu's under martial law with many people arrested and disappearing. We don't know what to do. No one's in charge, there's no one to rally us, to lead us ... We need you, Halwende."

I can't face Kalbum. His willingness to forgive me grates at my conscience too much. My cowardice incriminates me. And yet my anger grows, anger against Barak, anger over what happened to my family, anger for Eridu's citizens and the Rigel Empire. But it fights against my eagerness to return to Adala. I lower my head, trying to reconcile this conflict within me, and as my thoughts converge and set, I realize what I must do, not only for revenge but for the peace and prosperity of humanity. Someone must stop Shulgi. He will endanger Adala if he discovers Helheim, and I can't have that. I can't let him take everything away from me again. This must end, either in victory or in defeat and death. As I glance at Kalbum, I whisper, "I'll return."

Kalbum exhales after holding his breath. "We just need to devise a plan to sneak you back."

"I have a ship of my own."

"It's registered to you, though. They'll work out it's you."

I shake my head. "I've been working for someone else. It's filed under another name."

"Who?"

"It doesn't matter. Although they almost caught me on Santori, and they might have issued an alert for me."

"That could be a problem," Kalbum says as he rubs his chin.

"I'll have to take my chances. Do you have transport?" He shakes his head. "You can keep me company. And the others?"

"It's too risky to have more return at once. I'll place a notice on our network. Let them know. I won't mention you yet in case it leaks."

"Good. I can use a good night's sleep. Meet me at Q214 at the spaceport at ten tomorrow, and we'll head back."

Kalbum nods. "I'll be there. Where're you staying, just in case?"

"The Excelsior."

"Impressive," he says as he raises his brows.

"Privilege of my current position."

"Meet you at ten." He rises and leaves.

My pulse races as I consider the implications of my commitment. I've made the right decision, but it scares me. Not wanting to return to the bar, I hail a taxi and retire to the hotel to sleep.

A noise wakes me, and I rouse, trying to work out its origin. A fist bangs on the door of my room, and I am straightaway fully awake. As I view the security screen, I see Kalbum standing there, glancing left and right, worried. I let him enter. "What's wrong?"

"Someone knows you're here. There's an alert out, and Security will be here any minute. We have to leave now."

I wash my face quickly before stuffing my belongings into my bag and dress. "I'm ready. You've got transport?"

Kalbum nods. "Follow me." He opens the door and strides out. I obey, and we make our way to the foyer. Kalbum sees four men preparing to enter the hotel and pulls me in the opposite direction before they see us. We find a fire exit and leave through a side alley. As we slink along the lane, Kalbum looks around the corner, checking for guards. "I have a land scooter over there," he says as he points further along the street. "Just stroll over to it."

"At three in the morning?"

He shrugs. "You got a better idea?"

"No." So we leave the alley and amble toward Kalbum's scooter.

It seems to take forever to walk the short distance. With ten meters to go, a shout comes from behind us. "Hey, you!"

After glancing back, we bolt for the scooter. Kalbum has it in the air seconds later, and we head for the airport and the safety of my shuttle. With no clearance for departure, I energize the drive anyway, shooting off the planet to the anger of the spaceport authorities. Two hours later, we're on my ship headed for anywhere but Larsa. I've set a course in a random direction to put any pursuers off before I change the astrogation setting to Eridu and whatever awaits me there.

5

ERIDU

Kalbum knows his way around a ship, so he helps me on our journey to Eridu. We have the time to discuss a strategy for what we will do there, but I worry others may follow us, my venture ending before it even begins. This is an audacious plan, and many things can go wrong, but Kalbum trusts me and has convinced me I'm needed. Still, I doubt I will have any impact on future events.

After eight days of travel toward Eridu, we enter the system. I repeat what I did at Larsa and park my yacht in orbit around an outer planet distant from Eridu itself. We take my shuttle and descend to the night side of the planet. Kalbum directs me to a landing site far away from the capital. I worry that planetary control has detected my approach, but it doesn't appear to concern Kalbum. With his lead, I settle the shuttle on solid soil, inside a natural cave. No light shines in the cavern, and my flashlight illuminates little when I leave the ship. Kalbum leads me further into the cavern until we reach the back.

"Where're you taking me?"

"You'll see." He searches ahead and strides over to a rock, rummaging behind it. A small orifice appears in the cave's rear moments later. "This way."

Trusting Kalbum knows what he's doing, I follow him through the opening into a large room. The entrance closes again, and we stand in darkness until the place bursts into bright light moments later. Several land scooters sit on the floor.

"Where are we?" I ask as I scan my surroundings.

"A cache we've built up for secret missions. We're near a major town on the other side of the mountains. We'll be able to blend in and conduct our business from there."

"Won't people recognize me?"

"Maybe. What do you suggest we do for a disguise?"

"I'm not sure. I've got a jacket with a hood to cover my head. It won't last forever but should disguise me for now."

He looks at me and frowns. "That's the best we can do. I'll talk to someone when we get to Eridu City. Now, let's go."

We hop on a scooter. He starts it up and keys in a code on a device he carries, opening another door to reveal a tunnel. The scooter lifts us from the ground and sends us hurling along the shaft. I don't know where I am, but after five hundred meters, we burst out into the open air and rise, gaining speed as we zoom over the mountain range. A city comes into view a short while later, its lights illuminating the view in a dim yellow glow on an otherwise moonless night. He skirts the city and continues over the landscape for three more hours. The time-lapse and the planet's rotation bring us to the outskirts of Eridu City as the sole sun dawns on the horizon, the bright red flash welcoming the daybreak.

"Don't look up," Kalbum says. "There's surveillance everywhere." He speeds into an industrial precinct and past a set of warehouses. Zig-zagging his way between buildings, he slows and stops at a small workshop in the back of a dead-end alley. As he puts his finger to his lips, he hops off and raps on the door. I sit surveying the landscape. Warehouses line both sides of the alley. Excellent place for an ambush, I postulate as I wait. On hearing whispers, I glance back at Kalbum and see his mouth move. A lorry-sized doorway opens, and Kalbum returns, taking the scooter into the building, the door closing behind us. We hover for a moment and land. "We walk from here."

"Where're we going?"

"Don't talk." Kalbum strides to a rear exit. It clicks and opens, giving us access, and we step through it.

Inside another tunnel, we traverse it into an elevator, descending until we come to a stop and the doors open to a large chamber full of surveillance and communication equipment. They must have spent years developing this. I had no inkling of it, and I knew almost everything. Several people sit at terminals scanning the screens for important information to report. Kalbum leads me across the room and into an accommodation section with doors. Some are open and I see beds. We stop in front of one. "You can rest here. There's a refectory along the hallway if you're hungry but keep to yourself." He points the way. "I need to go for a while. Back soon." I nod.

The room I enter is cozy, but practical — a bed, a table, and a few shelves. A second door leads to a bathroom. I close the door and flop onto the bed, placing my hands behind my head, staring at the ceiling. What have I gotten myself into? Will I ever see Adala again now that I've agreed to this path? The picture of her crying before I left Helheim enters my mind, and my throat constricts. I must return, but I must end things here too.

After falling asleep for a time, I awaken, my stomach growling for nourishment. I sit up and rub my eyes before using the bathroom and then setting off in search of food. The refectory can fit twenty people, but it's empty now as I walk to a dispensing machine. I punch in the codes for an energy bar, a fruit bar, and a coffee and receive my order. In line with Kalbum's orders, I return to my room to eat and wonder where he is and what he's doing.

Kalbum returns after another two hours. "Come."

6

THE RESISTANCE

Kalbum leads me further into the underground complex until we arrive at another door. People only occupy the surveillance room. He stands in front of the entrance, and a scanner emerges from the wall. It is spherical and stops in front of him. He places his palms on it, and when it rises, he looks into a screen. It ascends and rests on his head for several seconds before the door opens and the scanner returns to its recess.

"Come," he says again. I follow him through and into an elevator. We rise and come out at ground level.

"Where are we going?"

"Not now."

I'm nervous over these clandestine movements where I have no control but decide to be patient.

The sun sets as we fly through the airways of Eridu City on a scooter, and I sit in silence while Kalbum drives us to our destination. We enter a residential district where skyscrapers penetrate the air like needles from a porcupine. The bustle of suburbia and the sounds of people hurrying to their homes filter up to us from below. On reaching the location, the scooter descends and coasts into a garage, settling into a parking space. The sounds and smells of the past return as I dismount and follow Kalbum through a crowd and into an elevator and descend into the planet's bowels. The doors open and we stride down a corridor and through several other doors until we enter a large room containing a group of people. They go silent as we enter. I halt and gaze at them, and they, me.

"At last, you come, Kalbum," one of them says as he walks toward us. "We were worrying."

"I didn't know we'd arranged a time."

The person stops in front of me and looks hard at me. He is my height and thin, an athlete in muscle tone but not bearing the bulk of extensive exercise. His searching eyes drill into me as he considers his words.

"Argandea," I say, sorrowful memories flooding me, ones I want to forget.

"Halwende." Argandea reaches out and pulls me into a hug, patting me on the back. I see him tearing up when we part. "It's been a long time. We believed you were dead."

"It was better that you did."

"Why? Why did you leave?"

I glance away, unable to maintain eye contact, but I gather my strength and return his look. "I had to disappear to remove you from the threat I represented. Too many died because of me. Even now, my presence here might place you all in danger."

"It's a risk we're willing to take. Come, I will introduce you to old and new friends. We must then eat, drink, and talk."

The room fills with voices again as Argandea leads me through the crowd. People stare at me as I pass. I nod, my nervousness plain, but continue following Argandea with Kalbum behind me. We enter an adjoining office where two others sit at a bench table talking. They stop and stand: a man, short and plump, in his fifties with graying hair and serious eyes, and a long-haired woman with green eyes, about forty, lithe, her head eye-height. She has a scar across one cheek. I choke back tears as I recognize them both. They react with emotion, too, as they move toward me. "Lugal," I say as I hug the man and "Ninsar," hugging her. I wipe the moisture from my eyes.

"I didn't believe Kalbum when he told us," Ninsar says. "Your return gives me hope."

I open my mouth to speak, but nothing comes out. Their faith in me is unbearable, bringing the tears back.

"About bloody time you surfaced, you old dog," Lugal says, the gruffness in his voice disguising his affection for me.

I smile and then laugh, shaking my head. "The suffering hasn't tempered you."

"A few battles can't rattle these ancient bones. Shulgi can send what he wants against me, and I'll get rid of them." I see the sorrow in his eyes, though, as if he's seen too many friends die.

"Where have you been?" Ninsar asks.

"I've been trading since you saw me last. At least most of the time. I crashed on a planet over a year ago and only recently returned."

"Didn't anyone recognize you?" Lugal asks.

"I kept to obscure trading routes. But the traders who rescued me recognized me. They captured me, but I escaped."

"Who would have thought," Lugal shakes his head and laughs, "you, a trader?"

"It's not that unbelievable," I say with mock indignation.

"Let's sit," Argandea says, bringing the reunion to the present. He talks to a person waiting aside, who sets food and drink on the table while we make ourselves comfortable and then leaves.

I sense a nervousness between us as we eat, neither they nor I wanting to break the silence, an occasional anxious eye darting toward me. The tension is palpable and tightening around my chest. To start the conversation, I say, "You look organized."

Sipping wine, Lugal says, "Looks are deceiving." He glances over to Argandea before taking another sip.

Argandea sighs and places his hands flat on the table as he stares into my eyes. "There are many groups. This is one of them. We work in isolation, though. Each group has its leader, but no one wants to be controlled by anyone else."

His admission shocks me. "But how do you coordinate yourselves?"

"We don't. And as a result, things go wrong, and we suffer. It wouldn't surprise me if we fight each other sometimes."

"This is how Shulgi and that traitor Barak maintain control," Ninsar butts in, anger in her voice. "While he can keep us separated, disunited, we are weak." I see her pleading eyes and understand what she wants. I realize how devoted she is to me, her trust unwavering. But she doesn't know everything — not the cowardice I displayed when I fled, leaving them to fend for themselves.

"There isn't anyone every group reveres and respects enough to follow," Argandea explains. "No one to replace you." He looks tired as if he has struggled with his demons as much as I have with mine.

I see the silent plea in the eyes of Argandea and the others, and I want to help. But I fear losing Adala forever. I chose to return here today to meet them, but I'm not sure I can choose to return permanently. I can't see how I can help them and have my new life with Adala, too. My world has shifted in the past year. I have put despair behind me and found happiness again, and I'm not prepared to risk losing it, not even for my friends.

"I must attend to other matters," I say as gently as I can. The deflation in their expectancy hits me hard. I am abandoning them again, but I have nothing to offer. Then, my emotions torn, I hear myself add, "Besides, I know nothing of your current circumstances and who's doing what. Or who your group leaders are. I'd need to become re-acquainted, or we would end up lost again."

Straightaway, hope returns to their eyes at my words. "We have time ... for now," Lugal says eagerly. "It's quiet at present."

As if to belie Lugal's statement, we hear shots ring out from the hideout's main room.

7

UNDER ATTACK

"**W**hat's that?" I ask, a knot of fear tightening my stomach.

Argandea, Lugal, and Ninsar stand alert instantly, laser pistols appearing in their hands from nowhere. Kalbum and I glance at each other. Shouts and cries of pain erupt from the other room as laser fire hits or misses its mark. Ninsar rushes to the door and cracks it open, peeping out. "Government troops," she says as she sees the action and prepares to surrender in defeat. She turns to Argandea. "There are too many. We must retreat and escape with Halwende. We can't afford for them to seize him. Not now."

I stand and stride to the doorway, peering through the gap. She's right. They outnumber us, and they'll shoot or capture us if we stay. Half the people already lie on the floor, dead or injured, the stench of blood and cauterized flesh sickening me. Why did they choose now to attack? Did they know I was here? Anxiety engulfs me as I look to Argandea to lead me to safety.

"We need to get to the emergency exit," Argandea says.

"But that's through the battle zone." Ninsar stares in disbelief.

"It's the only way. We're trapped in here."

Lugal strides over to a closet and opens it. A safe sits inside. He punches a code in the panel, and it unlocks. After removing two laser pistols, he throws one to me and the other to Kalbum. "You'll need these."

I catch mine and check it. Fully charged. On activating it, I wait for our course of action as the fighting outside grows louder and closer.

Argandea peeks through the gap and looks back at us. "We must run to an adjacent doorway. Halwende and Kalbum, you follow me. Ninsar and Lugal bring up the rear." We nod. "On my mark." He checks again. "Go!"

The door flings open and Argandea rushes out, crouched and gun outstretched, searching for assailants to kill while he waddles across in the unusual stance. I do the same. One attacker sees us and adjusts his aim, but I fire, and he drops to the floor.

Attackers and defenders shoot and engage in combat while we progress to our goal. The outcome is foreordained, but Argandea's people have an instinct to continue until he has escaped with his charge.

A laser flashes behind me and I hear a yelp, but I don't break my concentration to check what happened. The source comes into view, and I shoot at him but miss. The shot diverts the person's attention to me, and he aims. Argandea sees him and fires with more success, and the person falls.

We pass the halfway mark to our goal. It is taking us forever to reach it, but we continue. Two more inaccurate shots pass us. I hit the shooter, and more shots flash past me as I replicate my actions. We use tables for cover, but they are no match for a laser, disintegrating into splinters.

Our destination is before us, and Argandea opens a door.

"Don't let anyone escape," someone shouts from the melee behind us.

A barrage of laser fire blasts apart the door, just missing us. We lunge into the corridor and scamper away from the fight. Large crates litter the passage, and Ninsar and Lugal push two into the doorway to retard any chase. It won't be effective for long, but it's something. As I glance around, I see blood appear on Ninsar's arm and a grimace on her face.

We straighten and rush through the passageway, dodging stacks of boxes as we go with the shouts of the chasing enemy behind us. The corridor weaves and starts sloping upwards. I don't know where we're going, but I don't care. It's away from danger. My lungs are on fire as I struggle to get the air I need. The sound of running and exploding crates chases us. Ninsar and Lugal shoot at any movement in the dim corridor light.

Another barrier emerges before us, and Argandea stops, punches in a code on a panel, and curses. He stabs it again, and the door slides open. "Quick! In here." We dash through, and he slams his palm on a button, closing the door.

A passage disappears into the distance, and we continue running along it. Seconds afterward, fists pound on the door, echoing through to us, replaced by an explosion. As we round another corner, Argandea stops in front of yet another barrier and punches in a code. It unlocks first time, and an elevator opens as the pursuit gets closer behind us. We bunch inside, and the door slides shut, Argandea pressing a button to ascend.

Ninsar stands next to me, and I gaze at her arm. Blood leaks from her biceps, soaking her jacket as she holds her hand over the injury. "Are you okay?" I ask as I gasp for breath. The others gulp, too.

"I'll live," she says as she looks at me. "It'll match my other scars."

I smile at her dry humor and note it hasn't changed over the years. The adrenaline pumping through me reminds me of old times for a moment, but I soon return to the present. "What now?"

"I have an emergency scooter above," Argandea says. "We'll use that to flee."

"What of the fighters below us?"

Argandea grimaces. "They're lost, I'm afraid. The reality of our lives."

A wave of guilt floods through me as I realize my escape meant the sacrifice of so many lives. It recurs wherever I go; people die so I can flee like a frightened child. I close my eyes and lean against the elevator wall, feeling its motion vibrate through me. Why must so many lose their lives for me? I should have stayed hidden. The worth Adala gave me lulled me into a false sense of security, a belief that I could come out into the empire again and shed my alias as a trader. I was wrong, and now others are paying the price.

The elevator stops and the doors open. I open my eyes and peer out. A garage spreads before us, and Argandea raises his pistol before peering out. "Clear." He strides out and toward a scooter. The rest of us stay close behind him.

A storage cabinet lies under the seats of the scooter, and Argandea opens a hatch to gain access. "You'll have to squeeze in there." He looks apologetic.

"You've got to be joking." Kalbum stares at the confined space.

Argandea looks around, checking for anyone following. "Listen. A couple of passengers on a scooter is normal. Five are grounds for suspicion. I'll release you as soon as I can."

The space is tight, but we fit without overcrowding. Argandea closes the hatch and darkness surrounds us. The scooter starts and rises. The scent and nearness of Ninsar make me self-conscious, but I can't see her in the blackness. A sense of movement vibrates through the scooter and jolts bump us together when Argandea jerks a direction change. After the scooter shudders to a halt, we lie in the gloom for what feels like an eternity but is probably only ten minutes. The sound of Argandea talking to someone filters through to us. It sounds like a person in authority is questioning him, so I pat for my laser and ready it just in case, wishing I knew what was happening. Argandea appears to be negotiating. A tense period elapses before the scooter starts up again and we continue our journey.

After ten more minutes, we stop. But I don't know whether we've reached our intended destination, or they have escorted us to a place unknown. I have no alternative but to trust Argandea. There is movement outside, and after another minute, the hatch opens. I blink from the sudden brightness, wondering where I am and if I am a free agent or a captive.

8

YOU MUST LEAD US

"You can come out," Argandea tells us, and he comes into focus as my eyes adjust to the light.

The others crawl out, as do I, and we stand, stretching our legs. We are standing on a high hill overlooking the city outskirts. They stretch out before me, with skyscrapers towering into the air. We have come to rest on a plateau, and a house stands behind me. It is nondescript as if to camouflage its existence.

"Come inside," Argandea says, "and attend to that wound." Ninsar nods and walks inside through one entrance while Kalbum, Lugal, and I follow Argandea in through another.

"Where are we?" I ask, scanning the landscape.

"You don't remember? This is the old Susa district."

"But where are the houses?"

"Gone. Bombed to ruins, razed. This is what's left."

The revelation shocks me. As I peer through a window, I recall the past bustle of the neighborhood, so full of life and festivity. Now there's nothing. I dread to ask the next question. "And the people?"

"Dead, detained, or moved on to other places. Most moved, but we had many casualties."

My legs wobble and I must take the weight off them. A table and chairs stand nearby, so I stagger over and sit to digest the news before I collapse. All those people ... gone. The suffering must have been horrific. My shortcomings and cowardice caused this. My head droops in shame.

Argandea slaps my shoulder. "There is plenty you don't know. But first, we must move you to a safe location. We can talk there." The hand is one of friendship, and I gaze at it, then at Argandea. He smiles, but I sense sadness. Everyone conceals their suffering and pain, which they hide well, but I see it in moments when they think I'm not watching. "Come."

"I need to find my way back," Kalbum says.

"Sure." Argandea motions for me to stand. "Send a greeting when you get there."

Kalbum leaves.

I grip the table as I raise myself and follow Argandea and Lugal through several rooms and descend a set of stairs to a door. Argandea touches a scanner, and a sensor emerges to scan a retinal image. A click sounds from the mechanism, and it slides open. We enter a large room with desks and computers. A multitude of people sit examining the screens, taking actions with their fingers on keyboards. Ninsar is there talking to a supervisor, a bandage wrapped over the injury on her arm. They stop and look at us, and she smiles. It is hard to describe the smile. It's not a heart-thumping sparkle like when Adala beams hers at me, but one that nonetheless gives me a sense of pride and joy in seeing her. I return her welcome.

We walk over to them. "What's happening?" Argandea asks.

"The emperor is preparing for another assault," the supervisor says. "We don't know where he intends concentrating his forces."

"Do the other cells know?"

"We can't communicate with them at present. There is a blanket suppression on our frequencies."

Argandea slams his fist on the desk next to him. "How can we effect any meaningful defense if we're unable to contact the others?"

I consider the predicament, puzzled. "So, you don't know where he will strike?"

"No," the supervisor says, looking at me, frowning.

"He's one of us," Ninsar explains.

"Oh. They attack at random. And because we can't communicate, we can't reinforce whoever's under assault."

"Strikes are seldom by chance," I say. "Can you show me where the last few strikes were?"

"Sure, but shouldn't we concentrate on this one?"

"It's unlikely to be here," Argandea says. "We don't warrant such an attack, even if they suspect our presence."

The supervisor shrugs and goes to a screen and keyboard. He types and a map appears. After more typing, red crosses appear on the map. "These were the last ten attacks."

"We have units in each location?" I ask. He nods. The scattering looks random. I palm my cheek and scratch at the stubble of my beard. "So, you're saying these cells bear no particular significance? Personnel? Number of people? Strategic assets or locations?"

The supervisor glances at Argandea, who looks at Lugal and then Ninsar. Lugal shakes his head, and Ninsar shrugs. Argandea sighs. "Nothing." A satisfied grin plasters his face as he gazes at me.

"What?" I ask. I don't like the implication behind the smile.

"Good having a fresh set of eyes reviewing our intelligence."

His words unnerve me, but I let it slip. "You have tried other frequencies?"

"The ones we can access. As soon as we go to a different frequency, it gets jammed when they attack."

"As if there's a mole?"

Argandea goes to speak, but his mouth stops half-open. His eyes bulge and his brow droops. "As if there's an informer." He sighs and looks at the supervisor. "Keep watching and let me know if we have any problems here."

"Will do." He returns to his duties.

"Let's go somewhere private," Argandea says to me. He motions for Lugal and Ninsar to follow. We weave our way through the desks, leaving by a different exit. A staircase appears before us, and we descend four flights, entering another room. A table seating ten stands in the space with a large window overlooking the city. "Please sit."

I take a seat facing the opening and lean back in my chair. It's been so long since I've seen this city that I have forgotten its visage. Compared to Heimstadt, it's a metropolis full of people crashing in their rush to reach their destinations. With a start, I change my focus and gaze at Argandea, waiting for him to open proceedings.

The door opens. A man and woman enter, both young, vital, and fit. I don't recognize them, so I glance at Argandea, raising my brow.

"I hope this meeting's important," the woman says.

"It is," Argandea replies. "I have someone for you to meet."

They both stare at me with blank faces. "You had better introduce him then," the man says.

"Ishtar, Yarla, please meet Halwende." They both nod.

"Are we meant to recognize the name?" Ishtar asks. She holds her fists on her hips, looking from me to Argandea.

"It hasn't been so long since the massacre. Halwende was the leader, but he disappeared. We thought he had died in the onslaught."

"What's he been doing since, then?"

I turn away, ashamed that I survived. Why did I believe I could help these fighters? Why does Kalbum have faith in me? I deserve their skepticism. With a deep breath, I force myself to look back at Ishtar and meet her eye. "I needed to hide, and then I crashed on a distant planet removed from the empire." Why are these people here? Who are they? I have to find out. "What is this meeting's purpose, Argandea?"

Argandea looks at the others and back at me. "We are the leaders of the main resistance cells. There are other groups, but they are smaller and less effective."

I blink. "So, you five can't get along with each other?" It's incredible that they won't pull together for a common cause. Restless, I stand and wander over to the window, placing my hands behind my back as I gaze at the city's vista.

"He is the reason you took us away from our business?" Ishtar asks.

"Yes. You don't understand his importance. With Halwende we can put on a united front," Argandea replies.

"My people take orders from me." Ishtar sounds resentful.

"As do mine," Yarla says.

The acrobatics of the interchange play out in the window's reflection. Ishtar and Yarla stand with arms folded as Argandea holds his hands out and Lugal and Ninsar watch.

"And where has that gotten us?" Ninsar asks. "Our numbers continue to decrease. People are becoming demoralized. When did we last have an actual win to celebrate?"

"And when have you developed any plan for us to implement?" Ishtar retorts.

The pressure builds inside me as the argument oscillates. I don't want this life anymore. I crave my life with Adala, but events draw me to it. Still, this bickering must cease. "Look at yourselves," I roar. They stop talking and stare at me. "While you fight each other, it distracts your minds from the real enemy. Are you fighting for freedom for the empire's citizens or your own little fiefdoms?" I stare back, looking at each one in turn. Some drop their gaze, and others glare at me.

"You have a nerve admonishing us when you're the one who ran," Ishtar says.

I gulp as Ishtar's accusation stings my conscience, but I reply, "My presence at the time would have caused bigger problems."

"Enough," Argandea says, glaring at us. "This argument over the past is pointless. We must concentrate on the future. If we want things to swing our way, we must change. That reform must include you, Halwende, as our leader. You must lead us."

On seeing Argandea's pleading eyes and feeling the guilt knotting in my stomach, I turn and face the window, searching for a way out, an escape that absolves me of my responsibilities. "I can't," I finally mutter. "I have other obligations now."

"What's more important than returning the empire to its rightful ruler?"

Turning to them, I say, "You wouldn't understand."

"There you go then," Ishtar says, waving her hand at me. "Left alone yet again."

Ishtar's insolence grates at me. Not only because she speaks a version of the truth, but she refuses to consider other points of view. "Be careful whom you accuse of desertion."

She struts up to me. "Is that a threat?" she asks, glaring into my eyes.

"Friendly advice." I return the stare, withstanding her onslaught with ease. "You may require help one day."

She moves away. "Ha!" Turning her head back at me, she adds, "I can take care of myself."

I decide I've had enough and glance at Argandea. "I need to consider what you ask. It's not a straightforward decision, and you don't know the full implications of what it means to me."

With a sigh and drooping shoulders, Argandea says, "We can't make you do this. Consider your circumstances, but don't take too long. I sense time is short."

9

OLD FRIENDS

Depression overcomes me after the meeting as I watch Ishtar, Yarla, and Argandea leave the room. The chairs at the table look inviting, so I trudge over to one and sit, my head hanging low. My sixth sense informs me that Ninsar and Lugal are staring at me, so I glance up and into their eyes. "I ... I ..."

"Let's forget our worries for the rest of the day," Lugal suggests.

"And the impending attack?" I ask.

Lugal looks at Ninsar and returns to me. "Our cells know what to do without us if they're attacked."

"Aren't you concerned about leading them through the assault?"

He looks at Ninsar again. "There are more pressing concerns. Besides, we are contactable if we're needed." Returning his gaze to me, he says, "Let's go somewhere private where we can talk. Come with me."

I stare at Ninsar and Lugal. There is no choice. I must follow them. "Lead away."

We leave the house on a scooter and return to the capital, weaving across backwater airways into a less respectable part of the city. Our scooter lands half an hour later in front of a bar. It looks decrepit and the place I least want to enter. "We're going in there?" I ask, pointing at the entrance.

Lugal gazes at the building and at me, puzzled. "Yeah. We always go here, don't we?"

I glance at Ninsar, and she nods. As I shrug and shake my head, I gesture for them to lead the way. I sense an ulterior motive for bringing me here but don't understand what yet. The bar's interior is dark and noisy, with numerous patrons drinking, talking, and playing games. Several turn and check us out as we enter but then return to their earlier activities.

Lugal finds a table at the back, and we order beers. Happy to wait for his intentions, I stay silent. Although I sense Ninsar has an equal share in their connivances. They both sit and talk of nothing of import, distracting me to frustration until I've had enough. "Why have we come here?"

They both stare at me with the innocence of an unsuccessful thief. "Why do you think we brought you here for any other purpose than drinking?" Ninsar asks disingenuously.

I place my drink on the table and point my finger at her. "Because I know you, that's why."

She glances at Lugal and back at me, then sighs. "Look. I understand your irritation with Ishtar and the others. But we need you. Our little groups are fine on the surface, and we shout and celebrate our minor victories, but we're being strangled out of existence by the emperor while our leaders manipulate themselves to more recognition and power in a meaningless struggle to oblivion. You saw how strong Ishtar is. She is difficult to bring in line."

Uneasiness overcomes me as I gape at Ninsar and Lugal, unsure of what I should say. I dare not disclose Adala and my role with her or Helheim's existence, but I must reply. "Why do you think they'll take any notice of me?"

"Because of who you are," Ninsar says, her eyes emphasizing her plea.

"Do you really know me? Circumstances have changed since you saw me last."

"And yet here you are."

A disturbance percolates from the front of the bar. Troopers enter. Two stand guarding the entrance while two others weave through the crowd of patrons, asking for identification chips. I look anxiously at Lugal. He's scanning the room, taking in the change in atmosphere with the interruption. "Stay calm," he says. "It's a routine check. You've got your ID on you, haven't you, Halwende?"

"Yeah, but will it be valid, and is it on a list? Troops on Santori searched for me."

"Well, we can't fight four troopers unarmed. So, let's act unconcerned and see what happens."

My heart beats faster as the inspecting trooper homes in on our table, my hands dampening. I consider taking a mouthful of beer but fear my hand will shake, disclosing my nervousness. Thinking of my time with Sentinel, I recline and breathe deep, forcing myself to relax. "So, how do you earn a living?"

Ninsar smiles. "I run an electronic components business across the planet. It's profitable at present, despite the exorbitant taxes we pay."

I nod. "And you?"

"Don't ask what I do. You'll die laughing." Lugal has a gigantic grin on his face, his stained teeth just showing in the dim lighting.

"Chips," the lead trooper orders as he confronts our table.

We glance up at him — I presume it's a male — and we fish our IDs from our pockets. The soldier looks at them one by one; first Lugal's, then Ninsar's, and then mine. His eyes linger on the reader as he inspects mine. He stares at me and at the screen, and I sense my freedom is over, but, to my amazement, he grunts, returns my chip, and continues his check. I gulp and stare at the others. Lugal winks and grabs his glass, taking a swig of beer. I forget the troopers as we continue our chatter until a tap on my shoulder demands my attention. I glance up to see the same trooper who scanned my chip staring at me.

He bends and whispers in my ear. "I'd be careful where I'm seen if I were you."

My eyes bulge, but I nod, and he leaves. They rush out moments later, and the bar returns to normal.

"What was that?" Ninsar asks.

"I'm not sure. An alert must have registered on the ID scanner, but he overlooked it. Told me to consider my movements with care."

Lugal gazes at the doorway. "I wonder?"

"Wonder what?" I ask.

"Nothing. We should go."

"Don't I know you from somewhere?" bellows from above me. A hulk of a man stands behind me, rippling biceps extending from his shoulders.

"You talking to me?" I ask.

"I'm not talking to the wall."

"No, I've never seen you." I haven't. I'd remember a monster of his stature standing near me.

The man squints. "I'm sure I've seen you somewhere. A while ago."

I shrug and shake my head. "Sorry, can't help you."

As he scratches his chin, the man continues staring at me. "It'll come to me, eventually. You're lucky I can't remember because I only have terrible memories of whoever it was, and I don't like terrible memories." He walks away.

I stare after him as he disappears into the crowd, then turn back to the others. "What was that?"

"No idea," Ninsar says. "Just someone looking for entertainment. We should leave. We've had too much attention."

"Besides," Lugal adds, "we have somewhere else to go."

"Where?" I ask.

"You'll see."

10

SUFFERING

Lugal and Ninsar lead me outside and we hop on the scooter, traveling to another part of the capital and landing in the parking bay of a residential complex just as the sunlight begins to fade. "We can sleep here tonight," Lugal says. He leads Ninsar and me into a building, and we use the elevator to our apartment for the night. Several beds litter the floor in three of the rooms. There's a kitchen, bathroom, and living room extending to a balcony with a city view.

I'm restless and trapped. I know these people are my friends, but I'm at their mercy and have no independence except what they allow me. The apartment is spacious, but I feel claustrophobic in it, so I move to the terrace. The towering business district skyscrapers dominate the skyline as they silhouette the fading light. We are seven stories above ground and in a taller building in the precinct, with one- and two-story buildings predominating in the streets below us. Traffic is still heavy in the sky lanes, and the odd security sedan flashes by as I watch. Despite being born in this city and spending my early life here, I feel like a foreigner. The past year's events have transformed me.

"Credit for your thoughts," Ninsar says behind me as she moves next to me.

I turn my head, giving her a melancholy smile. "Just considering how much I've changed."

"You're the same Halwende. You've always been reluctant to commit yourself."

"And you're always blunt."

Ninsar releases a soft laugh. She touches my hand, and I jerk it away as if it were poison, instantly regretting the action. "I'm sorry." I have hurt her. "It's just that there's another."

"Oh?"

"That's all I can say."

"You've always withheld your thoughts, but you're more reticent than normal."

"I can say no more." I turn to gaze at the city again. She copies me. We both stare out in silence.

"You want to walk with me? Get something to eat?" she says.

I consider Ninsar and try reading her but decide she doesn't have an ulterior motive. "Yes, okay."

We both turn and go inside, where Lugal is busy talking with someone on his comm. He ends the call. "The raid's over. They attacked a small cell in an eastern town, but they scattered before the security forces arrived. They torched the township to the ground, though."

"The town's demolished?" I say, incredulous at the cruelty.

Lugal shrugs. "That's what they do."

"Nothing's changed." I grit my teeth in anger.

"We're going for a walk," Ninsar says.

Lugal eyes both of us but nods. "Be careful."

"Should we take a pistol or something?" I ask.

"They don't allow weapons on the streets," Ninsar says.

"Fine, but ..."

"Don't worry. We're protected."

I shrug. "Let's go then."

Ninsar and I descend to the street below, and she leads me toward a retail district. People loiter in the street, starved and miserable, fear in their eyes. The shops stand dilapidated, needing maintenance, with bored but hopeful keepers sitting inside waiting for customers so they can feed their families for one more day.

"This cafe is good," Ninsar says as we arrive at a shop with an alfresco dining frontage. Two attenders appear, giving us too much attention as they usher us to a table. Ninsar points to another table near the cafe façade, and one rushes to prepare it while the other leads us to it, apologizing for not suggesting it. She rearranges the chairs so both our backs face the wall. After ordering two beers, Ninsar looks both ways to check her surroundings. I wait for her to tell me what's on her mind. The beverages come, and Ninsar orders food while I take a sip, feeling thirsty. With the meal ordered, she takes her beer and sips. "What do you see?"

I glance at her, eyes wide with surprise. "What do you mean?"

"It's a simple enough query. Look around you. What do you see?" Her eyes stab me as I gaze into them.

On averting my gaze, I study my surroundings to understand the implications of her question. "People. Poor people, conducting their business." As I examine the street and consider each person, I realize something else is there. Something that shouldn't be there. "They are frightened."

As if on cue, a troop transporter comes into view overhead and lands nearby. I stare at Ninsar, alarmed. "Stay calm," she says. *Easy for you to say.* "They aren't here for us." The pavement becomes deserted.

"How do you know?"

"I know."

Six troopers disembark from the transporter and march along the street past us to a group of shops nearby. They blast a door to non-existence and four enter, shouts and screams emanating from the doorway. They toss three men outside, and the four soldiers return. Women and children appear screaming and crying. One man jumps up and runs, but a trooper lifts his laser rifle and blasts a hole in the man's torso. More howls come from the entrance.

My muscles tighten. I grip my chair in anger, my knuckles white.

The troopers grab their prisoners and restrain them before marching them to the transporter. The two men stare at me in despair as they shuffle past us. My heart leaps into my throat as it pounds with rage. Ninsar's reassuring hand restrains me as it grasps my upper arm. They pile into the transport, and it leaves.

I glare into Ninsar's eyes, angry beyond belief, but she displays desperation. We didn't come here by chance. She wanted me to experience today's events, and my anger unfairly redirects toward her. She wants me to understand the people's daily tribulations. "What was that?"

"Someone informed on them. Alleged complicity with the resistance more than likely, or just a jealous person wanting their removal."

"You don't act surprised."

She shrugs. "Happens every day. The more it occurs, the more people resent the empire. And the more recruits we receive, which repeats the cycle. It has to stop, but we can't find a solution."

I notice she doesn't mention what I know she wants to say, what I detect in her eyes, and I don't prompt her.

We eat our meals when they arrive and order a beer chaser as we sit in silence. I have nothing to add. My anger simmers, but there's no point in discussing an avenue for its release.

"Have you seen your old township since they renovated it?" Ninsar asks out of nowhere.

"No," I say as I study her, wondering where the conversation is leading. "Should I?" I don't understand why she brought up the place where I used to live.

"It might be cathartic."

Echoes of the past reverberate through my mind in an instant. The pain I want to forget keeps returning, no matter how deeply I bury it. Maybe Ninsar is right. I should visit my home and purge the despair from my soul.

11

HOME VISIT

The countryside is lush as we fly over the open plains away from Eridu City, a complete contrast to the ashes in my heart. Ninsar is with me. The landscape gives way to mountains, and we rise to a plateau. My heart palpitates as my hometown of Susa approaches. I deserted my home after the last disastrous battle — the pain was too rending — but Ninsar has convinced me I must return. Otherwise, the despair hanging around my neck will never dissipate. I wallow in my silence, and Ninsar gives me my space.

As we near where Susa should be, there is nothing but emptiness. No buildings stand: only debris litters the ground. Tears fall as I grieve the loss. Ninsar lands the scooter where she knows I will weep most. I step out and stumble over the debris. No undertaking to rebuild has occurred. No one is here. Ninsar walks in silence behind me. As I round the corner of what was once a pedestrian thoroughfare, I raise my eyes to my destroyed house, where my family lived, where my family died. Only a pile of rubble remains. My legs grow heavier as I draw nearer to the tragedy, and my tears flow more freely.

A patch of color amongst the debris of my home draws me to it. I clean away the debris covering the rest of the object, and my heart breaks. It is a doll — a doll I gave ... Charlotte ... on her sixth birthday. I collapse as the memories come flooding back; memories of joy and laughter with my wife Genevieve and daughter Charlotte; memories of my anguish when my people told me they were dead; and memories of my cowardice.

As I hug the doll to my breast and grieve in abject despair, a spark ignites in my heart. It takes hold and grows into a blazing fire of anger. My chest heaves as I grab the rage and exploit it to generate more. This crime cannot go unpunished, not anymore. I have hidden and dodged away from this until now, burying it deep within me, hoping I would forget, but seeing my house and this doll has made me realize I cannot escape the pain. I must confront it and use it to demand justice for me ... for my family ... for the people of the Rigelian Empire.

After wiping the tears from my eyes, they blaze with anger as I turn to face Ninsar. "We have work to do."

Ninsar bursts into a smile. "At last."

12

UNITED FRONT

Ninsar returns me to Eridu City and to the base where Argandea took me the day before. I get my bag and refresh myself while Argandea organizes the other leaders. Argandea and Lugal notice the change in me, and they both smile with approval. I grab a bite to eat while I wait and gather my thoughts for the meeting I have requested. Based on my earlier experience, it will be adversarial, the hostilities originating with Ishtar and Yarla. But I must convince them I'm a leader worth their loyalty.

An hour later, I stand in the room we used before, gazing out the window, immersed in thought. I hear the door open, and five pairs of feet enter. Ishtar and Yarla look unimpressed as I watch their reflection in the glass. It doesn't matter. What matters is their preparedness to work together. I turn and face them. "Sit."

Argandea, Ninsar, and Lugal comply, but Ishtar and Yarla peer at me with suspicion. Then they, too, sit. I check each person's eyes and detect friendship, competence, and loyalty in all but Yarla's and Ishtar's, which are awash with distrust. Ishtar's also display contempt. Never mind. I'll convert them both.

"Thank you for coming back," I say, still standing.

"It had better be worth it," Ishtar replies.

"I think it will be." I smile. "We didn't begin well. That is my fault. I had much to consider, both past and more recent events. It took a visit to my destroyed home and that ..." I point to the doll on the table, "... to give me focus."

"A doll?" Ishtar scoffs.

"It's not just a doll. It was my daughter's doll. I found it in the rubble. My daughter who died when Shulgi had my town demolished."

Ishtar's derision turns to sympathy as she understands the doll's significance. But she recovers her insolence. "What has that to do with us?"

"We ... I can no longer sit on the sidelines and let Shulgi bring this empire to its knees to satisfy his vanity and lust for power. From your earlier report, you have achieved little in curtailing his grip. I intend to change that. You will achieve nothing much while your resistance is fragmented." I raise my hand as I see Ishtar and Yarla agitate to voice a protest. "For us to get results for the empire's citizens, we must work together. Now, Ishtar and Yarla, you don't know me, so you have no incentive to trust me or follow my direction. Give me one chance, and I hope to change your mind. What do you say?"

Ishtar and Yarla stare at each other. Neither wants to show their hand first or be the first to cooperate. After a muted discussion, Yarla finally says, "I'm willing to consider what you offer."

Ishtar withholds her support a moment longer, but as the weight of everyone's eyes falls on her, she surrenders. "Okay, okay. I'll give you a go too. But you had better be good."

"And you had better follow orders," I say, challenging her with my stare.

I can see her itching to retort, but she desists.

"Well, that's settled," Argandea says. "What's on your mind, Halwende?"

Looking at each person before I speak, I ask, "What is your biggest problem at present?"

"That's easy," Ishtar replies. "Firepower. If we had decent weaponry, we could make more of an impact."

Heads nod.

"What do you have now?"

"Just small firearms: laser pistols, rifles, etcetera."

I gape at them. My arsenal is more equipped than theirs. "I'm surprised you've lasted this long. We must arm ourselves with proper weapons. Where are the empire's armories on this planet?"

Everyone looks at me as if I'm crazy. *Maybe I am.*

"I knew it was a mistake," Ishtar scoffs again.

I've had enough of her. "What mistake?" I put as much force into my words as I can. "Someone determined to take a risk to get results? Someone willing to put his life on the line to remove this tyrant?" Everyone's eyes widen. "Yes, I will lead from the front. I won't be hiding behind people sacrificing their lives when I'm not prepared to do the same."

"But you're too valuable to be in the assault," Ninsar protests.

"No, I'm not. Value has to be earned. If fighting in the frontline shows my worth, then that's what I'll do. That or die for the cause. Now, can someone please tell me where the armories are?" I stand, defiant, challenging anyone to go against my will. A smile materializes on Ishtar's face as if I've passed an initiation test.

Argandea pulls out his tablet and brings up a holographic map of the planet. He types commands and red spots appear in various locations. "There, as far as we know."

"Are they equally protected?"

They stare in confusion until Ishtar says, "I'm unsure of the other compounds, but these on the capital's outskirts are very secure. The heaviest artillery is in them." She points to the two.

"Artillery we could use?"

"Well ... yes. But they are impregnable." She eyes me with interest.

"And the others?"

"We have little knowledge of them," Lugal replies. "They are small and too far away."

"They are in remote locations. That could mean they're unimportant or they have very special equipment in them. Is there anyone who can find out?"

"I can put a few surveillance crews together," Yarla says. "They might convince someone who works there to talk."

"Good, do that. In the meantime, I want teams to reconnoiter the capital compounds. Uncover everything that happens in them. Even a guard visiting the can. Got it?"

"I'll organize that," Ishtar volunteers.

"Good. And I want you three developing attack forces. One for the assault and containment, one to cut off communications and protect the perimeter, and one for transport and extraction. Yarla and Ishtar, have a contingent of your groups support and integrate with the strike teams. Let's consider tactics then. We can refine them once we have more idea of the arsenal's security setup. We'll select a compound to attack at that stage too. Understand?"

Nods pass around the group as I check for confirmation. I see smiles and know I've convinced them.

13

ATTACK

Ishtar stands next to me, her strong jaw strutting out in profile and her eyes focused on the arsenal before us. I focus mine on it, too.

"This is either a foolhardy plan or ..." she begins.

I glance at her, unsure of what's coming next.

"... a courageous one."

Still unsure whether this is sarcasm, I say nothing.

"We must have bold plans to achieve inspiring outcomes," she adds. A hint of a smile crosses her lips as she turns to me. Her eyes meet mine, a spark of respect flaring in hers, and I know I have her approval.

"We need patience," I say, breaking the spell.

"Are you still bent on risking yourself?"

"I won't ask others to do things I fear doing. Yes, I will take the risk."

We return our attention to the arsenal, housed on a plateau up a cliff on the capital city's edge. The force field protection shimmers in the sunlight.

"Are your people ready?" I ask.

"Just waiting for the signal."

"Good. Let's get this done." I walk to the lorry and jump into it. "You set?" I shout at the false floor below me.

Two thumps are the reply.

As I start the drive, my mind wanders back to a similar audacious plan on Helheim. That assault succeeded, and I hope this one will too. I will die if it doesn't, never seeing Adala again. The truck lifts from the ground and I steer toward the armory gates, arriving before them ten minutes later.

"What's your business?" A questioning voice splutters from the lorry's comm, connected to the arsenal channel.

"I have to load a shipment."

"There's no consignment on my schedule for today."

"But I've got my orders. It is Monday, isn't it?"

"Yes."

"Well, they ordered me to pick up artillery today. They need it at the eastern base."

A heart-stopping silence buffets me as the security guard at the other end of the comm decides what to do.

"Show us your orders," the reply comes from the arsenal.

"Fine." Preparing the package on my stolen tablet, I send it across and wait, acting as if I don't have a care in the world.

"The paperwork is in order. When will Procurement ever get their asses organized? They could have told us in advance. We'll drop the gate shield."

"Don't blame me. I just work here." My heart thumps at a thousand beats per minute. I know there's no going back now.

The shimmer before me disappears and I coast into the compound, stopping at the security building.

"Pass through the scanner," the guard orders.

A scanning machine arches in front of the lorry, inspecting vehicles for weapons and other objects, including people. I nudge the rig forward. If the shielding around the lorry's secret compartment is faulty, we're dead. No alarms blare as the vehicle passes through or while I wait by the inner gate's force shield. After an eternity of waiting for the shield to drop or my life to end, the shimmer disappears.

"Go to warehouse 3," the guard instructs.

"Will do."

Before making the guard suspicious, I nudge the lorry forward and through into the arsenal's inner courtyard. Now that I've entered the compound, I can move to the next phase of my plan, my chest tightening as I think of it. I stop the vehicle and jump out.

"What are you doing?" the guard yells, motioning for me to get back inside the cabin.

"I need to ask you something important."

"What is it?"

His eyes bulge as I raise my hands. Before his mind reacts, I press the nerve suppressor button in my left hand and he drops, twitching as the disrupting radiation takes its full effect. Rushing to the guard's office, I peek into it. Two other guards sit in there. They have seen the first guard collapse and one has raised his laser pistol, aiming at me while the other reaches for the alarm button on the desk console. I dodge the laser fire, but the suppressor burst is too slow to prevent the alarm from activating. As I cringe at the noise, I rush back to the lorry and open the hatch to the concealed compartment. The hidden fighters scramble out and to their feet.

"I couldn't stop them," I say as the alarm keeps blaring away.

"We'll have to manage," the lead fighter says, directing his forces to the guard's office.

Within seconds, the technician in the group has the force fields off, allowing our waiting compatriots, with their arms and transport, to rush into the arsenal as shots fire from the other end of the vast courtyard.

There is little shelter from attack where I stand, so I weave toward the vehicle and grab my weapons still lying in the concealed compartment. I don my wrist lasers and belt up my maser as fallen fighters litter the yard. My heart falters for an instant before I realize the danger again, driving me into action.

Others shelter behind the lorry as it takes a pounding from the laser fire, and one fighter jumps in the driver's seat, edging it forward for a better position from which to attack.

Ishtar dashes across to me. "First thing to go wrong," she says, stating a fact of life.

"They saw the guard fall," I say defensively.

"Shit happens." She peers around the edge of the lorry, firing her laser. "We need more support in the courtyard, southwest," she speaks into her comm.

"Affirmative," it squawks back at her.

"Where can I help best now?"

Ishtar glances at me but doesn't speak straight away. "You should go somewhere safe."

"No."

She frowns and looks annoyed at my persistence.

"You won't coddle me. I intend to take part, making those deaths worth it," I say as I point to people on the ground, dead amongst the noise of battle.

The arsenal shakes as a loud boom thunders overhead. We both look up, a crease of concern on Ishtar's brow.

"Cannon fire from an orbiting destroyer," she says.

"They'll destroy the armory," I say, my voice wavering slightly.

"That might be their intent,' she answers calmly. 'We had better work fast. Check the guardhouse and call for help. We need a distraction."

Even though I know she is directing me to a more protected position, I obey, seeing the logic in her order. Crouched, I waddle to the lorry's rear and wait for a lull in the battle before dashing to the guardhouse. The noise is a standing wave, though its intensity has modulated. As I sense my opening, I aim my maser at the other end of the courtyard and fire as I run through to the guardhouse. An explosion wipes out several feet of the wall where my maser shot hit. I hurl myself through the doorway and grunt as a sharp pain emanates from my left upper arm. A cauterized chunk of muscle is missing from my arm, where a laser grazed it. With a curse, I rush into the guardhouse and to the console, holding my wound, careful to avoid the dead guards.

Another cannon shot rocks the arsenal as I gaze over the panel. The shield for the compound's roof is at sixty percent strength. Three or four more shots and it will fail. As I check over the panel, I see the shield's balancing screen and try to divert power to the roof shield, only to be prevented from doing so by a lockout.

Serum and blood dribble from my wound as I search the dead guards for an access card to release the lock. On finding only their identity cards, I rip one of them off and pass it across the panel's locking scanner. The light changes from red to green. *Poor security.* I rush back to the shield's panel and change the balance to strengthen the roof shield as another blast reverberates through the bunker.

A separate panel section houses buttons to open the warehouse doors. I stare at it, incredulous they have included such a crucial control in the guardhouse, the least secure part of the whole place. With a shrug, I press buttons and watch as warehouse doors rise, exposing the guards to our gunfire. The carnage is embarrassing until the defenders retreat to more sheltered positions. Still, the intensity of the battle abates as if a significant defensive barrier has fallen.

Our time diminishes before reinforcements arrive from elsewhere. We have timed their response and have Lugal and Yarla outside with their troops to cover our retreat if needed. But that would mean leaving the stolen weapons behind, which we don't want to do.

Another cannon shot reverberates through the depot as lingering gunfire abates. Transports rush to the warehouses, and loading begins. I sit, concentrating on proceedings at the depots, giving limited attention to the control panel and action near the gate. Everything proceeds as planned as fully laden lorries move out. The compound shakes again, and I notice the roof-shielding power is low. It may not survive another blast.

My nerves are on edge because I know time is running out. It has nearly elapsed when the final loaded lorries retreat. Ishtar and her troops fall out and, just as I prepare to join them, a gigantic explosion hits the arsenal. The roof shield has fallen and the outside compound roof collapses, a crack spreading across the guardhouse ceiling. Ishtar waves frantically at me to move. As I rise, the ceiling starts to fall.

Everything becomes so weird. Time dilates, and I see the events pan out in slow motion. Chunks of the ceiling give way and collapse as if under reduced gravity. Awareness of my predicament and imminent danger slowly trickles like molasses through to my brain. If I run, I can reach the reinforced exit wall, but I can't move. External forces hold me back. My hopes rise as the doorway is within reach, but then the first of the debris hits, pushing me to the floor. Panic sets in as I try outrunning it while knowing I can't. The pressure bears down on me, too strong in the end, and I drop to the ground, an enormous chunk of Plascrete colliding with my head. My last memory is the sight of my escape at my fingertips and Adala's face screaming in grief.

14

IN HIDING

S unlight filters through my eyelids as I regain consciousness, an incessant throbbing in my head. My last thoughts were of the ceiling falling and, for an inexplicable reason, Adala screaming as if she sensed my danger. When I open my eyes, a room containing monitoring equipment stands before me with many machines connected to me. Drugs make me light-headed. A window to my right provides a view of rugged mountains with snow-covered peaks and deep steep-sloped ravines vanishing into the distance. Sunlight highlights the mountain slopes with long shadows extending, but I can't tell whether it's early morning or late afternoon. Medical wraps encase my limbs, and my chest aches with every breath.

The door opens, and a short, overweight young man dressed in hospital garb enters; a nurse, I presume. "You're awake," he says as if telling me something I don't know.

I attempt a smile. "Where am I?"

"In the mountains." He checks the monitors and wraps, finishing with flashing a light in my eyes.

"In a hospital?"

"No."

"Talkative person."

The nurse stops and considers my comment. "I'm under strict orders."

"From whom?"

"Never mind."

With a frown of frustration, I give up trying to have a conversation with him and stick to the question-and-answer format. "How long have I been unconscious?"

The nurse thinks. "It would be five days now." He continues writing notes on the tablet he carries.

"That long?" I reply with a plaintive groan.

"That's it from me. Someone else will be along soon." He makes to leave.

"Wait."

"Yes?"

"Is it morning or afternoon?"

"Morning."

"Thanks."

He walks out, the door closing behind him.

I've only been awake a short time but am already bored. I have nothing to occupy myself, so I lie gazing at the outside scenery. No physical constraints prevent my departure, but I'm sure that nurse would lead me right back if I tried to leave. I'm not even sure I have the strength to raise myself. So, I stay where I am and sigh, turning my head to view the details of the landscape.

A matronly shaped woman comes in a few hours later and feeds me. Dinner consists of a blended vegetable mix that has the flavor of turnips and kale — the two vegetables I detest — but I'm hungry and comply. She knows I hate the vegetables since she tries to hide a smirk when I scowl after one more suck of the sludge. She helps me to a fruit juice later, which helps wash the foul taste away. After tidying the bed, she turns just before leaving to say, with a consoling smile, "The food may be more to your liking next time."

The ensuing solitude depresses me, and I close my eyes to sleep as a way of passing the time. I wake with a start when I hear a person approach.

"Hope he hasn't been too much bother," a familiar female voice says from beyond the door before it opens. Ishtar strides in, dressed in a formal military uniform emblazoned with the insignia of the resistance. She gazes at me. "About time you awoke!" Her jolly words have an undercurrent of concern.

Still groggy, I yawn, confused, but then I realize Ishtar can tell me how I got here. "What happened?"

She pulls a chair over and sits next to the bed, her face a foot above mine. "The roof collapsed when the shields failed."

"That I remember, but what occurred afterward?"

"That's a long story." Ishtar lowers her eyes in grief. She sighs and gazes at me again. "The lorries with the armaments started pulling out, but we stopped when the roof failed. It didn't damage us, but we knew you were inside the guardhouse. The shock paralyzed us for a few seconds, until I realized we had little time, so I ordered the lorries to continue to the rendezvous point while some of us stayed to search for you. We had almost given up hope of finding you alive when we shifted a large block of rubble and found a cavity under it — with you, miraculously, lying in it, seriously injured but breathing. We got you secured to a field stretcher and prepared to move out. That's when the army turned up ... We had to shoot our way out and elude their chase before bringing you here."

"And where is here?"

"It doesn't matter at present. Somewhere safe."

"Why the mystery about my location?"

Ishtar glances aside as if considering her words. "It's a safe house. Few are aware it exists, and that's how we prefer it."

My mind returns to the raid. "Were there many casualties?"

She glances away again, this too with unconcealed pain. "There were many — too many. But it's history now."

Her hurt transfers to me, and I gaze sadly out the window. I killed those people since I was the one who planned the raid and put them all in danger. My shortcomings killed them. The burden overwhelms me.

A mournful silence fills the room until a hand touches my shoulder, and I glance at Ishtar, my eyes pleading for understanding.

"We share the loss," she whispers. "We volunteered for the undertaking. It doesn't make the load any lighter, but they died to provide a future for their children."

"But I should have planned it better."

"We all should have done things better, but it's history now. Next time we will know."

I gaze silently out the window.

"We have a greater problem."

My head jerks backward, causing a sharp pain to dart through my skull. "What?"

"They had cameras in the guardhouse. They placed notices everywhere with your face on them. You're wanted, alive if possible."

What she says doesn't register immediately, and then I frown. "Why want me more than anyone else?"

"I don't know, but our informants at the palace tell us you've caused quite a stir."

Just then, the door bursts open. The nurse stares at Ishtar, his cheeks flushed red and fear in his eyes. "We're discovered!" he says between gasps for air. "The RSIU's coming!"

Ishtar's eyes bulge and she jumps up, ready for action. "Quick! Get Halwende to the emergency exit."

Danger and urgency seep through me. I jerk my head around, searching for an assailant. "Who are the RSIU?" I ask as I realize I don't like the sound of them.

The orderly enters the room, and she and the nurse pack up my equipment and move my bed, with me on it, out into the corridor.

"They're Emperor Shulgi's secret police: the Rigel Secret Intelligence Unit. They must have discovered this place," Ishtar says as she pulls her laser pistol out, scanning for enemies to shoot. She glances at me. "You've been absent for longer than I thought."

My bed whisks along the corridor as the nurse pushes it to a set of double doors, the orderly beside him and Ishtar bringing up the rear. He turns the doorknob twice clockwise, and a retinal scanner emerges from the adjacent wall. It scans his eye, and the door lock clicks. Opening the two doors to let us through, they wheel me inside, closing the doors behind us. The space is just sufficient for the three of us and the bed to fit. I sense downward movement and realize we're in an elevator.

Confined to my bed, I'm helpless, my injuries preventing me from aiding them. I rely on Ishtar and the others to rush me to safety. Moments later, explosions reverberate above us.

As the elevator comes to a stop, the opposite wall disappears, revealing a long tunnel cut into the rock. The orderly and nurse push me from the elevator, and the wall returns.

"We can't let the elevator return," Ishtar says to the nurse.

"I know," he says as he walks back to the reinstated wall. A panel insets into the wall. He opens the door, pressing keys until I hear a low-frequency buzz from behind the wall. It lasts twenty seconds and stops. "The shaft has filled. It will look unexcavated." He looks back at the elevator with eyes of regret. "I'll miss the place."

"Let's keep moving," Ishtar tells everyone, and the nurse returns to help the orderly wheel my bed along the tunnel.

Half an hour later, we arrive at a larger cutout cavern with a scooter stationed in it. The nurse and orderly detach the bed from the wheelbase and load me onto the scooter, securing the bed and me with straps. It is ridiculous, but I'm an invalid and must endure the indignity. The others hop on board. Ishtar drives the scooter through the tunnel for another ten minutes until we fly out into the open air. Our surroundings bear no resemblance to the prior scenery, so I wonder if we have traveled through the mountain range.

Ishtar hugs the ground at speed, too fast and too close for my comfort. But she's the pilot. The surface whisks past, and we descend from rocky terrain to a river valley far below the tunnel's exit. The scooter jerks in all directions, making me feel nauseous, and I stare hard at the sky to stop from being sick. After an hour, a tall, sheer cliff looms up in front of us, and I believe Ishtar has gone mad when she speeds toward it. A waterfall cascades from the top, the thunderous water overpowering the noise of the scooter as the wind whips past us. The cliff and waterfall come closer until we have no choice but to collide with the falling curtain, and I close my eyes and hold my breath, waiting for my impending demise. I should trust Ishtar, but I find it impossible.

A shower of water drenches me, and then moist air flows over me as I realize I still live and restart my breathing. But I can't open my eyes for fear of seeing the scooter collide when I do. With resolve, I crack open my eyelids again, the sight of a shadowy tunnel before me, the ceiling flying past overhead. Another half-hour goes by before Ishtar slows to a less neck-breaking pace as the passage widens into a rustic valley with luscious green grass and verdant trees extending into the distance.

The scooter veers to the left, and within minutes, we are hovering close to a homestead, Ishtar edging the scooter into a small shed next to it. The nurse and the orderly carry the bed through to the home-stead. A middle-aged couple emerges. They quickly get me off the bed and into an elevator, which takes me down to the basement, where they settle me on the floor. They then grip me firmly and lift me across to a bed. The couple set up my equipment before leaving me on my own.

Despite my doing nothing to help, the whole experience has exhausted me. I can only imagine how the others must be feeling. I am unaware of my location, but the room's single window overlooks the countryside with mountains in the distance.

Ishtar enters and sits on the edge of the bed, worry lines on her brow. "That was exciting."

I laugh.

15

UNEXPECTED VISITOR

Two weeks pass before I heal enough to venture from my bed. The only people I have seen are the nurse, the orderly, and the middle-aged couple who live here. They bring me food — decent food this time. The place is idyllic with its lush pastures and scenic mountains. It gives me peace despite my wish to return to my old life with Adala. Regardless of how often I ask where we are, the others remain secretive, refusing to reveal the information.

Recovered enough for exercise, I hike in the foothills near the homestead, where a copse of trees covers the pastures. A gentle breeze scintillates the shadows of the leaves as I settle by an oak tree to rest. Pigeons coo to each other while I close my eyes; the walking has wearied me. Apple blossom scent wafts past me from a nearby orchard. My thoughts return to Adala, and I smile as I recall her sitting next to me in the secluded garden we often used for our private discussions. She laughs, and her eyes twinkle, making my heart race.

"They said I'd find you here," a soothing voice says.

My eyelids shoot open in surprise, my hand searching for my maser pistol strapped to my side on most occasions but today left at the homestead. Recognition transforms alarm into joy. "Zabada! What are you doing here?"

Zabada, old and stooped — he must be in his eighties by now — smiles at me with a mentor's gentleness. He tutored me as a child and kept in contact as I grew into a man, but I lost touch with him years ago. "May I join you?"

"Of course. Do you need help to sit?"

His eyes flare in annoyance before returning to their usual mild state. "I may be gray, but I'm not feeble. I'm probably stronger than you are right now."

My cheeks burn the same way they used to when chastised by him for my misdemeanors.

He notices. "Oh, ignore me. I get grumpy in my old age. I see I drummed manners into you. That gladdens me."

Pleased by his praise, I wait for him to sit, watching him as memories of the past flash through my mind. "It's been a long time. Why are you here?"

"It has been a long time. When I was told of your return and your injury, I had to see you. It was foolish of you to take such risks. But I digress. I needed to talk to you while still able to. I fear my bones ache for eternal rest, and you must learn much before they do."

Zabada's words trouble me. He's old, but the thought of him dying places a great sadness in my heart. His news intrigues me, though. "What do you need to tell me?"

"That can wait. First, tell me what you've been doing."

I should not be surprised by his question as he was always keenly interested in my antics as a boy; but I sense more lies behind it now than fatherly interest. "I take it you know of the disastrous attack on the emperor's forces five years ago that almost wiped out the resistance?"

He nods.

"I was in the vanguard of that and went into hiding afterward. I was so ashamed of my failure, I just wanted to run away, which I did. I became a trader and conducted business at the empire's edges. But then I collided with an asteroid and crashed onto a planet."

Zabada's eyes sparkle with excitement. "And where was this?"

"Out along the route between Larsa and Santori."

He leans forward. "The planet's name?"

I hesitate, reluctant at first to concede that information even to him as it would be like betraying Adala's whereabouts and my relationship with her and the planet. But he has ever been my confidante, and I trust him with my life. "Helheim."

As he reclines, Zabada rubs his chin in thought and peers into my eyes. "This world has significance to you?"

I blush and turn away.

"Ah, love, I see."

With a shake of my head, I chuckle. "You always could see through my secrets."

"Not always, but it's easy with the obvious." He leans forward again. "Now come. Tell me what happened on Helheim."

I relate my adventures on Helheim to him but omit any mention of the portal room and the strange and powerful crystal. Every word interests Zabada as he soaks in the information.

"Grand Chancellor, ey?"

"Yeah."

"And is that your only relationship with Queen Adala?"

My cheeks redden again.

"Ah, I see I am becoming too personal." He gazes out into the distance for a moment, chuckling. "And who is this Queen Adala? What is her ancestry?"

"That's something strange. According to their records, she is a descendent of Alulim, son of King Alalgar. Now I'm descended from Dumuzid, Alalgar's son—"

"Don't mention this!" Zabada interrupts as he looks around in alarm, as though checking for potential eavesdroppers. "Your heritage must stay secret until the right time."

"Why?" His demand for secrecy confuses me.

Zabada does not reply for several seconds. He frowns as he considers what to say. "You must visit the library in the capital. There you will receive the answers to many secrets kept from you since birth for your own protection. Venture to the basement and find a sealed doorway. A room lies behind it, unknown and unvisited. Enter it and delve through the tomes."

This revelation baffles me, but I'm used to surprises from the portal room and the library in Helheim. "How do I get inside it?"

"The door will open for you. It will acknowledge you."

In frustration, I throw my hands in the air. "I wish you wouldn't speak in riddles. It reminds me too much of my childhood."

Zabada chuckles. "I can divulge little, and those childish puzzles were to prepare you for your later life."

I glance at him. "Helheim knows of my ancestry too — at least a particular chamber does."

"Continue." I've piqued Zabada's interest.

"This time, I will leave you hanging," I say, smiling.

"I have taught you well." He chuckles again.

We both sit in silence as we gaze over the countryside. It feels good to relax with my mentor and friend again. His foresight has always benefitted me, and I treasure it.

My stomach clenches as I glance at Zabada. "I must fight."

"I know. It is time to fight. But act with wisdom. Many citizens of Rigel will follow you, more than you think. Don't extinguish their spark of hope by rashly throwing your life away."

"Like what I almost did at the arsenal?"

"Yes. You planned it well, and it worked. But the leader must allow others to do their jobs."

"How can I ask them to do something I'm unwilling to do myself? They tell me many people lost their lives."

"They volunteered. They accepted the necessity. And they trusted their commander."

"Who nearly died."

"Who nearly died." Zabada glances at me. "Beware of General Barak. Don't underestimate his treachery or his web's reach."

I clench my teeth. "He will pay for his betrayal."

"Don't let that hatred fester either. It will cloud your reasoning and judgment, and Barak is a master at stoking hostility to cause mistakes."

"Are you hungry?" I ask, sensing my stomach grumbling.

"I could use a bite before I leave."

"Then come. We can talk more and reminisce while we eat."

We both stand and stroll back to the homestead. He has given me much to ponder.

16

RETURN

I stay at the homestead another two weeks before Ishtar arrives to collect me. By that time, my movement is unimpeded by my injuries, and I'm eager to conduct my research in the capital's library for the mysterious information Zabada alluded to.

Ishtar smiles as she approaches me. "Ready to join the world again?"

I sigh, my heart already regretting leaving this tranquil place, but I must. "Yes. I have something I need to do."

She raises her eyebrows as she considers my words. "What?"

"Later. Let's go." I farewell my hosts and the nursing staff, giving each a hug and thanking them for what they've done, amid their protests that it was no bother. I stride out with Ishtar.

The wind whips at my hair as we ride the scooter from the valley; the sky is blue and cloudless. Ishtar glances at me now and then as she steers us to our destination. I sit gazing out at the countryside or glancing at Ishtar, wondering what drives her to support me with such personal dedication. Several hours go by before we reach any civilization suggesting the outskirts of a city — I hadn't realized I was so far away. The first hint of dusk is darkening the eastern horizon when we slow, and the scooter is soon settling inside a parking garage next to a residential house.

"Home," Ishtar says as she jumps from the scooter and strides toward the entrance.

I scan the space and then follow her into the house. It is furnished sparsely in a characterless modern style, with oak synth-wood furniture and bold-colored cobalt blue fabric cushions. "Your place?" I ask.

"Mine?" Ishtar laughs. "Not on your life."

My eyebrows shoot up in surprise as I had thought her taste would incline toward contemporary fashion. "And what is to your taste?"

"Give me a farm any day." She smiles as if recalling a joyful memory. She then returns to the present and the dangers it holds. "This is a safe house, your residence for a short time. But I must show you something. Follow me."

I follow her into a bedroom and wonder what she is so intent on showing me. She stops at the mirror-faced wardrobe and turns the knobs of both doors simultaneously. A click sounds from behind the wardrobe; it slides left, revealing a tunnel entrance.

"Head into this whenever you are in danger." She points to the passage. "It leads to a junction where instructions will tell you your next move."

I nod. She steps back and rotates the doorknobs again, the wardrobe returning to its original position.

"I must go," Ishtar informs me. "But I'll return, and we'll meet the others in the morning. In the meantime, rest and sleep."

"I will. It's surprising how tiring doing nothing but sitting in a scooter can be. But I need to talk to the group tomorrow."

"Let's think of that tomorrow."

"Thanks for today."

"You're welcome."

She leaves me, and I settle for the evening, eating food I find in the kitchen and then sleeping.

I'm surprised when I wake rested without having roused during the night. I rise an hour after dawn, have breakfast, and wait for

Ishtar to return, which she does an hour later. We hop onto the scooter and fly across the city to an industrial district and into an abandoned warehouse, where she parks the scooter and jumps out.

"Follow me," she says.

Keeping pace with her, we stride to an office building at the rear of the warehouse, where stairs descend to a basement. The air is musty as we stroll through the cellar to a large disused air-conditioning outlet whose fan and bearings seized long ago. She opens the grill, and we step into the duct, the diameter enough for us to stand without stooping. As we maneuver past the fan blades, we continue walking, each step echoing throughout the conduit. Half an hour passes before we emerge into a large room with tables and chairs. Lugal, Ninsar, Yarla, and Argandea sit there waiting.

"You return at last." Argandea rises and smiles, reaching over to hug me.

I nod in greeting and return the hug before acknowledging the others.

"We had a significant win because of you," he continues.

"Many perished," I say, the sorrow of the loss escaping my repressed emotions.

"Yes, but they knew the risk when they volunteered. Thanks to them, the city is now in turmoil, and the palace is not happy."

Bottling my feelings again, I say. "Use your windfall wisely. But first, I must visit the library."

"What!" they all exclaim in unison, rising from their seats and leaning toward me.

"I must go to the library. Significant information waits for me there."

"This is Zabada's doing, isn't it?" Lugal looks annoyed.

"Who's Zabada?" Yarla asks.

"It doesn't matter who suggested it — I need to go there."

"But you are a wanted man. An alert is out for your capture," Ninsar says.

"Then we have to be sneaky. There is an unguarded rear entrance into the library," I inform them.

"What, not going in the front door?" Ishtar snickers.

Beaming, I reply, "Not this time."

Argandea rubs his chin. "It is dangerous for you to travel in the open."

"Then I must go in secret. I must go, regardless."

Argandea waves me to calm down. He opens his tablet and brings up a plan of the library. "Where is this entrance?"

With a frown of concentration, I search the screen. "There," I say, pointing to the spot.

They bend forward for a closer inspection at where I point.

"How do you know?" Yarla asks.

"I know."

"I don't like it, but if you insist, Ishtar will take you in a scooter with a concealed compartment," Argandea says.

"Thank you." I glance at Ishtar. "Let's go."

"We are in a hurry?" She raises her eyebrows and grimaces.

"Once I find out what's in there, we can plan our next maneuver to overthrow Shulgi."

We wrap up our discussion and have a quick snack before leaving to find a suitable scooter for the trip to the library.

17

TO THE LIBRARY

The scooter lands an hour after we take off from the warehouse. It's dark where I lie concealed, waiting impatiently for Ishtar to unlock the compartment. Daylight blinds me when the hatch at last opens, and I need several seconds for my pupils to adjust. As I crawl out, I scan my surroundings.

The sheer white library wall looms before me from the parking bay. Two other buildings stand opposite us. From memory, one is an art gallery, the other a museum of galactic artifacts. Comfortable that our position secludes us, my attention returns to the library. The featureless walls extend into the distance in both directions, but we walk to the left, skirting the wall until we come to a grate covering a four-foot diameter duct outlet with humid air gushing from it. The end angles to prevent rain from falling into it.

"Is this it?" Ishtar asks.

"Yes. No monitoring occurs in the ducting, and it passes the corridor we want to enter. There's an opening we can use."

Ishtar leans over the grill and sniffs, wrinkling her nose. "I don't think they need surveillance in there. Who would be stupid enough to go in?"

"We are," I say, giving her a cheeky smile.

She shakes her head and helps me cut the lock off to open the grate. We carry rope and suction cups with us for climbing, when needed, but, when we gaze over the first bend, we see the duct drops eight feet and bends again to a horizontal route. We both stand back, beads of perspiration forming on our brows from just standing in the air stream for that short time.

"We should strip off a few clothes," I say. The weather was chilly earlier, and we had dressed accordingly.

"Is that an invitation?" Ishar asks with a teasing smile.

I chuckle. "No. Just practical."

We both strip to our vests, and I crawl in first. Ishtar hands me the rope, a lamp, and a sack containing our clothes, water, food, and suction cups, and I slip over the cusp of the bend and disappear from her view, coming to rest when I slide around the next elbow and friction stops my motion. Ishtar bumps into me ten seconds later. After turning the flashlight on, I see the conduit extend into the darkness ahead, dim sunlight still filtering in from the outlet behind us.

"How did you know there wasn't another downward bend?" Ishtar asks.

"I didn't." She stares at me with wide, astonished eyes and shakes her head silently. "I mean, I wasn't sure."

We clamber on hands and knees along the duct, me in the lead and Ishtar following, making as little noise as we can. After sixty meters, we crawl past a half-open damper and come to a tee junction. I glance left and right and wrack at my memories, intuiting Ishtar is becoming more skeptical of my plan by the second. I decide on the right duct and start in that direction, only to be stopped after rounding another bend thirty meters along by a downward elbow. By now, we are both saturated with sweat. I change to a sitting position.

"I hope we aren't going that way?" Ishtar asks, gazing into the abyss with dread.

I nod. She groans, and I grin. After ferreting out one of the water canteens, I take a long swig and pass it to her, and she empties it, tossing it back into the bag. We assemble the suction cups and rope to abseil the ductwork and descend the vertical section ten minutes later, reaching the next horizontal segment after twenty meters.

Ishtar shines her light above her. "I wouldn't want to fall."

"That's the last."

"Good."

Leaving the ropes for our return, we continue crawling until we reach an outlet after two bends and two hundred meters. The air inlet is sixty centimeters square and covered by a grill. We both turn and sit, drinking the second water canteen while we rest.

"Now what?" Ishtar asks.

"We slip through there, and the entrance is along the corridor. But first I check it's safe." I pull a lens from my pocket attached to a telescopic handle and thread it through an opening in the grill, bringing my eye to the eyepiece to view the passage. After scanning in both directions, I inform Ishtar no one is visible. We both pull at the outlet, and it slides from the holding frame. I poke my head through and take another look for anyone using the corridor. Once I confirm there's no sign of anyone, I lower myself and drop the half meter to the floor, Ishtar and the pack close behind me.

Ishtar grabs her shirt from the bag and wipes the sweat from her face. "You sure we return that way?"

"Unfortunately. Let's go." I lead Ishtar along the corridor and around a bend. A door blemishes the smooth wall six meters away. "That's it."

We hear running approaching us, and Ishtar stares at me with frightened eyes. "I hope you can open this — and fast."

I gulp.

18

HELHEIM IS UR

I stand before the door, frozen into inaction as the running soldiers approach, not knowing how to open it. Recalling my experiences from Helheim, I say the first thing in my head. "Allow me entry." I feel stupid and fear our imminent capture. Ishtar gazes at me with disbelief, but I shrug.

To our surprise, a voice intones, "Who wishes entry?"

"Halwende of Eridu."

We wait as the footfalls of our pursuers grow louder. They must be just beyond the bend, and we hear them stop at the air inlet. "Around the corner," someone orders.

Just then, there is a click, and slowly the door swings open on its hinges. I grin at Ishtar's gaping mouth but waste no time. I grab her hand and rush through the door, closing it behind us just as the first of our pursuers round the intersection, hoping we have made no noise to give away our position.

Ishtar leans her back on the wall, and I stand listening. The soldiers have stopped by the door, and one of them tries opening it.

"It's locked," the person says. "They must have gone further along the passage." The running then fades into the distance.

"You're a walking disaster," Ishtar comments.

With a shrug, I reply, "Makes life interesting."

After regaining my breath, I turn and survey the room. Bookshelves line the walls with volumes of data chips sitting on them. A table and chair with a viewer stand in the middle. Dust covers everything. I walk along the shelves, reading the titles of the data chips. Ishtar does the same.

"What is this place?" she asks, fascinated.

"I'm not sure, but it stores the empire's history going back millennia." As I progress, I reach the back wall and see names of people — rulers — I'm familiar with from my family records. "I think these are chronicles of the royal family." My eyes glance across the titles until they stop, fixated on three data chips named *Alalgar*, *Alulim*, and *Dumuzid*.

On seeing my stare, Ishtar approaches, curious about what's caught my attention. "Who are they?" she asks.

I reach up and touch the volumes reverently. "Ancestors," I whisper, "my ancestors and ancestors of someone I know." I am in a trance.

"Who?"

"Huh?" I ask, coming out of my reverie.

"Who do you know?"

Frightened that I have let something slip, I blurt out, "No one," but still look at the tomes with awe. The data chips are each the size of my palm. I grab them, putting them in my pocket before continuing my search. As I near the end of the shelves, the names of planets appear on the data chips. I see *Eridu*, *Larsa*, and *Babylonius,* and then I see one titled *Ur* and am inexplicably drawn to it. I pluck it from the shelf. I take the Eridu chip, too. And right at the end of the shelving, I spy a chip titled *Recent History*. I snatch it too and stroll to the viewer on the tables. After inserting the chip called *Alalgar*, I read the entry.

BAD-TIBIRA BEGOT *Alalgar when five hundred and sixty-one years old, and after seventy-three years, he slept with his fathers, and Alalgar ruled the*

kingdom of Rigel. In Alalgar's two hundred and third year, he begot Alulim, and in his two hundred and eighty-ninth year, he begot Dumuzid, and they both grew to be strong in wisdom and knowledge of the gods.

The gods divulged knowledge of power and energy to Alalgar, showing him how to extract it from the holy rocks that shine blue with glory. At first, Alalgar used the knowledge for good and passed the blessings on to the nations in his kingdom; but, after a time, he became proud and demanded higher taxes from his citizens for the holy rocks, and his subjects became disgruntled.

It came to pass that the prophet Jushur visited King Alalgar and proclaimed, "Thus say the gods, 'We were merciful to you, King Alalgar, and gave you power and wealth. Because you were worthy, we endowed you with the gift of the holy rocks. But you have become proud and hardened your heart to us and our favor. So, there shall be wars, and we will wipe you from the face of the galaxy, you and your offspring, so that anyone that hears your name shall shake their heads in dismay.'"

When King Alalgar heard this prophecy, he humbled himself and shredded his clothes, crying and fasting, praying to the gods for forgiveness. Many days passed, but the king continued his repentance and did not eat.

Then the prophet Jushur returned and spoke to Alalgar, "Thus say the gods, 'We have listened to your cries and the humbling of your heart. And so, what we have said shall not come to pass, but we shall banish you from the royal planet, you and one of your sons. Your other son shall stay as a constant reminder to the citizens of Ur to share the holy rocks.

'And it shall come to pass that the royal planet shall vanish from the galaxy as penance. The royal planet shall return to the galaxy when one member of your lineage is worthy and returns to possess it again ...'"

I sit back, astonished as I realize the text refers to Helheim and its legendary disappearance into another dimension. It does not, however, explain the machinery that removed it from the galaxy or who built the machinery. It contains other implications I don't have time to explore right now.

Ishtar has been reading over my shoulder. "What a strange story. I've never read this. Have you?"

"No, I haven't."

"Any idea what it means?"

Wanting to keep my knowledge hidden, I say, "No." I pull the chip from the slot and place the chip titled *Recent History* in. I start reading.

~

A DESCENDANT *of Alalgar has been born to Puzur and named Sargon Halwende. This descendant shall fulfill the prophecy of the gods to Alalgar by returning Ur to the galaxy and reestablishing for the gods the reign of the royal lineage of Alalgar on the royal planet Ur …*

~

MY FACE TURNS WHITE, and I whip the chip from the slot before Ishtar can read it. I shove it into my pocket.

"Hey, what's it say?"

"Nothing of importance. We should go," I say, evasive.

Ishtar gives me a strange stare but says nothing further.

Suddenly, voices reach us from outside the room. "We had better check this one, too. Do you know what's in here?"

"No. It's always locked. No one's entered it for years."

Ishtar and I stare at each other, panic in Ishtar's eyes, and a tightness creeps across my chest. The soldiers bang on the door as if they intend to break it down with their shoulders.

"What do we do?" Ishtar whispers.

I search for another exit but find none. *There must be one.* Frantic for an escape as the banging becomes louder, I spot a square outline etching the floor. A strange hand-shaped mark lies next to it. Conscious that time is short, I rush over and cover it with my hand. The square hinges into a tunnel. "That's our exit."

"Where does it go?"

"I don't know. Away from here. That's all that matters at present."

Ishtar lowers herself into the pit, and I hand her the bag. As I prepare to lower myself, I look around the room with regret, realizing they will destroy the contents once they discover it and that so much priceless information will be lost forever. But I can't dwell on the loss as I dive into the hole, raising the square hatch behind me until it clicks into position just as the soldiers splinter the door and it crashes open.

With our flashlights on, we see that the tunnel only goes in one direction. It is high enough for us to walk in, so we stride off as confusion and anger ring out above us.

19

ESCAPE FROM THE LIBRARY

The tunnel continues on, and we follow blindly, not knowing where it goes. At this stage, I don't care. All I care about is that it's taking us away from whoever is chasing us. Then it ends abruptly with no apparent exit.

A blast reverberates through the tunnel from behind us. They have found the trapdoor and blasted it open. We must escape from this end, or they'll capture us.

"We're trapped," Ishtar says, panic filtering through her voice.

"There must be a way out. Otherwise, what's the point of the tunnel?" I search the walls and roof, frantic for a door of any description.

The surfaces are dusty, and I wipe away the grime, searching for anything as our pursuers close in on us. A handprint mark comes to view on the end wall, and I place my hand on it. Without warning, a hatch opens, and an optical scanner pops out. Ishtar and I glance at each other. I shrug and place my eye over the scanning lens. Seconds later, the end wall slides open, revealing the tunnel's continuation. We enter and the wall closes, saving us from those chasing us, for now.

We continue through the tunnel until we reach a tee junction and have to stop. With no idea of the direction we should take, I scratch my head. Then I remember the palace's secret passages on Helheim. They always had a map. I scrutinize the wall, seeking something similar. As I brush the surface clean, I get my reward: a diagram materializes.

"Can you read it?" Ishar asks as she regains her breath.

The map displays a maze of tunnels with black dots at designated locations, as if they are positions of other maps. There is a larger black dot at one spot. "This must be our current location," I say, pointing to the mark. Red dots scatter over the plan. I conclude they denote exits. After retracing from where we stand, I find a red dot for the library room exit. *The others must have used the maze to avoid detection.*

A loud explosion echoes through the tunnel behind us as dust falls from the roof, coating us and making us cough. I trace the map from our position to identify a suitable escape to our left. "This way."

We keep running for ten more minutes before I stop to check our location. There is another handprint on the wall. After placing my hand on it and undergoing the optical scan, a door opens, and we run on with shouts resounding from our rear. I spot the first soldier round the corner. As I push Ishtar through the door, a laser blast strikes my waist on the side. I cry out in pain but rush through the exit, closing it behind us.

"You're injured," Ishtar says.

I peer at my side to see how severe the wound is and touch the blood seeping from it, wincing as a sharp lance of agony rushes to my brain. "We have to keep going. It won't take long for them to blast through the door." After five minutes of climbing stairs, another barrier blocks our path, the last if my map reading is correct. The injury is hampering my movement by this time, and I limp with pain. Following the same procedure, the wall opens, revealing the building exit.

Our scooter is nowhere in sight. We both freeze, disoriented and desperate. I watch Ishtar scan the surroundings. "This way," she says as she runs. I try keeping up but fall further behind, and she turns, stopping when she doesn't see me. "It's just around the corner."

"I can't go any faster," I say as I pant, wincing and perspiring.

The door blows out, and soldiers rush outside seconds later. Ishtar grabs me, and half-pulls me, half-drags me along with her as laser shots ping past us, striking the ground with puffs of dust as we round the corner.

The scooter is thirty meters ahead, and we both rush for it as fast as I can manage, the pain threatening to make me pass out. Ishtar throws me in the flyer, and she jumps in, starting it up and rising just as the first soldier rounds the building, firing at us. The scooter shakes as a shot hits it, knocking a chunk from the rear but leaving it still airworthy. As I lie on the floor, the erratic movement of the scooter sends me sliding back and forth, aggravating the injury. It is bleeding profusely now, and I try staunching the flow with my shirt. I am light-headed, in danger of passing out any second as the scooter rocks from another laser hit.

Ishtar glances at me for a split second, concern for me etched on her face. She returns her concentration to flying and increases speed as she dodges and weaves around buildings, having left the ground-based soldiers far behind, on the lookout for any troop carriers or gun-scooters chasing us. As if on cue, two gun-scooters come into view, bearing down on us.

"Hang on," Ishtar says. "This might get rough."

Our scooter is unarmed, but I have my maser with me, so I pull myself up for a glimpse of our pursuers as they fall in behind us, attempting to lock on for a shot. Ishtar weaves in and out between the buildings to avoid them. She's an incredible flier, one of the best I've seen. After bracing myself, I take out my maser and line up the closest gun-scooter, firing. It disappears, but the other one takes its place and closes in.

My eyes blur, and I find focusing difficult. I squeeze the trigger and take a shot but miss, carving a piece from the building behind the gun-scooter. After pressing my thumb and forefinger on my eyelids and rubbing, I hope they refocus. But before I can discharge

another attempt, the gun-scooter locks on us and fires just as Ishtar
dodges. A sizeable chunk disintegrates from the rear of our scooter,
leaving me exposed to the gun-scooter and in danger of falling out.
The wind rushes past me, and my hair whips into my eyes, adding to
my discomfort.

The shot damaged the drive, which now whines as it tries to keep
the scooter in the air. Ishtar swerves and bumps the side of a building, bouncing me outside as I lunge my free hand at the interior side-
rail, grabbing it. I hold on tight, trying to climb back in. The gun-
scooter closes in on us, and I raise my gun, line up the assailant, and
fire. It disappears in a cloud of particles.

Meanwhile, the flyer is losing power, and we can't maintain our
altitude, smoke now billowing from our drive. Somehow, I crawl onto
the scooter and lie flat on the floor, gazing up at the cloudy sky
passing overhead in between the towering walls of the buildings on
both sides. I gasp for breath as the agony in my side floods me with
pain. My eyes blur again.

"Hold on," Ishar says. "We're going to crash. I'll make it as soft a
landing as I can."

Moments later, the scooter jolts, tossing me from side to side as it
skids across the pavement, losing momentum and speed. As I look
up, Ishtar desperately steers the vehicle away from structures that
could annihilate us. We come to a stop, still in one piece, as Ishtar's
concerned eyes gaze at my face and then my wound. She delicately
moves my shirt for a better view. "You need medical treatment," she
states as her eyes return to mine. "But first, we must escape."

She jumps off the ruined scooter and makes a call. Five minutes
later, two men appear from the shadows. They talk quietly to her and
then glance at me. An approaching noise makes them look up. "We
need to get under cover," one man says.

"Can you walk?" Ishtar asks me.

Somehow, I find a reserve of strength and sit. Making another
effort, I stand, with Ishtar's help, and struggle from the scooter. With
Ishtar's arm around my waist and my arm draping her shoulders, we
half stride, half run, following the two men in front. Moments later,

after threading through alleyways, darkness engulfs us as we enter a building. Each step sends shards of pain through my body. The two in the front switch on flashlights and continue jogging until we reach a stairwell, which we then descend, each tread a jarring agony for me.

A basement appears at the bottom of the stairs, and we cross it, passing through a doorway and continuing our journey to safety.

After passing through the entrance, I lapse into periods of unconsciousness. At one stage, I hear Ishtar telling the others that we must rest, and we stop. A wall cools my back as I lean against it, my delirious mind trying to make sense of my surroundings. Ishtar says something, but I can't understand her words. My last thoughts are of movement again as I drift into oblivion.

20

ANOTHER SAFE HOUSE

The chirp of birds and the steady beep of a heartbeat-monitoring machine greet my ears as I wake from a deep sleep. It takes several moments to realize I am regaining consciousness and a few more to remember what happened. My eyes are heavy as they struggle to open to my surroundings. Ishtar sits in the room's corner, her chin against her chest as she sleeps. Sympathy for her and my deep gratitude reach out to her as I watch her chest rise and fall.

Tubes poke into me, and sensors adhere to my skin from pouches and machines standing next to my bed. I raise my hand and gingerly prod at the site of my injury, now covered by a medical patch. The pain has subsided, whether because of painkillers or healing, I don't know.

As though she senses my looking at her, Ishtar stirs. Moments later, she opens her eyes, raises her arms, stretches, and glances over at me.

"You're awake," she says, halfway between a statement and a question.

"Just now," I reply. "How long have I been here?" I ask, conscious that I seem to be always asking someone this question.

She glances at the chronometer on the monitoring machine. "About twenty hours."

"And you've stayed all that time?"

"I popped out to debrief the others, but yeah, I've mostly been here. I feel it's my fault. I was supposed to be keeping you safe."

"You did keep me safe. I'm here, aren't I? And you couldn't have foreseen our pursuit."

She shrugs and gives a wry smile. "Anyway, looks like you'll live — again."

"Yes," I say, smiling back at her, "These hospital visits are becoming a tad too regular."

Her smile fades as she asks, "Who's Adala?"

My eyes widen in surprise. "What do you mean?"

"You were saying her name in your sleep."

My cheeks burn. I want knowledge of Adala and where she's from hidden, but I must respond to Ishtar. "Someone I know, that's all."

Ishtar creases her brow in disbelief. "She must be special from what you were saying."

"Why? What did I say?" My temperature skyrockets.

With a cheeky grin, Ishtar replies, "Something about your returning soon and being happy. Sounds like you're in love."

"Stop teasing me," I say, pretending to be grumpy.

She holds her hands up in surrender and laughs. "Hey, you're the one talking, not me."

The banter cheers me, even though it's at my expense. Ishtar is becoming a good friend as well as a valuable resistance leader. "When can I get out of here?"

"You'll have to ask the doctor that. But there's no hurry. You need to stay hidden for a while until Security stops looking for you."

The forced rest dampens my spirits. Then panic tightens my chest. "Where are the chips?"

"Stay calm. I placed them in the drawer there. No one threw them away."

"You didn't look at them, did you?"

"No. It's obvious they're for your personal viewing only."

After calming down, I say, "Thanks." I think for a moment. "You couldn't organize a viewer for me?"

Ishtar smiles. "I can try."

We sit in silence until Ishtar gets fidgety. And I could use a rest, my stamina fading.

"I have things to do," she says. "Looks like you'll live, so there's no point in my staying here."

"Thanks for being here when I woke."

Ishtar stands. "Just recuperate. We need you."

I nod in appreciation, even though I doubt they need me as much as she thinks.

"I'll see you again when I can. Might bring the others with me next time."

"I'd like that."

She leaves me to my own devices, and I soon fall asleep, waking up a few hours later. It is dark outside, and diffused light from the ceiling gives the room a dimmed, subdued tone. A meal sits on a portable table, ready for me to tear open and heat up. After finding the controls for the bed, I change it to a sitting position, pull the table over me, and place the pack into the heater. Within a minute, steam and the aroma of stewed lamb are wafting across to me. I remove the tray from the wrapping, devour the food, and wash it down with orange juice. A cup of coffee lies there, too, so I heat that and sip it. The taste is nothing to get excited about, but I finish drinking it without complaint.

21

TRUE IDENTITY

Several days go by before I'm allowed to rise and walk. I am going insane with nothing to do, and Ishtar still hasn't organized a viewer. Maybe the doctor won't permit it until I recover. They bring me a sweatshirt and jogger pants to wear instead of the hospital gown and, once I regain my balance, I change into them and go exploring.

The building is a countryside residence as before but somewhere different. It sits high in a mountain range, overlooking a valley with vast pastures in the flood plain of a river that threads its way through the middle. Cedars grow around the house, and warblers nest in one of them. A dove coos above me.

I look beyond the forests and see the last traces of snow lingering on the ground. I amble outside onto a small terrace, where the chill of the air hits me. I hug myself, tucking my exposed hands under my armpits for warmth. Despite the air's bite, I enjoy the freshness on my cheeks and laugh in sheer delight at being alive. The sights and sounds and smells bring back so many pleasant memories, especially from my childhood, and I ache for a simpler life. A bench seat stands next to a flower bed in the shade of a tree, the plants just sprouting as spring takes over from the winter ice. After strolling to the bench, I sit and study mother nature spread out before me. Once again, the setting and charm of the scenery remind me of the times Adala and I sat and talked in the enclosed garden at Helheim. How I miss her! My heart aches for the comfort of her smile and the thrill of her lips on mine. Yet, I sense I must resign myself to a significant wait before I see her again. I sigh, but the expression reflects both sadness and joy.

"There you are," Ishtar says as she comes toward me with Argandea in tow. "We've been searching everywhere for you."

I beam with delight at seeing them. "I doubt I'd get far if I wanted to leave."

They both come over and sit.

"It's good to meet you again," Argandea says.

"It's wonderful to see you, too. But this bliss overwhelms me," I say as I wave my hand at the view.

They chuckle.

"Enjoy it while you can," Ishtar says. "It won't be too long before you return to us and further work."

"You've caused a big stir in the capital," Argandea says. "They're calling you 'The Phantom'."

"Ha! I don't think I'll be here much longer. The wound is healing well, and these people prefer their solitude. Another week and I'll be fit to return and help you again."

We talk for an hour before they leave. I then retire inside for warmth and to find a viewing machine.

With the viewer tucked under my arm, I grab the chips from my bedside drawer and settle into a comfortable lounge chair in the sitting room.

Time flows by as I read of Alalgar, Alulim, and Dumuzid. These people's history and everything they did astounds me. I marvel at how people sourced Alulim's biography, though, since he stayed behind on Helheim when it moved to another dimension.

Next, I delve through the accounts of Eridu and Helheim. The latter I now know is the ancient planet Ur that featured in the stories and fables of my childhood. I wonder why they changed the name to Helheim. Perhaps they forgot their lost past when they left the galaxy.

The reason for their departure saddens me, as the data chip describes the people's greed and the destruction wreaked on the planet in minute detail. Flerovium, the blue crystal prevalent on Helheim/Ur, was the source of the fighting.

Last, I return to the chip titled *Recent Events,* my hands shaking as I insert it, recalling what I read last time. After rereading the extract, I marvel at the name Sargon Halwende. I know of no other person named Halwende but me, and I crashed on Helheim when it returned to our space dimensions. Was my being there a coincidence, or did my presence trigger a switch, my landing there predestined? The implications send a shiver down my spine. What puzzles me is that Puzur wasn't my father's name, but my parents mentioned a Puzur, telling me how important this person was and that I needed to research his history when I reached adulthood. Apart from that, the mere mention of his name resulted in whispered chastisement.

I continue scrolling through the list of Puzur's lineage, freezing when I see who he can trace his family back to — Dumuzid, my ancestor. It cannot be a coincidence. As I read, my understanding grows that this story and prophecy are about me. But my reuniting Helheim and the Rigel empire to its past glory is absurd. I am a failed nobody.

"Ah, so you are reading," Zabada says from the doorway.

I jump, in danger of falling from the lounge, looking around in panic before I sigh, recognizing the person. "Where did you come from? You nearly gave me a heart attack."

"I apologize." Zabada chuckles with amusement. "May I join you?"

"Of course. You might enlighten me. These words baffle me."

Zabada ambles into the room and sits in a chair opposite me. "And what are you reading?"

"A chip from the library called *Recent Events.*"

Nodding sagely, Zabada says, "Ah, the crux of the matter. What is it that confuses you?"

"This information infers that a Puzur, a descendant of Dumuzid, is my father and Sargon is my real name."

A hint of alarm clouds his face. He stands, walks to the door, and closes it, returning to drag his seat closer. He then sits, gazing at me. "Do not mention those names where people can overhear them," he whispers. "Those words could get you killed. It is true, your actual name is Sargon Halwende, but we withheld it when you were born so others couldn't find you and kill you, bringing the royal line to an end. And yes, your biological father was Puzur. We hid that knowledge, too. I fear the discovery of the library crypt will allow the emperor to discover his existence. Only the chip you hold reveals your identity. Keep it well hidden."

"But that's absurd. It says I'll reunite the kingdom under one rule. I'm a nobody."

Zabada stares into my eyes before answering. "Have you ever sensed that you have a higher purpose?"

I scoff at the suggestion and reply with bitterness. "A higher purpose? I was just a general, and the emperor destroyed my entire unit and killed my family. I ran like a coward. How can I expect the people to follow me now?"

Zabada nods but replies, "The season was not yet right. What you suffered was immense. No one can blame you for running. Times have changed. The groundswell of demand for change is growing, with the empire's citizens willing to follow a genuine leader and die for him if needs be. Your time is fast approaching. But only you can enter your heart; only you can decide the path of righteousness. And that requires patience and the dice possibly rolling again."

Zabada's words puzzle me. "What do you mean? You're almost prophesying. How do you perceive this?"

He gazes at me kindly. "I have eyes and ears."

After pondering his words, I shake my head. "I can't do this."

"What you achieved on Helheim is a foretaste of your potential."

My eyes widen in surprise. "How do you know about Helheim?"

He smiles and repeats. "I have eyes and ears."

"Then you know of Adala?"

Zabada nods.

"I cannot allow any danger coming to her. Never."

"This is true."

Thinking again, I say, "I need you if I do this."

"I will be here."

"How will I find you?"

"I will find you."

"I can't absorb this now. Give me time to consider it. But I'm coming to understand the overall perspective here, and it scares me."

"Good. It should scare you. But I must leave you to recuperate. Farewell until we meet again."

Zabada rises and leaves without looking back. I stare open-mouthed after him as he slowly fades from my sight.

22

RALLYING THE TROOPS

It takes a further two weeks before I am fit enough to leave my alpine haven and return to the others. Ishtar conveys me to a different site in her scooter, and we go into a subterranean basement below a factory owned by a sympathizer. Ninsar, Lugal, Argandea, and Yarla, who are talking together around a table, stop and glance toward us as we enter the room.

Argandea rises and strides over to me. "Good to see you well again."

"I'm pleased to be back." I shake Argandea's hand and follow him to the others. Both Ishtar and I sit.

"We were just discussing the state of affairs," Lugal says, bringing us up to speed on their conversation, "We think we could raid another arsenal. The fallout from the last raid has settled down now."

I nod but say nothing as they gaze at me, expecting my ... what? Approval? Judgment? Suggestion? As I turn away and stare at the bare basement wall, I meditate on who I am and know I must begin acting on my destiny. But I can't decide on our next step, and that frustrates me. As a counterbalance, I yearn to go back to Helheim and Adala. My heart sighs as I return to my friends. "An arsenal is a good start."

"But …" Argandea says.

"We need to consider our overall goal. While we just fight here on Eridu, we gain little when destroyers orbit above us, ready to blast their cannons on any position we hold."

The others glance at each other, uncertain.

"What do you suggest then?" Ishtar asks.

I look at the people around the table and see confusion but loyalty in their eyes. "To win this war and overthrow the emperor, we need command of our own fleet."

Amazement and chatter break out, and I wait for my words to sink in and the chatter to stop.

"But where would we get a navy?" Lugal asks as the spokesperson of the group.

A devilish smile crosses my face. "We steal one."

Astonished eyes stare at me across the table.

Ishtar laughs. "I don't know what your injuries have done to you, but I think you've gone mad."

"Only bold and seemingly crazy ideas can achieve our goals. Think. What have you achieved by fighting on the ground? You're barely maintaining a resistance movement. I dare say, for each recruit you gain, you lose someone, either by death or disillusion." Downcast eyes confront me, confirming I speak the truth. "Why should anyone follow an outlaw band that gives no prospect of changing their lives? They need to hope things will change. That requires us to take the battle into space. That is where the emperor's strength lies. I'm not saying we just go up there and sacrifice our lives. We start small and plan to grow our navy, so we have a fleet matching the emperor's."

Argandea shakes his head. "How?"

"I have a yacht in the outer system, a powerful vessel with a weapons system." I hold up my hand. "We use that and its shuttle to board one or two of the destroyers orbiting the planet. Then we take them to a secure hideout and plan our next move."

Lugal chuckles. "You make us sound like pirates."

"Maybe we are." I smile in response. "But we need experienced pilots who can steer these vessels and sailors to run them."

"We have naval personnel in our ranks." Ishtar peers at me. "We must review their records and assemble crews."

The others nod. They warm to the idea as it coalesces.

"Any ideas about where to hide them?" I ask.

Argandea rubs his chin. "We have a sympathizer on Larsa who owns mining operations in its asteroid belt. I can see if he's willing to harbor a couple of destroyers."

"We need somewhere out of the way. Few must know of it," Ninsar says, excitement putting a sparkle in her eyes.

"Could we steal a troop transporter or two?" Yarla asks. "Boarding a vessel would be much easier with them than a shuttle. We'd have space for fighters and crew on them."

"Where can we get them?" Lugal paces the room, thinking.

"There are regular transfers of personnel from the fleet to the planet. We must hijack them."

"Don't they have transponders on them? And how do we take them over without raising the alarm?"

"We'll need a tight plan," I say. "I agree with Yarla. The troop transporters are ideal. If we can confiscate any ferrying to the vessels we want, we could surprise the destroyers before they realize they're being attacked and boarded. Let's start working out the details."

ISHTAR and two ex-naval crew members go with me to my yacht. It's a tight fit in the small shuttle I arrived in, but we manage. The six-hour trip passes without incident, and we board my ship. I smile as the others stare, open-mouthed, astounded at the vessel's opulence.

"You sure you don't need a shipmate to help you?" Ishtar asks once she recovers from her stupor.

I chuckle. "This belongs to a queen, but she won't mind my using it in the meantime. Let's settle and find us two destroyers to capture."

I enter the helm to fire up the drives and steer the ship closer to Eridu. Approaching the planet makes me nervous, but it's the only way to detect the vessels. Ishtar directs me to one of Eridu's outer moons, still distant from Eridu and outside the orbital surveillance zone of the destroyers. Once up to speed, I cut the drives to decrease the risk of detection until I need them again to slow to a stable position above the moon.

"Don't they have any reconnaissance of the moons?" I ask.

"They patrol the inner ones but don't worry about the ones out this far," one of the naval crew tells me.

"Slack," I comment.

Once at the moon, I settle on the surface instead of in orbit, as it's small. I find a lava tube suitable for me to park the ship out of sight of any passing snooping ships. It still gives us a view of Eridu and the ships circling it. After switching to my passive sensors, I take a sweep of Eridu and soon complete a 3D holographic chart of the planet and the objects orbiting it, locating a dozen potential vessels. The ex-naval men gaze at the map with interest.

"Four destroyers are circling." The junior one straightens and turns to me. "The other ships are commercial and merchant vessels."

As I rub my chin, I glance at Ishtar. "Two too many." I turn back to the others. "Are there normally that many?"

They both shake their heads. "No," the senior one says. "They deploy two. It may be a rotation of duty, and two may leave soon. Although corvettes should be present, I don't detect any. I hope they aren't lurking in the shadows."

"If it's a ship rotation, then the crews of the arriving vessels will have transporters descending to the planet for personnel R&R," the other person says.

"Let's wait then and see what happens," I say.

After an hour, two destroyers pivot away from orbit and leave Eridu. Another two hours elapse before transporters exit the remaining ships headed for the planet's surface.

"OK, inform Argandea the transports are coming and prepare to start the plan," I tell Ishtar.

They prevent me from taking an active role in the campaign, despite my protests. They say I am too important to risk but leading from the front is in my nature. Frustrated, I pace the helm impatiently while the others go about their duties.

The plan's success depends on confiscating the transporters without raising the alarm — neither on the planet nor the destroyers. The transporters must dock simultaneously. Once the troop carriers berth, they have the equipment to block communication with the surface. Chatter erupts on our secure comm network from the two teams at the naval personnel transfer terminal, but the wait is agonizing.

Ishtar glances at me and grins.

"What?" I'm unsure of what she's thinking and resent what I presume she's thinking.

"Go get a coffee or something. You're making everyone nervous."

"I'm not used to waiting behind the action, relying on others."

"You should have more faith in those following you," Ishtar speaks her comment in jest, but I sense a hint of chastisement, too.

I should trust people more, but it's difficult since that trust has betrayed me in the past, with disastrous results. I know Ishtar, Argandea, and the rest of them are excellent leaders, and I *do* trust them, but it's a change that's tough for me to make. So, taking up Ishtar's suggestion, I go to the galley and, sitting at the bench table, prepare myself a coffee. Nerves are tying knots in my stomach. How many people have I sent to their deaths?

23

PIRACY

"It's started," Ishtar announces on the ship's comm.

My thoughts instantly return to the present after an indulgent period of mulling over my past misfortunes. Shaking off the self-pity, I jump from my seat in the galley and stride back to the helm, more nervous energy stored in me than I can consume. A cacophony of chatter blasts from the operations comm as Ishtar and the others lean over the unit to hear every word.

"What's happening?" I ask.

Lines of concentration etch Ishtar's forehead as she deciphers the noise. "They're overpowering the transporter terminal and moving in to secure the ships."

I nod and listen, pacing the helm in frustration. *This is infuriating!* Settled in the command chair, I close my eyes and wait, listening to the comm.

"Transporters secured and taking off," Argandea reports over the comm. My eyelids swing wide open, and adrenaline pumps through me.

Ishtar glances my way and smiles.

I bring up the navigation screen and watch the two ships rise from Eridu toward the destroyers. As I lick my lips, I pray everything proceeds smoothly, but I know it won't. The transporters request permission to board their respective ships and are both accepted. As soon as they land, their hatches open, and intense fighting breaks loose on the warships. Shooting and screams of pain broadcast from the comm with no update of progress on securing either helm.

Tense minutes elapse before Argandea announces, in between gasps, "Helm of Rigel Destroyer Utu secured."

"Well done!" I say to him over the comm. "One captured, one to go."

We wait for news of the other destroyer, but we only hear fighting. I don't like it. It's taking too long. "I'm going over there," I say as I rush to the shuttle bay.

"No," Ishtar yells behind me and then whispers, "Shit."

As I hurry to the craft, I hear running behind me. Ishtar draws up next to me. "You can't go there," she says between breaths.

"They need me," I say, rotating the lock to open the hatch.

"I'm coming too then."

We both climb in, and I close the hatch. Two minutes later, we're on our way over to the destroyer. After five minutes, our shuttle passes through the atmosphere's force field, and I settle the shuttle on the deck, turning off the drive and opening our hatch.

I bolt out with Ishtar behind me, our masers drawn. "Any news from Lugal yet?" I ask a resistance member in the transport dock.

"No."

The sound of shooting and death filters through from the corridors ahead, and I rush in that direction. Before long, we're in the middle of a standoff between the crew of the destroyer and Lugal's party. The defenders are tucked away behind bulkheads with an ideal view of the passageway. Every time someone tries to advance, a barrage of laser fire drives him back.

I move to a wall display and pull up the ship's corridor map. After a quick study, I trace a route to gain access behind the defenders. Not seeing Lugal anywhere, I step over to the person in charge. "I need two people. You keep them busy while I sneak up behind them."

He nods and picks out volunteers to follow me. I rush off with them and Ishtar in tow. We weave up to the next level and zigzag through corridors before descending to the operating floor again. From there, we rush toward the fighting and stop around the corner from the enemy. I get Ishtar and one raider to cover our backs as I and the other raider move forward. Since I have a line of sight, I pull my nerve stimulator from my pocket and blast them with that. They drop to the floor in seconds, and the fighting ceases.

The team leader takes control, directing his soldiers to restrain the prisoners and striding up to me. "Thank you, sir."

"Do you know where Lugal is?" I ask.

He shakes his head. "He headed to the helm, but I haven't received word from him."

"Thanks, I'll go look." I move in the helm's direction, but Ishtar and the others barge in front of me, and two cover my back.

"This time, you have protection," Ishtar instructs me. "I'm not having you injured again." She leads us to the helm with the sound of more fighting ahead as we approach.

Two entries service the helm, and our people cover both, but they cannot break through because of the fierce defense. I'm nervous, as it's taking too long. Soon Security on the planet will suspect something's amiss up here.

"Anyone got a flashbang?" I ask.

One looks through their kit and finds one, handing it to me. A hand seizes my arm, holding me back as I make to rush to the helm. "No, you don't," Ishtar says as I glance behind to the hand's owner. She grabs the flashbang and rushes forward.

My gut tightens as I see her risk her life instead of me. The incendiary armed, she dives and throws it through the doorway, a flash and blast issuing from inside moments later. We advance. After a few short bursts of gunfire, we secure the helm, and the battle is over.

Lugal comes in through the other door and stops dead in his tracks. "What are you doing here?"

"You needed help," I say.

"I couldn't stop him," Ishtar says, apologizing.

"Well, you're here now. Let's get moving." Lugal shouts an order, and his people rush forward to crew the helm and start procedures to steer the vessel out of orbit. "Destroyer Enzu secured," Lugal speaks over the comm.

"Prepare to leave orbit and enter hyperspace," Argandea replies.

"Roger," Lugal acknowledges.

"We'd better get back to your ship, Halwende," Ishtar tells me. "I doubt the crew we left there can fly it."

"Good point," I say. With my attention returning to Lugal, I say, "See you at the rendezvous."

"Will do."

Ishtar and I sprint back to our shuttle and return to my yacht.

On board, I rush to the helm and prepare for departure as I watch the destroyers rotate and leave the planet. Minutes later, fighters follow in pursuit.

"That doesn't look good," Ishtar says, standing behind me.

"The destroyers have more firepower than a squadron of fighters."

"But are there personnel on board to use it?"

Missiles stream out from the destroyers, searching for the fighters. Most hit their mark and destroy the ships, but several fighters avoid the projectiles and continue toward our warships. Drops of sweat dot my forehead as I urge the destroyers into hyperspace before the fighters can cause any damage. My knuckles whiten as I grip the armrests of my chair.

Laser fire shoots out from the fighters, but the beams deflect from the shields. I breathe out in relief that they could activate them. Moments later, missiles streak out from the fighters toward the Enzu. Defensive fire comes from the destroyer and stops every missile but one. The remaining projectile strikes the destroyer in the midsection. I groan as I watch in dread. *Jump!* Seconds later, our destroyers disappear as they enter hyperspace. Not realizing that I was holding my breath, I gasp, breathing again.

"Let's move," I say as I ramp up my drives and turn to leave.

On seeing another ship, the fighters veer off toward me, but I outrun them and enter hyperspace before they have time to fire at us.

I EXIT hyperspace with Ishtar and the others watching through the front window of the yacht. We enter normal space on the edge of the Larsa system six days later and rush toward the asteroid belt. Two hours later, I approach one particular asteroid that looks like a cracked-open fortune cookie and reduce my speed. A large cavity looms before us moments later, and I steer into the entrance. The stars disappear as we enter the cavern, but I dispel my fear of losing my view of space as I marvel at the two destroyers before me, the only dampener being a large hole in the hull of one of them.

"Let's go inspect the damage," I say as I lock the yacht's controls and jump from my seat, heading for the shuttle.

"I hope it's repairable," Ishtar muses as she runs behind me.

We land in the hanger of the Enzu, and I rush to the helm, where Lugal stands with Argandea, their faces beaming.

"We did it," Argandea says to me.

I nod in recognition and turn to Lugal. "How many did we lose?"

Lugal's smile dampens. "Ten and fifteen wounded."

"And the ship?"

"Significant damage to the cargo compartments, but nothing vital is lost. Nothing we can't fix."

I breathe easy. "Not as broken as I was expecting."

"I've arranged for resistance members to congregate on Larsa, and we'll pick them up from there to crew the two vessels."

"Have we vetted them?"

"Yes."

"Good." I look around and see that others in the helm have gravitated into groups, talking and comparing notes as they laugh and smile. I'm glad to see them enjoy our success today. "We did a good job. Let's celebrate tonight with something special. Inform me of the arrangements, and I'll meet you there." I turn and let them bask in their triumph, but I know we have struggles ahead before we can pose a real threat to the empire. I only hope I survive to see Adala again.

∼

As I enter Destroyer Utu's general assembly compartment at seven that evening for a celebratory dinner, laden bench tables stand before me. The chefs have arranged a buffet service along one wall. The room is abuzz with laughter and chatter as I walk toward Ishtar, Argandea, and Lugal. They have changed clothes, each impeccably dressed, as am I, attired in the Grand Chancellor's uniform of Helheim. Not that the others are aware of the clothing's significance. They hold champagne flutes, and a passing caterer shoves one into my hand.

"Welcome, Halwende," Argandea says as the others turn to face me.

"Cheers," I say, raising my glass.

"Cheers," they repeat, and we sip.

After a while, the caterers inform us the meal is ready, and we file past the buffet, grabbing what we want and sit. Argandea has arranged a separate table for himself, Lugal, Ishtar, and me. I would have preferred to mix but leave it at that. Maybe it's proper for there to be a separation between the leadership and the rank and file. The food is sumptuous, and I go back for seconds in between drinking wine. As the celebrations end and people drift to their beds, I, too, have thoughts of leaving and returning to my yacht. I say farewell to the others, but Ishtar follows me, and we stroll together toward my waiting shuttle, discussing nothing in particular.

Just before I turn to board, Ishtar grabs my arm and looks into my eyes. "We can christen the yacht?"

Sorrow grips me as I understand her intent. "I have someone else. Under different circumstances, I might agree, but let's leave things as they are. We work well together. I don't want that to change."

Ishtar turns bright red and rushes away, leaving me feeling miserable at causing her embarrassment. I continue to the shuttle and my yacht for the night.

24

LET'S DO IT AGAIN

Over the following days, people busy themselves repairing the damage to the Enzu. Argandea, Lugal, and Ishtar arrange transport for more crew to board both ships.

Ishtar has been avoiding me, so I decide to confront her and mend the rift between us before it becomes irreparable. Even the others notice an abyss developing. I corner her in a conference room, where she is reviewing personnel files.

She looks up as I enter, but her gaze darts to the tablet again as I come forward and sit opposite her. A wall of silence separates us as I wait for her to finish what she's doing, but I know she wants me to leave, so I break the impasse. "Did our misunderstanding embarrass you?"

"Why should it?" Her voice is gruff, but her eyes betray her discomfort as she peers at me.

"So, you're not embarrassed?"

She looks away, biting her bottom lip to prevent her mouth from jerking in a lament. Tears threaten to flow as she returns my gaze. "I shouldn't have made a pass at you."

"Why not?"

"You're my commanding officer, and it could compromise our operations as we move forward."

"I'm not your commanding officer," I say as I search deep into her eyes. "But, yes, it might affect the future. That's irrelevant, though. As I mentioned, I have another." I shrug. "Who knows? If I wasn't already in a relationship, we might have one to explore. Still, you're too valuable to me, and to this cause, for a rift to develop between us. Please, let's forget it happened and carry on from there."

Ishtar stares at me for seconds before giving a tremendous sigh and shaking her head. "I think the wine got to me, and I wasn't thinking straight."

I shrug again. "Hey, no harm in trying."

She laughs at my comment and shakes her head. "Yeah, no harm in trying," she whispers as she prepares to return to her work.

As I reach over, I place my hand under her chin, getting her to gaze back at me. "I may not be your commanding officer, but people turn to me for direction. I need talented leaders to support me, and I consider you one of the best."

Ishtar's cheeks tinge pinkish-red as she replies, "Thanks. I won't disappoint you ... ever."

"I'll let you continue your work." My quest accomplished, I rise and leave the room, satisfied we have repaired our friendship.

WEEKS PASS as the ships fill with personnel and supplies. We're now ready to plan our next mission. In the interim, I've been pondering what it might be. Yarla and Ninsar have joined us, and they sit opposite me in a conference room on the Utu, together with Lugal, Argandea, and Ishtar. The mood amongst the leadership has changed. Before, they operated as individual units, and their demeanor was desperate. I now sense hope and purpose. My only concern is that their deference to my authority has caused this change, which I find daunting.

Argandea calls the meeting to order. Even though they glance at me, he undertakes the role of the senior member of the group. "We're now a pimple on the empire's nose after confiscating these two destroyers. Now that we've made them notice us, we need to do more to increase our strength."

"Yeah, let's do it again." Yarla leans forward with an excited smile. "There are destroyers orbiting Larsa."

Ishtar shakes her head. "They won't fall for the same trick twice. I can assure you they've strengthened their security at their personnel transfer stations."

"Well, what then?" Yarla's mood darkens.

"That's why we're here." Argandea glares authoritatively at them.

"So, who has an idea, then?" Ninsar asks.

They glance at one another, no one able to offer any suggestions. It perturbs me that, with the collective brainpower they possess, none is considering our final goal. It's as if annoying the empire with raids and piracy is their new purpose. The room stays silent for a while longer before they turn their attention to me.

"You've said nothing yet," Ishtar comments.

A stylus lies on the table in front of me. I pick it up, flipping it between my fingers as I ponder. After considering my words carefully, I make eye contact with them. "I had a joyride back to Eridu last week. Not the planet, but Isin." Isin is the Eridu system's outer gas giant.

Their eyes bulge. "But the shipyards are there," Ninsar says.

"Correct," I say. "There's a fighter carrier and a battle cruiser being prepared for handover to the fleet as we speak. They'd be nice to have."

The room erupts into a chorus of confused chatter. As it dies, Lugal says, "That's impossible. We can't achieve such an undertaking."

I stare hard at him and then at the others. "We must, and we will. With that firepower, we stand a chance of damaging the emperor."

"You're crazy," Ishtar says as she smiles, "crazy enough to pull off such a stunt."

"There is one thing I've learned while I was away. You only hit where you aim. If you choose small goals, you gain modest outcomes. But you will achieve monumental results with objectives that target our fundamental purpose — the overthrow of the emperor and the removal of oppression from the empire. Confiscating these two ships gives us a stepping-stone along that path."

"You're still crazy," Ishar says.

I shrug and ask, "Who wants to try?" I survey the team as they turn and gauge each other's responses before answering.

After a time, Argandea replies. "If we develop a workable plan, I'm for it."

I break into a smile.

25

ATTACKING THE SHIPYARD

Through back channels, Argandea has located disenchanted naval officers at the shipyards willing to help us steal the two vessels. The arrangement doesn't impress everyone. They fear the exposure is a tremendous risk to the organization, but we decide to accept their aid. With the damaged destroyer repaired and their transponders deactivated, we position them near the yards in readiness for the attack.

Another decision the leaders reluctantly agree with is my direct participation in the action this time. Against their better judgment, they give way and include me in the plan, which is fortunate since it requires a person with the audacity and knowledge to impersonate an admiral.

My yacht can house a small troop transporter in its storage bay, so I fly out with Ishtar and a contingent of twenty fighters dressed as naval personnel. We emerge from hyperspace and communicate with the shipyards.

"Permission requested for Admiral Heinrich to dock with Eridu shipyard," Ishtar says.

"We have no notice of an admiral's visit," the comm officer at the shipyard says.

"I have no control over your incompetence. The admiral will note this inefficiency and raise it with the advisory council if you impede his inspection."

Worry lines appear on the officer's face. "I'm only doing my job. I'll speak to my superior. Please wait." The screen goes blank.

Ishtar, in naval uniform, glances over to me, out of the officer's view, and smiles.

Five minutes later, the comm officer comes back. "My superiors inform me that I may grant the admiral permission to dock for his inspection."

"About time," Ishtar says. "We were preparing to leave and complain. RN (Rigel Navy) Rosalind out." Ishtar breaks communication.

I laugh. "Really? *We were going to leave*?"

Ishtar shrugs. "Let them think you're annoyed. They might let other matters slip."

It's time for me to dress for my part.

~

AN HOUR LATER, we dock at the shipyards in the troop transporter we've fitted out for a four-star admiral. Ishtar and the others stand fidgeting behind me as the hatch opens.

"Here goes," I say as I shrug myself into shape for the role of an arrogant admiral.

An honor guard of twenty spacers in full parade uniform awaits me as I stride across the connection tube and onto the shipyard deck, ignoring them.

"Attention," the petty officer shouts to the recruits, who obey in unison.

At the end of the line, a man dressed in a captain's uniform salutes as I pass. "Captain Eshme at your service."

I stop and salute, looking bored, and glance back at Ishtar, who stands behind me. The others in my company march out and place a protective detail around me.

"Captain Eshme," Ishtar says. "Your personal attendance pleases the admiral." We know who is present at the shipyard through our informants.

"It is my pleasure," Eshme says.

"At ease, captain," I order as I walk off to inspect my surroundings with my guards surrounding me.

Ishtar follows me. Eshme, hesitating over what to do, panics and rushes to catch up to her.

"If I may inquire, we wish to know where your admiral comes from," Eshme says. "There is no mention of him in the personnel database."

Ishtar halts and drills her eyes into his. I stop, too, and turn to see drops of sweat appear on the captain's face. "It is a new appointment," Ishtar says. "The navy hasn't caught up with the paperwork yet — typical."

"Noted," Eshme replies.

"Well," I say impatiently. "Are we inspecting these damn ships or not?"

Eshme gulps. "This way, sir."

We walk to a waiting personnel scooter, large enough for six. I climb on, along with Ishtar, Eshme, and the driver. Two of my detail follow. The others board a troop transport scooter.

"What is the population of the shipyards?" I enquire.

"There are over three thousand at present, sir," Eshme replies.

"I meant the exact number, not an estimate."

"I do not have the exact number on me, sir."

With a huff of disapproval, I cause Eshme to frown with worry. Ishtar bites her lip when I glance at her, struggling to contain herself.

We stop at the connection tube for the fighter carrier and disembark.

"This way, sir," Eshme says as he leads the way into the vessel.

We board and walk to the fighter deck. A full contingent of fighters is stored there, which I find negligent. Why have a fully equipped ship ready to be stolen in the shipyard? After inspecting the helm, I say I've seen enough, and we continue to the battle cruiser. I prefer this vessel. The fighter carrier is a much larger ship, but this one is lethal with its armaments and missiles. After an hour, we end the inspection at the helm of the battle cruiser.

I glance at the operating stations and sit in the captain's chair. "Let's take them for a spin."

"What, sir?" Eshme asks.

"You heard me," I say as I glare at him. "I wish to observe their performance."

"Sir, we don't have the personnel on board for that at present."

"They can't be that hard to fly. I reckon even I could do it. In fact, that's what I intend doing," I say as I bring my maser up and point it at Eshme.

Eyes popping, Eshme gulps and raises his hands. My guards secure the helm and rush to capture the rest of the ship. "You'll never get away with this," Eshme mutters.

"Oh, we will. What you didn't notice is a contingent of my body-guard staying behind at the fighter carrier. They now occupy that vessel."

"You can't fly a fighter carrier with a handful of people."

"You're right. That's why we have transporters coming over to help them."

On cue, rebels file into the helm, taking positions in the respective seats to power up the ship and leave the shipyards. They smile at me as they pass by.

"Now, I need you to contact traffic control and get approval to leave. Tell them we're test-flying the ships. If you do that, you will live."

"They'll never allow it," Eshme says. "It takes a higher authority than me to gain that level of permission."

"You'd better think of something fast then, for your sake." I watch beads of sweat appear on Eshme's forehead. The stress is palpable as he licks his lips while he thinks.

"OK, I'll try it." He sits in the copilot's chair and opens a comm channel.

"Traffic Control here," a person answers.

"Traffic Control, Captain Eshme here. I need taxi routes for Battle Cruiser Nergal and Fighter Carrier Dagan for another trial."

The controller looks at Eshme, surprised. "We don't have any test runs scheduled for today. What is the authorization for this?"

"Admiral Heinrich has requested us prove the two ships' performances."

"One moment, please." The controller leaves his seat, and we wait for his return.

Another person comes to the screen moments later. "This is Superintendent Pardok. I have no information on any Admiral Heinrich. I refuse permission for tests, and I see you are powering up both vessels. Power off at once, or I shall inform Security to lock the ships in port."

I knew we'd have to fight but had hoped the bluff would outlast escaping the yards.

"The admiral looks disappointed. I hope you have authorization for your refusal of the admiral," Eshme replies.

"Let me handle this so-called admiral." The link closes.

Eshme stares at me, knowing he has failed, but I can't shoot him for trying. "Take him to the brig," I order the two people guarding him. On opening a secure channel, I ask Ishtar, "Are our personnel aboard the vessel?"

"Yes," she replies.

"Secure the hatch." To the person at the weapons systems terminal, I say, "Power-up weapons and put the ship under general alert." Moments later, an alarm resounds throughout the ship, and lights redden to accord with the high alert level. After switching to another channel, I ask, "Argandea, you ready for departure?"

"The last personnel are coming on board now through the fighter bay doors. We've secured the hatch," Argandea replies.

"You need to prepare for fireworks. There'll be resistance to our withdrawal."

"In progress."

"Good. See you at the rendezvous."

"Confirmed."

As I recline in my seat and chew my cheek, thoughts of all the possible avenues of failure flash through my head.

"Sir, two destroyers have emerged into view from the shipyard's rear side."

"Any signs of other attack ships in the vicinity?"

"No."

I want to keep my destroyers in reserve and consider our probable strength in defending ourselves from the enemy. After making my decision, I comm Lugal and Ninsar.

"What's happening?" Lugal asks.

"We have company, so things'll get rough soon. Power up to standby status and wait for my word."

"Will do," both say.

"Let's leave," I tell the pilot. The effects of motion reverberate through the ship moments later, with the starfield changing as we rush away from the shipyards.

"We have a comm from a destroyer," the communication person tells me.

"Ignore him," I say. "Full speed ahead. Shield status?"

"Shields on maximum strength."

Seconds later, we rock as a maser blast hits the ship.

"Weapons, open fire on those two destroyers."

Masers shoot from us moments later, striking each destroyer, but with their shields raised, the damage is minor. Never mind. They know we mean business now.

"Missiles fired," Navigation alerts me.

Now we'll see whether the money was worth it. We can't avoid the missiles and don't have other ships to help destroy them. I watch on my screen as five projectiles streak toward us. Our ship defense fires masers at them, but one makes it through our defenses, detonating on our shields as it strikes. The vessel rocks in response. "Damage?" I ask.

"Nothing major. Port shield at 65%."

"Impressive blast." We can't allow another missile to penetrate our defenses, and a similar strike on the fighter carrier might cripple it. I make my decision as another barrage of missiles ejects from the destroyers. I open the comm channel again and say, "Lugal, Ninsar, take out those destroyers."

"Consider it done," Ninsar says, and they both end communications.

I check how the carrier is doing and notice it powering from the dock, heading away from the enemy destroyers. One destroyer diverts its attention from chasing me to take on the carrier. I curse as it closes in on the ship, hoping Argandea has enough firepower to avoid serious damage.

To my surprise, a dozen fighters stream from the carrier headed toward the destroyer and start peppering it with maser fire as it nears them. As they make a pass on the destroyer, they target one location on it and release their missiles, which explode moments later. The size of the blast destroys the shield in that section, the destruction penetrating the hull but not deterring the destroyer from its pursuit.

Meanwhile, another shudder reverberates through our ship, and damage-control sirens blare. "Damage report!" I shout over the commotion.

"Hull breach into the accommodation compartment."

"How long till we can jump into hyperspace?"

"Ten minutes," the pilot replies.

"We may not have that long. Full power to the drives." I contact Argandea. "How long before you can jump?"

Argandea looks to his left as he asks the question. "Twenty minutes."

Nodding, I say, "Hope I can stick around for you."

As I sign off, a gigantic explosion comes from the damaged pursuing destroyer after the Utu fires a barrage of missiles at it, breaking it in half before it disintegrates to nothing as its reactor blows. The shockwave blasts past us, causing convulsive shudders throughout our ship. Our pilot turns our vessel to shelter our damaged side away from direct attack, providing us with the protection of the starboard shields.

With its sister vessel destroyed, the one remaining attacker calls off its pursuit and pulls away from us. I instruct the others to stand down unless we're attacked further, and we power from the shipyards.

Argandea comms through to me. "Ready to jump, Halwende."

"Good, jump at your pleasure. I'll join you soon." Two minutes later, the fighter carrier disappears from normal space. "Prepare to jump," I tell our ship. Then I contact our destroyers and instruct them to do the same.

"Ready to jump," the pilot tells me.

"Jump!"

26

HOPE

After depositing the fighter carrier and battle cruiser in a safe location, we all meet back at our secret base in the asteroid belt of the Larsa system. On entering, I hear shouts and cheers as the resistance celebrates our audacious capture of the two military ships. I step into our main conference room to a standing ovation of the resistance leaders. Unable to stop the huge grin spreading across my face, I accept the accolades and slaps on the back before sitting at the head of the table and pouring myself a glass of water.

After a sip, I say, "Thanks, but the operation's success was because of the combined efforts of all of you."

"You should have seen the expression on Captain Eshme's face when you said," Ishtar continues by imitating me, "*Let's take them for a spin.*"

The others burst into laughter.

I let them have their fun for a while longer. Once the celebrations abate, I ask, "How many did we lose?"

Sobering, Argandea replies, "Fifty, mainly because of the damage to your ship. I lost three fighters."

"We shouldn't have lost any, but they were light losses considering. Well, let's celebrate tonight and think about our future tomorrow." With that, I rise and walk out, leaving them to their revelry.

Other thoughts sit prominently in my mind as I stride to my shuttle and head for the *Queen Rosalind*. Homesickness for Adala suddenly engulfs me again, and I grab the tablet from my cabin, powering it up and bringing up a hologram of her. I sigh as I stroke her face in the image. How I wish I could stroke it in the flesh and kiss her full lips again, the memory giving me pleasure.

I go to my personal galley and pour a large whisky, sitting on the lounge in my quarters as I continue gazing at Adala. After taking a sip, I down the rest in one gulp and get another. The fire of the liquid instantly sets me alight, and I realize I haven't had a full-on drinking session since Sentinel and I went on a binge together back in Helheim. I chuckle as I recall our misplaced words about my getting a spanking from the queen. The chuckle morphs to yearning for her again. Despite knowing I will regret it in the morning, I continue drinking until I stagger to my bed and flop on it, asleep before my head hits the pillow.

OVER THE NEXT FEW WEEKS, we all busy ourselves repairing the damage from the fighting and training up the first batch of new fighter pilots.

I stride into the conference room after Yarla's return from Eridu. He had traveled there to speak with the other resistance leaders on the planet and check the general atmosphere. All the leaders are sitting and talking amongst themselves while waiting for me. They fall silent when I arrive.

"Don't let me stop you," I say.

"We were just killing time," Argandea says.

"Let's get started then, Yarla. What do you have to report about Eridu?"

With eyes brimming with enthusiasm, Yarla says, "I couldn't believe I was on the same planet we left. Everywhere I went, people were talking about the hijacking of the two ships from the shipyards and what it might mean. There's new hope in the air as if they sense imminent release from the chains of tyranny. Even the stock markets have a sense of optimism."

"What about the security?" I ask.

Yarla's enthusiasm is tempered with concern. "It's tightened significantly in the capital. They're rounding up more people than ever for questioning, some never to be seen again. The emperor is livid about what's happened. He's executed the shipyard managers, including Captain Eshme, I'm afraid, although Eshme should have seen it coming and disappeared. He's executed several admirals too. I think he just wanted some entertainment with them. I can't see what they had done to deserve it. But that's our emperor." Yarla gazes at me. "Your hologram is all over the empire, ordering your arrest. The reward has increased tenfold."

Ishtar whistles. "I might turn you in myself for that amount of money."

"Don't kid yourself," Argandea says. "You'd never see the money."

"I'd be lucky if that was all I lost," Ishtar replied, causing the others to chuckle.

"Anything else?" I ask.

"Support for the resistance is growing. That's the reason for the increased security, but it isn't dampening the enthusiasm for change. It's growing."

As I sit back, I rub my chin in thought. "We aren't ready yet. We're still too weak to consider a full attack on the military."

Eyes bulge all around. "We could never overpower the military," Lugal says. "I was thinking more like a covert operation to capture the emperor."

Shaking my head, I say, "We could never do that. He has too much security around him. We couldn't even bombard his palace to assassinate him. It's too heavily shielded."

"But he never leaves the palace," Ishtar responds. "That's how trusting he is of his *loyal* subjects."

"So, what do you suggest?" Argandea asks as he eyes me.

"I really don't know yet. That's why I've stayed on my ship so much. I've been brainstorming ideas, but each one is fatally flawed, and failure is not an option this time."

"Well, we'll need to think of something soon before we lose the momentum we've gained," Ninsar says.

"One other thing," Yarla says as he looks back at me. "Tirigan has suggested that you come and provide some moral support for the remaining leaders on Eridu."

"No!" Ishtar shouts.

I hold up my hand at her as I consider the suggestion. "Who's Tirigan?"

"He's one of the minor cell leaders. You can't have met him yet."

"That may be a good idea."

"I don't like it," Ishtar says. "I'm going with you if you go. You're now too valuable to go on your own."

27

BETRAYAL

My shuttle descends toward Eridu, coming to rest at the resistance's secret landing site. Once we land, Ishtar opens the hatch and rushes to a scooter. By the time I shut down the spacecraft and lock it, she has the scooter ready and is impatient for us to leave.

"You're in a hurry," I remark.

"You know I'm not comfortable with this. Let's do this and leave before the emperor's spies discover you're here."

"Relax." I give her a pat on the shoulder. "I'll be careful. Nothing will go wrong."

"Famous last words."

After a chuckle, I glance at Ishtar and see she doesn't find the circumstances funny, so I shrug. "Let's get on with it then."

Ishtar raises the scooter and speeds through the tunnel and out the other end, racing across Eridu's countryside toward the city and Tirigan's location. Given the fine balmy weather, she retracts the scooter's roof and the wind whips at our hair. Three moons shine overhead, and the resinous scent of pine from the woodlands just below us wafts upwards. It reminds me of my youth when I explored the woods and climbed the trees to figure how high I could reach before the branch threatened to break and send me tumbling to the ground, and probably to a broken neck. The fleeting reminiscence departs, and my concentration returns to the present.

The downtown lights come into view on the horizon, my heart pumping faster. I fear we're entering the lion's den, but I'll never betray my feelings to Ishtar. Another ten minutes and we breach the outskirts. Ishtar veers to the right, and we enter a part of the city given over to industrial buildings, cannon-blast damage peppering them. We slow and five minutes later approach a decrepit warehouse cloaked in darkness.

"Tirigan's headquarters," Ishtar advises.

I nod. "Doesn't look like anyone's home."

"It's only for appearances."

The scooter descends and touches the ground beside the three-story building. We disembark and stride to a side entrance where Ishtar places her palm on a detection pad. Nothing happens for a few moments, and then the noise of the door unlocking prompts Ishtar to push it open. After we enter, she swings the door closed with a clang, and the locking mechanism engages again.

"No welcoming committee?" I ask, raising my eyebrows.

"Don't worry, we're being watched."

As if pulled by a puppeteer, I glance up, searching for cameras. But they have camouflaged them well.

Ishtar leads me along a corridor and then down steps. We pass through two more doors and enter a basement full of personnel sitting in front of screens. They are monitoring the building and exterior. A small office occupies the far corner. A wiry man with a hawkish nose emerges, walking over to greet us.

"Ishtar," the guy says. "Good to see you again. And this must be Halwende. I'm Tirigan." He extends his hand to me.

"That's correct," I say as I shake his hand and scan the room. "I see you're serious about security."

Tirigan chuckles. "You can never be too careful."

"Which is why I disagree with this visit," Ishtar interjects.

A quizzical expression crosses Tirigan's face. "You doubting my ability to keep your new champion safe?"

"Of course not," Ishtar replies defensively. "It's just that Shulgi has eyes and ears everywhere with what's happened ... and he's not my champion."

With a frown, Tirigan says, "Yes, you've made operations here much more troublesome since your shipyard antics."

"You disapprove?" I ask.

"No, not at all — it's just our movements are more difficult at present. Enough of this. Come with me, and I will get you some refreshments." Tirigan turns and strides to a door next to his office and opens it, ushering us through ahead of him into a general mess hall with tables and couches for relaxation. "Sit," he says as he gestures to seats nearby while he veers to a cabinet in the far corner, from which he collects a bottle of whisky and three glasses. He pours shots and hands Ishtar and me ours. "To removing the emperor," he toasts.

"To removing the emperor," Ishtar and I repeat.

As he glances at me, Tirigan says, "I've organized for you to speak to my people tomorrow morning. You can rest here tonight. I'll give you a tour before you return to your headquarters. That sound good to you?"

"Sure. I'd like to assess their sentiment myself. What do you think?" I glance at Ishtar.

Ishtar frowns. "You know my thoughts. The longer we stay here, the riskier it is. But I won't change your mind, so we'll go with that."

Tirigan finishes the rest of his drink in one gulp and stands. "Bunks are in there. I'll see you both tomorrow." He strides out the door, leaving us to our own resources.

With Tirigan out of the way, I gaze at Ishtar. "I never took you for a worrier."

"I'm not. Just ultra-cautious. You remember how I was when you first came."

I nod.

"We now have a charismatic leader to lead us. I don't want that hope jeopardized."

As I stare at her, I weigh my words, flipping the coin on whether I can trust her. "There's more at stake than taking control of the planet."

Ishtar frowns. "What do you mean by that?"

"You'll find out in due course. I'm off to bed." My back cracks as I rise, and I stretch it further before venturing off to explore the sleeping arrangements and get a good night's sleep.

SOMEONE IS SHAKING ME AWAKE. As I open my eyes, Ishtar's face confronts me.

"What?"

"Time to get busy."

I glance at my watch, surprised to see it's already nine-thirty. "I must have been more tired than I realized." With no further talk, I rise, rub the sleep away, stretch, and get ready to meet the day. When I enter the mess room, the aroma of scrambled eggs and fresh coffee makes my mouth water.

"Eat fast," Tirigan advises as he enters. "We leave in fifteen." He strolls over, grabs a coffee, and sits with us at the table.

He doesn't need to coerce me to eat as I shovel the food down to satisfy my grumbling stomach. After pushing the empty plate away, I sit back, sipping my coffee as I let the meal settle. Ishtar does the same.

The door opens, and one of Tirigan's underlings pokes his head inside the mess. "We're ready, sir."

Tirigan downs the rest of his coffee and stands. "Shall we go then?"

I do the same. "Let's."

Tirigan strides through the entrance and leads us to a covered scooter. We take off flying to another section of the city. Ishtar is on alert, her attention shooting from side to side as she surveys our path for trouble.

After forty minutes, we approach a vast warehouse, and Tirigan slows the scooter. He talks into his comm as we get closer, and a concealed door opens just before we reach it. We dart through, and he lands the scooter. "Follow me," he says as he jumps out and over to an elevator. Moments later, we are descending in silence.

The elevator doors open to a large room filled with people; the noise of their chatter reverberates like a soundbox. We step in, and the doors close behind us. I feel trapped and glance behind with trepidation. I see Ishtar has the same concerns. But deciding my concern is baseless, I smile at Tirigan. "Lead the way."

Tirigan steps into the crowd, which parts to let us pass. We aim for a podium at the rear and climb the steps to the stage. As I scan the room, I confirm three other exits, two possessing double doors.

A microphone stands in position on the dais, and Tirigan approaches it. "Hush, please," he shouts into it, bringing the crowd to instant silence, their attention drawn to us. "We have special visitors today. Ishtar, whom you already know, and someone I'm sure you are eager to meet — the person whose name is on everyone's lips: Halwende!" A murmur goes through the mass. "I felt it proper to invite him here to give us a talk on what we can expect in the future. So, I'll hand the speaking over to him. Halwende." He steps away, gesturing for me to approach.

I take the three strides I need to bring myself to the microphone. "Fellow rebels, a long and sorrowful path has brought us here today. Many families and friends have died or just disappeared. I'm sure each one of you has a story of grief to share. But I haven't come here to mourn past events. I have come to give you hope for the future. Delivery is in sight, friends. I will strive to lead you to it, to remove the shackles of our current tyranny, to show you a world where freedom will allow us to live our lives in peace without fear of arrest for our beliefs or our disagreements with our leaders."

As I talk, I glance at the elevator and notice the light above it is flashing. I frown, taking a moment to steal a glance at Ishtar. "I promise to lead you to this dream with my last breath if I must. Will you follow the path I tread?" I finish, and a great shout comes from the crowd.

The doors to the elevator open and imperial security forces stream into the room. The other doors open, too, with more troops trapping us. Panic grips everyone as they rush to escape but have nowhere to go. A few fall and are trampled.

The soldiers club the occupants and head toward Tirigan, Ishtar, and me.

"Quick!" Tirigan shouts as he grabs Ishtar's arm, pulling her off the dais and into the crowd.

I stand frozen for a moment as I watch Ishtar retreat from me, her eyes frantic and one hand reaching out for me, before my brain clicks and I am running in the same direction. I have no weapon with which to protect myself and feel naked. No one else is armed either, but, to my amazement, the imperial soldiers appear interested only in me and restrain from using their weapons.

Rough hands grab me as I reach the edge of the stage. I struggle to evade them but in vain. My eyes latch onto Ishtar's as she recedes further away, pulled along by Tirigan. She shouts my name in despair. Knowing I cannot escape the clutches of the guards, I stare once more at Tirigan. He smiles as he disappears through a concealed door with Ishtar, and as I fall into unconsciousness from a blow to the head, I know Tirigan has betrayed me.

28

CAPTURED

Darkness surrounds me as I regain consciousness, a thumping headache searing through my skull. Is it nighttime, or is the gloom deliberate? Silence fills the air, too. As clarity returns to my mind, I replay the events leading up to my capture. The whole exercise was an elaborate trap by Tirigan, and I fell right into it. Is he the only traitor in the group, or were they all in on it? I'll never know unless I escape from wherever I am. There's no point in dwelling on it, as that won't help me now. And since nothing's happening, I may as well rest while I can.

When I move to find a more comfortable position, I realize I am shackled at the wrists and ankles and am lying on a hard, chilly surface. I can't tell whether I'm on the floor or on a ledge, with a deadly drop next to me. Having been on my side, I change to lying on my back. It surprises me I haven't received a beating yet. They may deliver it later. Ishtar's despair flashes through my mind. She was always against my risking myself, and she was right, although she couldn't have suspected one of their own.

Adala's enchanting face recedes from me even further. How I wish I were with her, holding her in my arms or watching her sail her yacht on Lake Brandensee, her hair flying in the wind. I may never see her again now. But I must find a way. She will be in immense danger once the empire realizes her existence and her lineage.

Time is meaningless as I lie on the cold, hard surface in darkness. It could be seconds or hours since I woke, and I sense that the solitude is part of the torture they intend for me. There is nothing I can do but wait for them to collect me and make their intentions known.

As if on cue, an immense light fills the room, blinding me as I shield my eyes from the glare with my forearm until they adjust to the intensity. I now see I am lying on a concrete floor in a bare cell three meters by two meters — they're sparing no expense in accommodation. The sound of a motor starts, and one side rises to the ceiling, revealing a force-field barrier preventing my escape. I sit and shuffle backward, leaning against the wall, away from the force field, waiting.

The wait is short. A door opens opposite me, and a tall, stocky man walks through, about sixty years old with thinning gray hair and wearing a military uniform. General Barak. He glares at me. "We meet again at last, Halwende."

My muscles tense with anger and I spit out, "Traitor. Murderer."

"Contraire. It is you who is the traitor ... and a coward, I might add," Barak says with an unpleasant smile.

My jaw aches as I bite hard, gritting my teeth and throwing darts at him with my eyes.

"You've been a very slippery fish to find. Now that I've cornered you, we'll have a chat. But not here. It's too confined, don't you think? I'm sure we can find a more accommodating room for our discussion."

"I'll kill you for what you did to Genevieve and Charlotte."

"Oh, I doubt that. Don't believe I enjoyed that subterfuge. I didn't, but it had to be done. Let us save our reminisces for later, shall we?" He turns and leaves me alone again.

Two guards enter five minutes later. One lowers the force field while the other keeps a maser trained at my chest. They behave with cool disinterest as if it's just a job, but I know they'd shoot me without hesitation if I tried to escape.

"On your feet and come out," one orders gruffly.

My shackles, magnetically coupled, allow independent movement of my limbs up to a point, after which I can't separate them further. I can only shuffle my feet as I move to obey. The shackles also prevent me from standing straight, causing me to hunch over as if in obeisance. As I shuffle slowly toward the guards, the one without the maser raises a truncheon and smashes it into my ribs, which seems counterproductive if walking is what he wants me to do. Clearly, these guards are selected more for their sadism than their intelligence. Stars come to my eyes as the pain radiates through me, and I keel over, gasping for breath and wrenching my stomach contents onto the floor.

"Uh, shit," the maser holder says to the other guard, "why'd you do that for? We'll have to clean it up." He turns to me and says, "Now move!"

Truncheon Guard prods me with it, offering his own motivation for obedience. I shuffle toward the door, still recovering, and continue along the corridor, moving with the prodding, as if I'm a horse obeying a mouth bit. We reach an elevator, which opens to the guard's handprint. Inside, the elevator descends and stops moments later, the doors opening again. Again, Truncheon Guard prods me to move.

After five more minutes of shuffling, we enter a pristine-clean room that in the center has just one item of furniture: a padded dental chair. The guards push me to it. They tell me to sit and strap me into it. My blood freezes since I know the chair's exact purpose. Once secured, Truncheon Guard smashes it onto my forearm, eliciting a scream of pain from me, as he follows the first stroke with a hard smash to a kneecap of equal strength.

"Stop that!" the other guard says. "You know they don't want him damaged."

Truncheon Guard shrugs. "Traitors deserve punishment."

"Let those who can afford to punish them do it. I want to go home to my family in one piece."

"Let's get out of here, then. We've done what they asked."

The guards leave me alone, waiting for what comes next, the anticipation of pain and torture playing with my sanity.

After what feels like hours, they return.

"What'd they want us to bring him here for, if they do nothing?" Truncheon Guard asks the other guard.

"How should I know? It's not our business. Just do what we're ordered and keep out of trouble, will you?"

"Yeah, yeah."

They approach me, and Truncheon Guard can't resist shoving the truncheon into my groin, causing me to urinate and him to burst out laughing. "It's amazing how many can't hold their piss."

The other guard glares at him as he unstraps me. "You'd piss too if you sat here the time he has. We'll have to clean that up now, too."

"Stop getting panicky. They've got janitors for that."

When released from the chair, they lead me back to a different cell that has a minute window, a latrine bucket, and a concrete bed. After the guards raise the force field, I sit on the cot and contemplate what just happened.

We go through the same ritual for the next five days. But if they think they can break me, they are disappointed. The sixth day promises to be no different. Then, the door opens, and General Barak strolls in, smiling.

INTERROGATION BEGINS

"We're going to have a chat," Barak says, a glimmer of a challenge to me in his expression. He closes the door and circumnavigates me sitting helpless strapped to the chair.

"It should be a brief conversation," I say.

Barak laughs. "You will tell us what you know before we finish. Or at least your mind will enlighten me on what it knows."

His last sentence sends shivers down my spine. It suggests he has no hesitation in using the mind probe to extract the information he desires, a device few can resist. Its efficiency is notorious, and it has no regard for the damage it inflicts to the brain. Many recipients return to civilization as blithering idiots, burdens on society until an untimely death removes them.

"It's been five years since the last battle with your pathetic mob," Barak says. "What did you do afterward? Your name only resurfaced from oblivion a few months ago."

"I've been minding my own business," I say, a hint of defiance in my tone.

"You've been trading across the outer planets, from what my informants tell me. But then you disappeared two years ago, and no one knows where you went until you re-emerged with the resistance movement."

"I had a vacation." Barak's knowledge of my movements unsettles me. I watch him, maintaining my guard.

Barak chuckles. "A vacation. Very good. And where was this *holiday*?"

"Nowhere you'd care to visit."

"And yet I want this information. It may interest my emperor."

I feign impatience. "Look, I crashed. You happy? I sat marooned there until someone picked me up again. And before you ask, I can't remember where." I haven't told a lie, just omitted rather a lot. But I need to be careful what I divulge.

Barak moves closer to stand towering in front of me, studying me for too long. "I think you know, but you don't want to tell me."

"I don't."

"Maybe your subconscious remembers then." He strides away and clicks his fingers at the room's side window.

Two technicians rush in with a device that terrifies me. They set it up beside me and put a skullcap on my head, wires extending from it to the machinery. After several minutes and checking their work, one technician says, "Ready, sir," to Barak.

Barak nods and glances at me. "You sure you can't remember?"

"My mind's a blank."

Barak roars with laughter. Once he recovers, he says, "It will be." He nods again to the technician who looks at me, fear and pity in his eyes, before returning his attention to the mind-probe equipment and flicking the switch.

A hum fills the room as the machine progresses through its start-up sequence. My heart races as it anticipates the moment of torture approaching, but I take deep breaths and prepare my consciousness, locking away my most precious secrets until I am ready. Watching the technician, I see his finger descend on the button to start the probing. The button depresses, and I blank out.

～

LIGHT RETURNS as I regain consciousness, and my eyes flutter open. I am in a cell with a padded bed this time. *They must still want me alive.* They've removed my restraints and changed my clothing to a version of a medical orderly's outfit. My final memory flashes by me, and my hands jerk to my temples by reflex. I've heard rumors that the mind probe leaves burn marks on the recipient's head afterward but, apart from a splitting headache, my scalp feels as it always has. More importantly, I am sane and myself.

After rising to a sitting position, I check myself. All I find are bruises on my wrists and ankles where the straps held me to the armchair. They are tender, though, and I wince when I probe them with my fingers.

I then inspect the cell. It is larger than the earlier one with a flushing toilet, a basin, a tap, and a table and chair. A plate containing bread and salad sits on the table, a glass of water beside it. The sight of the meal makes my stomach grumble. I try to stand but fall back onto the bed as vertigo overpowers me, gasping for breath to recover from the sensation. After bracing myself, I try again with success as I overcome the sensation's return. Taking small, precise steps, I manage the distance from the cot to the table and fall into the chair with relief. I hungrily consume the food, washing it down with the water.

As I finish my meal, the door beyond the force field swings open, and Barak enters. "Open it!" he barks at the guard. After fumbling with the control, the jailer switches the force field off, and Barak confronts me.

I watch him approach, alert and suspicious. He stops a meter from me and glares. "How did you conceal your memories?"

"What?" I understand what he's saying, but I'm as confused as he is.

"We have gaps in the mind-probe extraction. How did you prevent us from removing your subconscious thoughts?"

My eyes widen. I didn't realize that was even possible. "I don't know."

He lashes out with his fist and connects with my cheek. A cracking sound comes from my jaw, and the pain dims my vision.

Blood leaks from my mouth. "Where were you for eighteen months? And what did the library contain?"

Suppressing my relief, I look at him with a vacant expression. He doesn't know about Adala or the information I discovered on the library's chips. "That's impossible with the mind probe."

"Well, apparently, it is possible. Never mind. I have the technicians busy increasing the power for it to break whatever lock you have on those memories, and I will have everything soon." He goes to leave, but I cause him to pause.

"Why did you turn?"

Barak stops and faces me. "You'd never win against the emperor with the measly forces you had. I had to consider my prospects, and there was no future with you."

"But why exterminate all those people?"

Pain crosses Barak's face when I mention the slaughter. "I ... wish that hadn't happened. The emperor ordered it, and I couldn't go above his orders. My position was too precarious."

"And my family?"

"The emperor commanded it to show my loyalty."

I stare at him with disgust and, just for a moment, a flicker of shame crosses his face before his stern façade returns. "If I were you, I'd rest. You will need your strength for the next probe." He turns again and leaves. The force field slams back on straight afterward.

Terror soaks through me as I contemplate another probing with greater power.

30

HUMILIATION

After the guards deliver another meal and while waiting for my next interrogation, I doze fitfully. During wakeful moments, I am aware of darkness engulfing the landscape outside, which matches my gloom as I lie and wait.

My heart jumps into my throat when the door jerks open and two different guards enter. Their insignia denotes them as members of the emperor's guard. *Why is the emperor's guard is interested in me?* After a brief discussion with the on-duty guards, the force field ceases, and the guards approach me.

"On your feet," one commands.

To resist is useless, so I obey and stand while they shackle my wrists and ankles.

"Come," the same guard orders.

He moves out, and I follow him, the second guard bringing up the rear. At least they have no interest in battering me along the way. Intrigued to know where they are taking me, I scrutinize my surroundings. We ascend far above the level of my cell into the main palace and the private residential suites of the emperor, which intrigues me even more. *Where are we going?*

Music and laughter emanate from behind the huge oak doorway

ahead as if a party is in progress. We stop at the entrance, and the lead guard talks to another standing by the doors. He nods and raises his head. After a few seconds, he speaks to the ether — he has a sub-cranial communication implant which he uses to communicate with the recipients — and after more delay, he nods to my guards and places his palm on the bio-sensor. At once, the doors open and the full noise of the interior blasts through to me.

A decadent party is in progress. The room has couches and cushions scattered over the floor. Naked servers weave their way through the maze to serve the drunken men lying on them, sometimes having to stay for more service than they expected. Male guests have one or two women with them, some in various stages of the sex act. The entire scene disgusts me. A band plays music in the corner, oblivious to the depravity before them.

The guards lead me to a central pillar and shackle me to that, then remove themselves to three steps behind me.

The stench of alcohol, perfume, and body odor saturates the air as I stand and wait for whatever transpires.

A few minutes later, a man lurches to his feet, a man the entire empire knows: Emperor Shulgi. His flamboyant dress is untidy and hangs half off him. He motions for the band to cease playing and addresses the guests, his words slurred, "Ladies and gentlemen, we have a special guest with us today." He staggers toward me, and the crowd quietens, eager for events to unfold. After negotiating the distance between us, he stares at me with unfocused eyes and pats me on the cheek. With his arm around my shoulders, he says, "Meet my one and only friend: Halwende."

"I'm no friend of yours." I spit out the words.

A gasp rises from the audience.

Shulgi lets go of me and wags his forefinger at me, tutting as he does. "Unfortunately for him, this traitor, coward, and thief got caught."

Laughter fills the room.

After tottering to regain his balance, his eyes turn evil. "We must punish thieves." With a speed belying his intoxication, his fist slams into my stomach, making me hunch over, and his knee flies up into my face breaking my nose with a cracking sound and bringing stars to my eyes. Straightening, Shulgi then kicks my groin before he loses his stability and sprawls on the floor. My knees buckle, but my shackles prevent me from collapsing. As I gasp for air, the audience increases the volume of their derogatory laughter, enjoying the entertainment at my expense.

Painfully, Shulgi struggles to a standing position and grasps my shoulder to balance himself. "Now," he says, "Deliver your own punishment for his crimes. But don't damage him irreparably. He is still of value to me. And, women, you may experiment with him, although I may've damaged the goods." To emphasize his point, he boots me in the groin again before staggering back to his cushioned throne on the floor to be surrounded by women as he flops, the music restarting and the party continuing again.

After the second kick, I vomit on the marbled flooring and hang from the pillar, drained of energy and complaint. As the cavorting progresses, people stagger over to me and use me as a punching bag. With my lower garments disrobed, several women venture over to inspect my genitals, making degrading comments as they fondle me before tiring and returning to their present partner for the evening.

Amidst the torment, I sense one person approach me, pretending to behave as the others have. But as I open my puffed and bruised slits of eyes, I see concern and a hint of anger as she pretends to grope me in imitation. It only lasts for a moment before she too rushes to rejoin the celebration.

Somehow, I stay conscious, but my facial skin is already puffing from the evening's battering. My chest and ribs cry out in pain with each breath. They keep me there well after midnight, the revelry continuing unabated, but most have passed out and lie comatose on the floor. At last, my removal from the party relieves me of my misery.

The two guards unshackle me from the pillar and drag me back to my cell, as I am incapable of walking after the beatings I received as part of the evening's entertainment. I lose consciousness as my body falls onto the bed.

31

WHERE IS UR?

"I hear you attended a wild party last night," Barak says as he enters the interrogation room. "Wish he'd invited me."

"You wouldn't have enjoyed it," I rasp through my split, bruised lips.

Barak chuckles. "Well, let's start our business, shall we?" He snaps his fingers at the technician, who quickly positions the upgraded mind probe over my skull.

My senses numb in anticipation of the excruciating pain to be inflicted. No words can describe my powerlessness. With the flicking of a switch, energy flows through my neural pathways, coercing the information they contain with all the delicacy of a sledgehammer. My muscles spasm and lock as agony courses through them. I moan and shout until the session reaches a climax and the anguish suddenly disappears, leaving me limp and dripping in sweat, my head lolling in exhaustion, saliva dribbling from my mouth.

"The results are the same, sir," the technician says.

"That's impossible!" The anger is plain in Barak's voice. "You must have calibrated it wrong."

"No, sir. We set it up correctly, and I used full power."

"But how? No one can hide their secrets from the probe."

When I hear of their failure, I raise my head, and Barak looks over at me. "Who are you?"

I whimper and flop my head.

"We will try again tomorrow," Barak says. "In the meantime, tune this thing to peak condition."

"Yes, sir."

Barak leaves, and within ten minutes, I am back lying on my cot in my cell, almost unconscious from exhaustion and pain.

A meal arrives. My stomach grumbles at the aroma of spicy beef stew. As I twist my head, I open my eyes, seeing the wisp of steam ascend from the bowl. Groans escape my lips while I swivel and rise from my bed, shuffling the distance to the table and my food and collapsing into the chair. Too much energy has drained from me for me to eat, but my hunger encourages me to reach out to my reserves. The first mouthful sends a surge of ecstasy through me as the flavor hits, hinting at the nutrition to follow. With slurping gusto, I devour the meat and ration of bread allowed me, satisfaction coursing through me afterward. I flop back, my arms dangling at my side, as the feast digests.

I must have dozed because when my eyes open again, I'm still reclined, but my head is tilted back. The bowl has gone. As I let a sigh escape, I rise and stagger to my bed, falling asleep instantly.

The routine repeats for too many days for me to count — wake, meal, probe, meal, sleep — with the same inconclusive results, sending Barak into a rage every time. Until one day, it stops, and I'm left to rest and heal.

This disturbs me. Did I give what they wanted? Did I tell them the secrets of the resistance? Or worse, did I divulge Adala's existence? I pace the prison in trepidation, my mood spiraling into despair with each day of silence from my jailers.

The door opens and the force field lowers as two guards enter my cell. They inflict no harm before or during my march to a different interrogation room from the other times. This one has four chairs and a table and, although spartan, has an air of peaceful efficiency. My stomach cramps with dread as I wait.

After thirty minutes, the door opens, and Barak and Emperor Shulgi enter together.

"Stand!" Barak barks at me.

After I refuse, he yanks the seat from under me, and I fall rear first to the ground where I stay.

Shulgi sighs. "Let him have his pathetic rebellion." He peruses the room before sitting. "Give him his chair back. I can't talk to him lying on the floor."

Barak throws the seat at me, making sure it hits me as it clangs over the floor. "Sit!"

Seeing no need to upset my captors further, I obey. In any case, it's uncomfortable on the floor. I rise, reposition the chair, and sit facing Shulgi, wearing a neutral expression.

Shulgi's eyes pierce me as he sits silently studying my disposition with a bemused smile. The lack of sound unnerves me, but I stay unflinching as I wait. Eventually, he asks, "Where's Ur?"

The question stabs my soul, as it's obvious I've allowed vital information to leak from my mind. That Shulgi's asking where it's located suggests I haven't disclosed everything, so I console myself with that knowledge and keep my expression neutral. "Where's what?"

Shulgi bursts into livid anger as he slams his fist on the table. "You know! You informed us it exists."

I shrug. "I don't know. Our parents told us tales of a fabulous city called Ur as children. Weren't you told the fables of our prehistoric mythical world?"

Uncertain, Shulgi glances at Barak, who shakes his head. "No. This isn't the memory of fairy tales. It's buried in your subconscious. Something you want hidden. Now, where is it?"

"I don't know. You extracted a myth from my brain."

Barak strides around the table and slams his fist into my jaw, toppling me from the chair. "Answer us!" he shouts.

I flinch as I check my mouth, wobbling my jaw to make sure it's not broken.

Shulgi stands and moves over to Barak. "We must know its location," he whispers, but the words float to me. "It is a threat to our plans. It could be a great asset to my empire." He turns his head and glances at me. "Get him to talk. I don't care how. Just get him to talk." With that command, he leaves the room.

"With pleasure." Barak glares at me, his intent displayed in his expression.

32

LILITH

The next days are a blur of probing, torture, and pain. Despite the torment, my secret thoughts stay intact, to Barak's increasing frustration.

There is nothing to compare to the abuse I endure. Masers set at minimal energy spray their beams over my flesh and burn, the smell of cooking meat filling the air with its stench, the inquisitor taking delight in carving artistic patterns on my skin.

Apart from the physical maltreatment, mental suffering includes light deprivation interlaced with intense light and strobing for hours on end. My sanity is brought to breaking point. On other occasions, they strap me to the floor in an isolation cell, leaving me to starve and wallow in my excrement.

Without notice, the torture stops, and I lie in an infirmary bed for several days, my wounds healing and my mind returning to soundness. Nutritious food provides renewed strength to my body. It's as if the inquisition failed, so they are trying another tack to entice me to divulge my secrets.

A woman enters my hospital room. She searches the entire room before sitting in a chair near me.

"Who are you?" I ask.

She bows her head and clasps her hands tightly in her lap. "I'm Lilith." She raises her head and gazes timidly at me. "Do you recognize me?"

"You look familiar."

"I attended Father's party three weeks ago when he had you brought in for entertainment."

Her face refreshes in my memory. She was the one who showed concern for me. "I remember. You're Shulgi's daughter?"

Lilith lowers her head. "Unbelievably, yes."

Her presence now stimulates my interest, and I raise myself on the bed to a half-sitting position to see her better. "Why do you attend his parties? You don't have the indecency from my recollection of the partygoers."

Her visage is pained as she bites her lip and steals a glance at me. "He forces me to go. Says it will educate me on the pleasures of power. I hate it. The decadence. They're sick. And they only come to stay in Father's favor."

"You joined in with fondling me if I recall."

Lilith turns bright red. "I had to do it. Father was watching. He might have forced me to do more degrading things if I had refused. Please forgive me. I tried to be gentle." She shows panic. "Did I hurt you?"

I chuckle. "By that stage, I was beyond pain." With nothing further to add, we sit in silence until I recall her unusual actions when she first entered. "What were you doing when you arrived?"

After gazing at me with a confused face, Lilith says, "Oh ... I was checking the room for bugs. It's a certainty Father has surveillance in here, and I discovered two such devices. It's irrelevant, though. I carry a signal jammer on me." She smirks. "It frustrates Father no end when he checks up on me and finds nothing."

"But why are you here?"

Lilith's expression changes to loathing and disgust. "My father is evil. His treatment of his subjects in the empire is despicable." She then becomes inquisitive, interested. "I researched you. You're causing Father headaches. You've suffered much with the death of your family years ago. Then you disappeared, and everyone thought you were dead. The resistance movement lost direction without you and fragmented. They have regenerated under you."

"What makes you think that's my doing?"

Lilith raises her eyebrows. "Come on, it's obvious even to me."

"Well, it's changed with me here, hasn't it?"

"Yes, it has." Lilith rubs her chin, pondering and glancing at me.

We sit in silence, thinking our own thoughts for a few seconds.

"You still haven't told me why you're here," I say.

A troubled look shades Lilith's face. "I ... wanted to know who you are ... whether you're as virtuous as your reputation." She bows her head again. "Whether you're worthy of my help."

The implications of her words worry me. She is placing herself at significant risk if she helps me. I'm sure her father would execute her without compunction if he felt she was a traitor. Someone of her stature within his sphere to inform on Shulgi's actions to us would be invaluable, though. It still depends on me escaping, an impossible occurrence at present. I find the nerve to ask the futile question. "What help were you considering giving?"

As she stares into my eyes, she suggests, "I could make it easier for you to escape."

"Your father would kill you if he found out."

Sorrow fills Lilith. "I am already dead inside me. Completing it would be a relief."

"What nonsense!"

"You don't realize what it's like being Shulgi's daughter. I have no friends, no real friends. My father terrifies any friend I try to make or turns them into spies."

Her desperation reaches out for sympathy, and I understand how life is for her. The constant checking to search for those watching her every movement, eager to offer any information back to Shulgi to gain his favor. Lack of any genuine friends leaving her in a world of loneliness.

Sincerity is obvious in her eyes, so I decide to trust her. "What did you have in mind?"

After nibbling her cheek for several seconds, she says, "How long will you stay here?"

"I don't know. My presence here surprises me. I'm almost fully recovered, so if the purpose was to bring me back to full health again, I must be due to return to my cell soon."

"That's when you'll escape. When they move you. They won't be expecting it."

Her naivety appalls me. "Right, I give them the jump and run away. Then what? Ask them to open the door for me?"

"Don't belittle me. Of course not. I need to devise a plan, but that's the opportunity."

Her determination encourages me. "And what of you? You must come with me."

"No. Your escape will be more likely to fail if I'm with you. My father will tear the planet apart if I disappear. I'll risk staying. I'll be of greater value to you if I stay."

"You're a brave woman."

"Just tired of this tyranny." She stands up and says, "I must leave before people investigate the electronic static. Be ready."

33

ESCAPE

My recovery is complete three days later, but I see no more of Lilith and hear no more about her plans for my escape. This unnerves me as I have placed myself in her hands. I will trust her, though.

The guards come for me mid-morning and escort me from the infirmary back to my cell, one on either side of me. My nerves are on edge in expectation of a disturbance.

We follow a corridor through two sets of doors and enter an enclosed courtyard where windows offer a view of the exterior. The royal palace has prominence to my right in its vast splendor, and lush parklands fill the surrounds on my left. Just as we near the courtyard's far end, a door opens, and a guard I've never seen before enters. My guards stop in their tracks, confused by this stranger's intrusion.

"I shall take him from here," the man says authoritatively and, without giving them a chance to query the order, he raises a maser and stuns them. They flop to the concrete floor.

While I'm still struggling with this rapid turn of events, Lilith appears. She frisks the unconscious guards until she finds the restraint controls, which she uses to remove the restraints from my wrists. The fake guard quietly calls in another man, also dressed as a guard, and the two men silently drag the unconscious guards through the door.

"Come," she says to me, and I follow the way she entered.

"Where are you taking me?"

"No talking." She grabs my hand and leads me through an adjacent corridor.

We stop at another doorway, and she looks both ways before waving her hand to open it. We enter a large, unused chamber full of furniture covered in dust sheets. Her accomplices with the unconscious guards follow us and shut the door.

"We can talk now," Lilith says.

"Where are we? Who are your helpers?"

"They are my loyal friends and have agreed to help me. And we're in a special room." Lilith glances at the others. "Dump of them through there." She points to an exit. "You may then return to your business."

Her accomplices nod and drag the guards away. I wonder what they intend to do with them. Lilith does not strike me as a killer, but to let them live to tell the story could be dangerous for her, even though they did not see her.

Seconds later, we are alone.

"There is little time," Lilith says to me as she grasps my hand. "They will miss you soon. A scooter waits for you outside the palace grounds. Use it to make your escape."

As Lilith finishes speaking, the thunderous sound of running guards roars past the door we just entered, sending a shard of fear through me and, judging by Lilith's changed expression, through her too.

"Time is shorter than I'd hoped. Quick!" Lilith leads me to a corner of the room and moves a chest of drawers. She lifts a section of the floor, revealing a set of stairs descending into darkness. "Down there. Follow it, and you will emerge outside the palace compound."

The sight astounds me. "How did you find this?"

Lilith smirks. "I enjoyed exploring as a child and stumbled on it. I use it to sneak out when life here becomes unbearable."

"Are you sure you won't come with me?"

"No, I cannot. Now go."

"You're a brave woman. I won't forget this, and I hope we meet again under less dangerous circumstances."

A sparkle of hope flashes across Lilith's eyes. "So do I."

With no further conversation, I make my way down the steps, the hatch closing over me as soon as I'm below the floor line. The sound of the chest being slid back in place comes to my ears moments later. Just as I wonder how I'll negotiate the darkness, lights flicker on, revealing the rest of the stairs below and allowing me to descend the remaining distance.

A long passage greets me at the bottom, so I continue to trust Lilith as I follow my path of escape to freedom. Concern for Lilith surges through me as I glance back up the steps before I start along the corridor. Many minutes and bends later, I reach the other end, not knowing where I am. I smile as I see a maser pistol with a holster lying on the ground at the foot of ascending stairs. I pick it up and strap it around my waist. With a slow exhaling of breath, I calm my nerves and begin the ascent to my unknown destination. After several flights, a door blocks my route. No handle or device is visible to open it. I know a way exists, so I prod at possible secret mechanisms with no success. With thoughts of betrayal entering my mind, I become frantic to locate the lock. I pat the walls and door from top to bottom, seeking any hint of a switch. Stretching, I slide my fingers across the lintel surface and feel a slight indentation in the middle. After pressing that point, the barrier glides open to the countryside and a scooter.

Wasting no time, I rush out and jump on the scooter, starting it and taking off toward the nearby mountains. The door is closed when I glance back, concealed against the granite escarpment. I doubt I could find it again. Its existence intrigues me, and I wonder who built the tunnel and why.

As I gain momentum, I hear airborne vessels approaching and

search the sky for them. Two fighters and a troop carrier streak into view before I reach cover in the mountains. I have no choice but to surge up to maximum speed and hug the terrain, hoping the protection of the topography will allow my escape. Maser fire zips past moments later and blasts into the landscape ahead as I make my desperate dash to freedom. *How did they find me so fast? Did Lilith betray me? Or was Lilith betrayed, and is she now paying the price?* With no time to ponder the options, more maser fire singes my scooter's paintwork. I'm no match for them in the open, but I appear to be holding them off, hugging the ground. I just need a place to lose them while I regain my bearings enough to find my Lander and eventually get back to my ship — although the prospect of ever seeing my ship again seems too distant in the future to contemplate in my current predicament.

I weave and swerve from side to side in a desperate attempt to escape. With no weapons and no backup, I sense my fortuitous bid for freedom will be short-lived. A sharp bend through a ravine in a stream bed approaches, and I brace for the maneuver as the scooter banks to take it. Too late, I realize I'm traveling too fast, and the scooter slams into the gorge embankment, throwing me through the air. The scooter continues without me, fast losing control, and crashes.

Luck clings to me as I brush the grass-covered cliff at an angle, slowing my speed. I bounce off and start rolling moments later. The uneven ground pummels me with bruises as I roll to a stop and gasp for breath. I flex my limbs, checking for breaks, pain flowing to my brain, but I'm still intact. Before I recover, I hear the troop carrier preparing to land, and I know I need to keep moving even though I have no destination.

Fear urges me to my feet, and I run away from the carrier and any pursuing soldiers. I follow the stream bed, searching for anywhere I can hide or use as a barrier to take my stand. Rushing around a bend, I stumble to a complete stop.

An old man stands in front of me, fishing. He smiles and reels in his line as if there's no rush. I hear the splash of men running through the water behind me. "Come," he says as he packs his creel and starts walking toward a cliff face twenty meters away.

I stare at him as if he's mad, my frantic brain racing for any other means of escape other than following him.

When he turns and sees my hesitation, he says, "I suggest you accompany me if you want to live in freedom."

With one last glance over my shoulder, I make my decision and follow his suggestion, making my way toward him over the pebbled stream shoreline. My destination unknown, I stare in amazement at his calmness in the face of the imminent arrival of a squad of soldiers, but he exudes an aura of trust.

After checking that I'm following him, he continues his ambling. We reach the wall and I look behind me, hoping the man does whatever he intends to do with more haste and in time for both our escapes. My chest heaves to regain my breath as I stare at him. He searches the cliff face and says, "There," as he puts a palm on a smooth indentation. A door slides open, and he ushers me inside. He follows, and the door whooshes closed.

"Who are ...?"

"Shh!" The man places his creel and fishing rod on the ground and places his ear on the barrier.

"Where's he gone?" we both hear from behind the door as pounding footsteps rush past before they stop in unison.

"He must have run further ahead," another voice says. "Keep going."

The splashing and stamping start again and fade into the distance.

The man glances at me. "Let us continue." He stoops and retrieves his equipment before ambling further into the tunnel. I have no choice but to follow him. Lights flicker on as we move through the passage. The slow pace helps me regain my breath and shed the adrenaline coursing through my veins, although my bumps and bruises still afflict me. After what seems like many minutes, he stops and leans against the wall. The walk has taxed his stamina.

I use the opportunity to ask him again, "Who are you?"

"I'm an old man hoping to catch a fish." A sparkle in his eyes suggests his words carry two meanings.

"Seriously, who are you?"

The man straightens and resumes his slow walk. "Just a while longer and I'll answer your questions."

34

THE OLD MAN

The tunnel weaves through the subterranean space to a destination unknown to me. Half an hour later, the shaft opens to a cavern with a cathedral-like domed roof towering above. Stalactites suspend from the ceiling surface, chandeliers reflecting the lighting that illuminates the volume. Several couches stand in the far corner, and a table and food synthesizer occupy a bench, which the old man heads toward.

"Ah! Time for a break," he says as he drops his rod and creel to the floor and flops onto a lounge.

I don't disagree with his comment and collapse on a couch opposite him.

"There's a meal dispenser over in the corner there if you're hungry." The man points in the direction.

The adrenaline has drained from me, and my fluids need replenishing, so I stand again and wander to the machine. I turn and glance at the old man, raising my eyebrows. "You want a drink?"

"Water will be enough."

Water is my choice too, so I order two glasses and wait for it to cycle through twice, delivering a glass of water each time. Clutching both glasses, I return, hand one to him, and retake my seat before sipping at the chilled fluid, enjoying the cool sensation of it running down my throat. After draining the contents, I place the glass beside the couch and gaze at this enigmatic man.

With an unperturbed expression and amused smile, he gazes back at me. "Now that we have peace, I can concentrate on answering your questions." He eyes me as if gauging my temperament. "The Princess Lilith is an associate of mine. She transmitted to her trusted collaborators that she was embarking on a dangerous venture and might need help in the field. Which took me fishing and you to me, chased by those unfriendly soldiers."

His revelation astounds me. Lilith's reach is greater than I comprehended. That she can broadcast information without the emperor's knowledge is revealing, too. She has more resources than people realize. "You must be very devoted to Lilith."

Sadness crosses his face. "She and I go back to her infancy and happier times. Let me just say I'd give my life for her and the ideal she desires."

The mysterious words pique my interest. "Does her cause and that of the resistance movement cross paths?"

The man's smile spreads. "Not every one of this movement's goals agrees with hers." He eyes me with curiosity. "You align with her interests as you do mine."

These remarks take me aback. "What do you mean? How do you know me? I haven't seen you before today."

His amused, enigmatic grin returns. "Ah, but you have ... many years ago, but you were too young to remember. I believe Zabada is a good friend of yours?"

Nonplussed and speechless, I stare at him. I regain my voice. "Yes, he was a mentor when I was a child. I met him again just recently."

"So he told me. He mentioned he suggested you visit the library, which I understand you did. Did you find what you sought?"

I lower my eyes and wonder what else this man knows. "It taught me a history lesson."

"An up-to-date one, I believe."

After shaking my head, I raise it and stare at him. "Possibly."

He returns my look as if again considering what intelligence is useful for me. "Did you peruse the technology section?"

A panic attack grips me. My eyes bulge in alarm. "Is there something important I missed? They breached the room, and we left it unsecured."

The man waves his hand to calm me down and replies, "The information is safe. There's no harm done, and what you didn't take is again secure."

I relax at the news. "I only had time to view the few data chips that drew my immediate interest."

The man nods. He leans over and opens his creel, rummaging around inside until he finds what he's looking for and extracts it. Two chips of data sit in his hand. "You may find these interesting, especially since you have been to Ur."

What other knowledge does this person have? "How could you know that?"

"I perceive many things." He holds out the chips for me, and I grab them, puzzled by their importance. "View them at your leisure — but to use the information, you must return to Larsa."

"Why? What's there?"

"Resources, my boy, resources. You will understand once you read and when you get there."

Tucking the chips into my pocket, I recline and review the man's words. Why did he believe I'd find technology interesting? Something keeps tugging at me while we talk. The puzzle bursts into my mind. "How did you know I'd use your route?"

He smirks. "I didn't. But I took a lucky guess. It's the course I'd take if I were being chased, so I stationed myself there. Besides, I enjoy fishing. Haven't caught a fish in ages. Looks like it will be a while yet."

"Do you have a name?"

"That is unimportant."

So, this enigma wishes to stay anonymous, although he says we've met once before. My memory recognizes him on the subconscious level. I'm just not able to bring the recollection of him back into recall. Feeling that we have exhausted our conversation, I ask, "What now?"

"I suggest we grab a bite to eat and continue on our journey. We still have a hike before we reach our destination. Do you own a Lander nearby?"

The question catches me unprepared. "Yes, and I know its position. But I'm unaware of our present location. What has happened to Ishtar? And Tirigan's a traitor."

"Ishtar has returned to the others with the unfortunate news of your capture. I learned of Tirigan. I thought his acts of treachery were minor and harmless, but I was mistaken. We will take care of him."

My stomach grumbles, so I accept the man's suggestion and stroll over to the food synthesizer and dial in ham salad sandwiches and an orange juice, taking them to the table when they pop from the machine. The man prepares his own meal and joins me. We eat silently, the earlier discussion having exhausted our curiosity about each other for the time being. The man's identity still frustrates me. What's more annoying is his knowledge of me, even of things I haven't told my trusted allies. And what is his involvement with Lilith, the resistance, and Zabada? It's as if there's a secret cabal operating on the sidelines, only emerging when the occasion needs it. Yet, I owe this person my gratitude for assisting my evasion of recapture.

"It is time to leave," the man says as he rises from his chair and ambles over to his fishing rod and creel.

With reluctance, I follow his lead and stroll along with him from the cavern and into another passageway. I wonder how long this underground warren has existed. The rock walls are smooth, and the lighting is secured for long-term use. How extensive is this network on Eridu? It seems I am entering these places with eerie regularity. The width of the tunnel allows me to walk alongside him, which I do, although we stay silent for now.

After twenty minutes, the man says, "You will learn useful information on the machinery you saw in Ur and how it provides power in those files. You must guard the details of that technology with your life. Its existence has remained a secret for many centuries."

"Why are you revealing it, then?"

The man stops, as do I. He turns and gazes at me. "The person has arrived who will use it with discretion." With those enigmatic words, he returns to his ambling along the tunnel.

It is another twenty minutes before we reach a smaller cavern. A scooter sits in the middle of it, and he heads for it with me in tow. We hop on, and he pushes power into its drive.

"Can you show me where your Lander is?" he says as he pulls a tablet from a side panel on the scooter and sets up a display of the planet's topography.

I study the layout, and after a minute, the location comes into view. I zoom in on the region. "There," I say, pointing to it.

"Good, let's travel there."

"Won't Security still be looking for me?"

"Let me worry about that. You just rest and enjoy the ride." He grins with gentle warmth.

Sensing I have no choice, I take up his suggestion and sit in the passenger seat. The man bears an assurance that unnerves me. And yet, his elderly wisdom gives me confidence in the future, regardless of any immediate tribulations I may meet.

The scooter rises and we fly forward through the cavern. Moments later, we emerge into the countryside, the blazing sun blinding me until I adjust to the intensity. We hug the ground as we race across the surface of Eridu, the old man at ease with low-level flying. He uses the uninhabited terrain to avoid inquisitive eyes.

It takes two hours to reach our destination, and the sun is sinking as we enter the cave housing my Lander. A sense of relief flows over me when I see it. The scooter settles on the cavern floor, and we jump out.

"An exquisite-looking Lander you have there," the old man comments.

I grin. "Came with the ship."

"And a magnificent vessel, I hear."

I shake my head and laugh. "Do I have any secrets from you?"

"I am sure you do."

After strolling to the Lander, we stand facing each other. The man grabs my arms and gazes at me with piercing and sincere eyes. "You must travel from here with caution. Do not place yourself in danger unless it's unavoidable. There is too much at stake. Don't contact the others until after you have visited the site on Larsa." He removes a hand and places his palm on my cheek. "And most importantly, stay alive for the sake of the realm and the one you love on Ur."

I cannot talk. His words have transfixed me, especially the reference to Adala. How could he learn of Helheim's existence, the planet beyond the reach of the galaxy for centuries, and of her? When I find my tongue, my mouth feels dry, but I say, "I will." He releases me. I go to enter my Lander but stop and turn. "Why shouldn't I contact the others yet?"

"They'll distract you from what you need to do."

I nod. "I hope we meet again."

"So do I." He smiles and leaves. I watch him hop back on the scooter and zoom from the cave moments later.

With a sigh, I board the Lander and take off, heading for my yacht.

35

THE ENERGY SOURCE

I pass the time on my trip to Larsa studying the chips the old man gave me. They contain diagrams and technical specifications. Above all, they reference Flerovium, the same material identified as the cause of the original conflict with Ur, now Helheim. Flerovium is an element on the 'island of stability' with an atomic number of 114 but only stable for short periods under everyday conditions. But scientists discovered a long-term stable form of the element with a particular crystal lattice. When experimented on, they found it possessed an extreme, almost limitless, energy that they could tap and use. Even a tiny crystal could power a ship the size of the *Queen Rosalind* for a century. The crystal was rare, the only deposit discovered found on Ur.

I sit back and ponder this revelation and the temptation this substance poses for anyone wanting to control its supply. No wonder people fought wars over it. Egon had understood the blue crystal he forced slaves to mine for him had value, but he never tapped into the energy contained within it.

As I return to the diagrams, I understand their significance. They detail the means of tapping into the crystal's energy. One identifies the method of connecting the substance to the power supply for a ship's drive equipment and using it as the energy source for the shields and weapons. This has mighty ramifications for transportation — and warfare. Under current technology limitations, shields and weapons need recharging time, but this technology would allow instantaneous re-energizing of these systems, providing continuous protection and firepower for anyone possessing such technology. No wonder they hid it.

Near the end of the chips' data is a reference to the place that has the only known crystal deposit, apart from Helheim — Larsa. The information is unclear about whether the hoard is natural or placed there as a secret cache. A diagram identifies a particular mountain on Larsa with a hidden cavern where the Flerovium is stored. The old man wants me to discover and use the crystals in my fight against the empire.

A few days later, my ship maneuvers into orbit around the Larsa star, concealed in the asteroid belt but away from the secret base the resistance has there. Traveling in the Lander, I spiral through the planet's atmosphere and land at the spaceport under an alias. The old man's words to not put myself at risk echo in my mind as I stride through the arrivals lounge of the spaceport. I nonetheless fear they might spot me despite my pseudonym, a fear that proves unfounded as I sail through immigration without complications.

After hiring a scooter, I fly away from the spaceport, heading into the countryside, eager to find the mountain and the mysterious cavern ensconced in it. Torrential rain blurs the way ahead but does not impede my progress because I have dialed my destination into the scooter's computer, and it maintains speed despite my discomfort at flying blind. The rain ceases, but an overcast sky holds the gloom. An hour later, the peak comes into view, and I am soon landing at my journey's end. I hop out and scan the area. The scooter has landed far into a ravine, with cliffs towering above me on both sides. The restricted access to my location unnerves me, there being just one exit if things go wrong.

Steeling myself, I review the schematic on my tablet and search for the cavern entrance along the left cliff face. The diagram mentions and details the inscribed symbol of the House of Alalgar on the rock face, but I cannot see it and hope erosion hasn't erased it. As I pass my fingers across the wall, I detect a slight change in the wall's evenness and trace a section that appears artificial. On a hunch, I stride back until I lean against the opposite cliff face. Immediately, the detailed ensign of the House of Alalgar rises from the otherwise smooth surface. I consult the data on my tablet again and return to the wall, where I carefully place my palm over the sign of the blazing star of Rigel.

A noise and faint vibration come from the cliff, and moments later, a section of the cliff slides away to reveal a doorway leading to a dark tunnel. With a sigh at having to enter yet another dark tunnel, I stride through the orifice, hoping I'm not stepping into a space that will trap me until I die. Once I pass the threshold, a blue light radiates from the ceiling ahead and the entrance slams shut, leaving me bewildered. So much for avoiding being trapped. Since I'm now inside, I might as well explore where the passage leads, so I stroll along the passageway in the hope that movement will trigger lights. It does. After several turns and fifty meters, I arrive at a closed door, emblazoned once more with the same House of Alalgar sign.

Now that I'm getting the hang of how things work, I immediately place my palm on the star of Rigel, and again, the barrier slides open, revealing a vast cavity. My mind boggles as I step inside and take in a panoramic view of the cavern.

No other entrances mark the walls of the vault. Tall closets line the side to my left; shelves line the right wall, books and data chips stacked on them. A baroque-style table and chairs stand near the back, together with two cushioned armchairs. I raise my head to view the ceiling and see the House of Alalgar emblem spanning it in illuminated gold and splaying its golden silhouette over the floor. My mouth falls open in amazement. *Who built this place? And how can they have kept it secret?* After recovering from my trance, I navigate the room, my footfalls echoing throughout the chamber as I cross to the table. Marquetry embeds the same golden emblem into the tabletop.

"Welcome, Sargon of the House of Alalgar," a disembodied voice booms in the chamber.

I jump and wonder how whatever the device is that has detected me knows who I am. "Who are you?"

"I am the keeper of the vault."

Not this again. I recall the portal room under Adala's palace and the unwelcome transference of responsibilities when its keeper knew my name. "Why does this vault need a curator?"

"To keep out unwanted intruders and help you with your enquires."

Resigned to talking to nothing, I ask, "Where is the Flerovium stored?"

"A small stockpile exists in the closets. I can guide you to larger stock if you need it."

"I'll see what the closets contain."

"As you wish."

I stride over to the closets and open the first one I reach. A blaze of blue light confronts me as crystals luminesce out toward me. The ones I mined as a prisoner on Helheim didn't radiate to this extent. "Why do they shine?"

"Energy saturates them."

"How do they become saturated?"

"I cannot answer that query."

Cannot or will not? I ask myself.

Reaching in, I pull the closest crystal to me. It is the size of an apple and has hexagonal facets. "What quantity does a spaceship need to power the drives, shields, and weapons?" I ask as I refract the room's golden light off the crystal surface.

"What you hold in your hand suffices to supply a battleship's energy for twenty years."

My eyes boggle at the massive abundance of energy stored in the substance. Then I raise my eyes to the ceiling. How does it know what I'm holding? Knowing I won't get an answer, I grab two more crystals of a similar size, close the closet, and stroll back to the table with them. I place them on it for now.

Wishing to explore the rest of the room, I move to the shelving and begin investigating the contents. Old tomes of paper-based writings sit on one shelf. For books undisturbed for maybe four centuries, the layer of dust that coats their covers seems too thin. But since the vault has remained sealed all that time, I surmise there has been limited opportunity for dirt to enter. As I read their titles, they appear to contain historical treatises of the Alalgar realm. I have little interest in them at present. Moving on, I see data chips occupy the next shelves. They have the same titles as those in the Eridu library, and I wonder which has the originals. With one bank of shelving left, I spy a jewelry box at the top, just out of reach. I jump and grab it, a puff of dust exploding into the air where my hand disturbed it.

When I brush the residual dust off, the same insignia decorates the marquetry lid. The box is of wooden construction with gold inset insignia and hinges. A gold clasp holds the lid closed. After returning to the table, I sit and place the box on it, fiddling with it as I contemplate whether I should open it. My inquisitive nature wins the battle, and I swivel the clamp from the eyelet. The lid resists for a moment until the pressure I exert breaks the seal. A gold signet ring sits inside as I raise the lid, its polished radiance reflecting the light of the room. The ring's bevel has the emblem of the House of Alalgar embedded in it. The jeweler has used Flerovium as the scribing material, a blue luster gleaming from it. Temptation draws my hand to the ring, and I pull it from the box, gazing at it in fascination.

"This ring belongs to you, Sargon."

The sudden sound of the voice unnerves me, and my shaking hands juggle the heirloom in fright. The implications of the words annoy me. "Why? Why does it belong to me? I didn't ask for it."

"You are the living heir of the great King Alalgar, ruler of the realm of Rigel. You are the rightful claimant to the throne."

I shake my head and sigh as I place the ring back in the box, close the lid, and refasten the clasp. I wonder if I'll ever rightfully wear it. Now realizing I must keep moving and need something to carry the items I wish to take with me, I return to the closets, looking for a suitable container. Most of the closets contain Flerovium crystals of various sizes, as well as a few house gadgets whose purpose I cannot fathom. As chance has it, I find a suitable bag in the last closet I check. Velvet cloth sits next to it on a shelf, and I take four pieces to wrap the crystals and box, both to protect them and to ensure they won't rattle and create unwanted attention.

With no further reason to stay, I collect the Flerovium and box and retrace my steps to the outside and my ship.

36

MODIFICATIONS

On returning to the *Queen Rosalind*, I deposit the box containing the ring in the secure and indestructible safe on board. I leave two crystals there, too. Staying in the asteroid belt, I take the remaining crystal into the engineering section and the reactor room for the ship, which houses the power source. The instructions for installing the crystal in the power circuit are straightforward. I have it installed after three hours. I keep the existing power supply in parallel because I'm unsure of the crystal's behavior.

With a wipe of my brow, I move to the engineering control panel and add the suggested code from the chip into the controls. Once I reboot the software, I'm ready to trial the new setup, so I return to the cockpit to verify the weapons and drives. The shields are difficult to check without someone firing at me, but they can wait until later.

As the yacht's maser powers up, I look for a suitable target to prove the enhanced weaponry. A small asteroid floats nearby as we both orbit Larsa's star. Once the maser is at full strength, I line it up and fire with destructive results. The original maser power would have caused significant damage to the rock, but, with the enhance-ment, the asteroid disintegrates, minute particles of dust radiating out from where it used to exist. How the hardware for the maser copes with the extra power escapes me. I can only assume the code I entered reconfigures the flux load.

Now that the maser testing is complete, I concentrate on the drive's capabilities. As I fire them up, I immediately feel the extra available power when I direct energy to them to pull out of orbit, almost colliding with an asteroid as I do so. With a correction to my flight path, I avoid the collision and speed away from Eridu. I appreciate the inertia compensation as I watch the acceleration climb far higher than I've ever experienced before, with no hint of discomfort. The yacht can out-pace any ship in the empire. After putting the maneuvering thrusters through their paces, I realize I can out-maneuver any vessel in the empire too. But what about hyperspace? There's only one way to find out. I lock in a course for Santori and, after flying to a suitable position, enter hyperspace. The speed is mind-boggling, and I expect to arrive at Sartori in less than two days instead of the usual six. With nothing further to do, I set the yacht's autopilot and relax for the rest of the trip. When I reach Santori, I turn around and return to Larsa and the resistance hideout, uncertain of what my reception will be on my arrival.

I consider it prudent not to mention the crystal and what it can offer the ships. Withholding information makes me uneasy, but I sense the rebels could not handle the technology responsibly in the short term. I keep it in reserve for now. With the yacht parked in asteroid orbit, I get on board the shuttle and fly to the base.

"Please identify yourself," a strident voice asks over the comm.

"This is Halwende, requesting permission to enter."

"Halwende?"

"You heard." I can be as abrupt as the next person, and the terse response suits my purposes.

"Permission granted. Please use the course sent across to you ... and welcome home."

Not what I'd call home, but it's enough for now. Thoughts of Adala distract me for a moment.

It takes another twenty minutes to traverse the distance and land the shuttle in a landing spot in the resistance fortress. I notice they've been busy improving the asteroid defenses. Ishtar, Argandea, and Lugal come into view as the hatch opens and I disembark. Even before I reach the bottom of the stairs, Ishtar rushes forward and pulls me into a hug, which embarrasses me given her earlier infatuation.

"I thought we had lost you for good," she says as she gazes soulfully into my eyes like I'm her long-lost lover.

"I'm not that easy to obliterate," I say, gently extracting myself from her arms.

"Welcome back," Argandea says, his smile disguising his relief.

The memory of my experiences sobers my thoughts. "You realize Tirigan is a traitor?"

Ishtar recoils in shock. "But he rescued me!"

"The soldiers were only interested in me. I knew by Tirigan's eyes just before you disappeared that the entire event was a trap."

"We told you not to go." Ishtar huffs in disgust. "You might listen next time."

I smile. "Maybe."

Argandea frowns. "That is disturbing news. Fortunately, he doesn't have much knowledge of our organization."

"How did you escape?" Lugal asks.

"I had help." I won't tell them who helped me, as I don't want to place her in danger.

"Well, let's discuss things over a drink, shall we?" Argandea pats me on the shoulder and starts walking away.

"Sure." I move to follow him with the others next to me.

We file into a private lounge, and Argandea goes to fetch our drinks once he takes our orders. Afterward, refreshments in hand, I tell them as much about my imprisonment and escape as I think wise to divulge. My story complete, I ask, "And what news do you have?"

Argandea raises his eyebrows. "Very little. We've been practicing defense and offense drills with our new ships, but it's difficult doing that on the empire's doorstep."

I nod in agreement.

"Several naval personnel have defected to our cause," Ishtar inter-jects, enthusiastic over the turn of events.

"You sure they aren't spies?" An uneasiness grips my stomach.

Ishtar straightens her back, affronted. "We have scrutinized their credentials."

I hold my hands up as a peace gesture. "Just checking."

"They've brought a few naval ships with them. Our fleet's build-ing," Argandea says.

I frown. "Why did they defect? They know the price for treason."

"Sick of killing innocent people is the most common reason given."

An uneasiness still grips me, but I let it slide for now. "We'll learn soon enough how untrustworthy they are."

As if on cue, the base's claxons announce a call to general stations. An attack is imminent.

"We'll see if your practice has paid off," I say as we rush into battle.

37

SURPRISE ATTACK

As we rush into the command center in the asteroid, I search for the tactical officer and walk her way. "Status?"

The woman cranes her head toward me and blushes when she sees who is asking. "A battleship, five destroyers, and a fighter carrier, sir."

I frown, musing on the implications. "Rather small force for an attack."

"They may underestimate us," Lugal says.

"Or it's a diversion for the main assault."

"Well, whatever," Argandea says as he reviews the tactical display, "we're committed to engaging them."

"Yes, we are." As I rub my chin, I consider the possibilities of trying out my newfound weaponry capabilities. *A perfect chance to test my ship if I can slip away.* After gazing across the center, I say to Argandea, "You're in charge of the defense," and try leaving.

"Where are you going?" Argandea looks alarmed at the responsibility suddenly placed on his shoulders.

"I just got back. And you know what your fleet's capabilities are. Besides, I have a couple of issues to resolve."

Argandea, Lugal, and Ishtar stare at me in shock as I leave the room. Perhaps they are thinking of the past and see this as another abandonment. I can't help it. My services are of little use in the command center, and the newfound power of my ship may make the difference between victory and defeat.

Without delay, I rush to my shuttle and take off, intent on reaching the *Queen Rosalind* before shots are fired. She comes into view twenty minutes later, and I land. The display in the ship's cockpit shows no one's interested in following me, either.

"What are you up to?"

With a jump, I swirl to face Ishtar. "How did you get in here?"

"I stowed away on the shuttle, of course. You need to be more aware of your surroundings. Well?"

Heat radiates from my face. "Well, what?"

"What are you doing?"

"Nothing. I just thought you could use another ship. Mine has weapons installed, too."

Ishtar's eyebrows rise, and I know she doesn't believe my words.

"You don't know everything."

"Obviously not."

"Now, if your inquisition is over, stop distracting me and help."

"Whatever you say." Ishtar strolls to a chair next to me and straps herself into it.

I do likewise and power up the ship. With a glance over at her, I wonder if she will notice the ship's improved performance. Resigned to whatever happens, I energize the shields and push energy into the thrusters to move the yacht from its resting orbit. The acceleration pushes us both back in our seats until the inertial compensator catches up to the force.

"Wow-ah! What've you done to the ship?"

"Just tuned it a little."

As I steer the vessel to the base, the enemy ships appear on the screen. Moments later, fighters stream from the carrier and position themselves into attack formation. Within seconds, ours spew from the base to join in the conflict. They can conduct their own battle. I intend to go after larger prey as I locate one of the enemy destroyers and veer toward it with increasing speed. Ishtar is staring at me, which I spy from the corner of my eye, but I concentrate on my own intentions. The shields are at full power, so I energize the maser cannons and bring up the targeting display on my screen as a secondary readout to my navigation, which I can transfer to when ready to fire. Adrenaline pumps through my body as the rush of battle fills my psyche.

The targeted destroyer sees me and changes course to challenge my attack. When we move within range of each other, the destroyer fires two missiles, streaking toward me at incredible speed. Flipping to the targeting display, I lock onto both of them and fire my masers, destroying the projectiles in an instant. A smile crosses my face as I realize the ease with which I destroyed them.

My concentration having lapsed, a maser strikes my yacht, sending violent shudders through it. But, when I review the status of my shields, the hit has barely reduced their strength, and they return to full power within seconds.

"What the hell've you done to your ship? That should've taken us out, or at least weakened the shields."

"Are you here to help me or give a running commentary?"

"Help, you idiot."

"Watch out for fighters sneaking up on us, then."

"Aye, aye, captain."

I turn and glance at her, giving a wink as she brings up the tactical display. Returning to my duties, I decide to return fire on the destroyer and send off two shots to the main thrusters in quick succession. The first one destroys their shields, the second takes out the thruster, crippling the destroyer and removing it from the battle.

As I gaze at the tactical screen, I see the resistance fighters are holding their own against the empire's, so I decide to chase the battleship. I sense Ishtar staring at me as she realizes my intent, but I concentrate on the best means of disabling the battleship. This will test the capabilities of my ship's crystal-reinforced power supply. With stolid determination, I line up the ship and fire a shot. My display says it dented the shields, but they still have plenty of energy before they fail.

The battleship fires ten missiles toward me. Now I have a battle as there are thirty seconds to impact. My hand flashes across the operating panel and keys in a sequential aim-and-fire command for the maser cannons, starting the sequence. The masers take out three in quick succession, but the rest of the missiles use diversionary tactics to split up into random trajectories, testing the capabilities of my targeting controls. I take out two more, leaving five and fifteen seconds till they collide. A bead of sweat sits on my brow as the projectiles close in on us.

"Are you sure about this?" Ishtar asks, gripping her seat.

"Hold tight."

I destroy two more missiles with ten seconds left as the rest turn and weave to avoid my masers. With five seconds left, I destroy another. Then I run out of time. The last two collide with my ship and detonate. Ishtar shrieks beside me as the ship rocks from the impact. Any other ship would have disintegrated into particles of dust, but my shields hold.

After regaining my composure, I check the shields, and they have already recharged to seventy percent. Not wanting to go through a similar ordeal, I target the masers on the battleship and start firing each maser with alternate shots, wearing away its shields until they fail. One more blast to the thrusters, and it's taken from the battle.

"That's impossible," Ishtar says as she stares at me in disbelief.

I shrug and grin. "Lucky shot."

A blinding flash lights up space as the battleship disintegrates. Even I'm left speechless by the annihilation.

"How did you do that?"

"Must've hit the reactor."

After seeing the battleship's destruction, the still-functioning destroyers and fighter carrier retreat and vanish moments later, leaving a stranded destroyer for us to overpower and confiscate.

The overwhelming power of my vessel staggers me. It frightens me, too. Now that the empire has seen my ship's capabilities, they'll be warier next time and attack with greater force. As only my ship has these abilities, it leaves the whole resistance vulnerable, but I juggle conflicting choices over the solution. If I offer crystals to the other ships, I fear their captains will become overzealous and uncontrollable to the point of using that strength against us. I still mistrust the others after Tirigan's betrayal. Not only that, but the empire might overpower and capture one of the converted ships, only to discover the technology and convert their entire fleet, leaving us at their mercy again.

As I glance at Ishtar, I know she suspects how I destroyed a battleship, but she says nothing. "Let's return to base," I say as I plot a course back to the asteroid.

An hour later, the leadership team assembles in the main conference room on the asteroid base to discuss the aftermath of the surprise attack.

"We must evacuate," Argandea says, after a discussion about the base's vulnerability now that the empire knows it exists.

"But where shall we go?" Lugal asks, devoid of any suggestions himself, his shoulders sagging.

"There is a disused mining base in the outreaches of Eridu," Ninsar suggests.

"That is too near their center of power," Argandea says.

"Don't we have assets in Uruk?" Ishtar asks. "It's a quiet backwater with little military presence."

"That could work." Lugal's depression leaves him, now hopeful of a solution.

A general murmur of agreement circles the room.

I have no disagreement with the suggestion, but I gaze at them, wondering if anyone else has considered what we should do before we leave Larsa. The others' reaction suggests they just want to retreat before another attack, with no thought to the possibility that we could strike them. So, I speak up. "We must put the empire on the back foot before we leave."

Conversation ceases as they draw their attention to me.

"What do you mean?" Argandea asks.

"The armed forces on Larsa are licking their wounds at present. Or worse, they're a wounded predator, infuriated by the sting of the injury we've just inflicted. We must make sure it's in no condition for future attacks. We need to conduct a counter-offensive against them before we leave. Destroy their capabilities here. That way, we stoke the fire under the emperor and Barak. Enrage them to the point of making mistakes."

"You want to attack the bases here in Larsa?" Lugal stares at me, incredulous.

I shrug. "Why not? We have to let them know we aren't playing anymore. They sought to damage us. Two can play that game." As I glance at Ishtar, I see her eyes sparkle with excitement.

"I agree with Halwende," Ishtar says. "Let's do this and kick ass! I'm sick of being on the defensive. It's time we became a problem for the empire. There are many dissatisfied citizens, even military personnel, too scared to fight the tyranny they live under because they don't see any organization worth fighting with. Let's give them someone to support, a force to rally behind."

My mind swells with pride as I listen to Ishtar and realize I couldn't have said it better myself. Of the leaders, Ishtar displays the most aggression, and I admire it. The others glance at each other to gauge their reactions.

Argandea sighs. "This makes me nervous, although I admit a point must arrive when we change from defensive tactics to embracing the challenge of offense. Maybe that time is now. Who agrees with this strategy?"

Ishtar's hand shoots up. Lugal raises his, as does Ninsar. Yarla holds out for several seconds as he rubs his chin, thinking, but his hand rises in the end too. With the others having voted, I raise mine to join the agreement. I can't help but smile at the group's solidarity. And yet, I realize the responsibility just placed on my shoulders.

"Much as I fear the consequences of failure, I will agree to this course of action," Argandea says as he gazes into each of our eyes. "Let us plan what we must do."

38

COUNTERATTACK

Our ships gather into formation and gain speed as we head for the empire's military bases around Larsa. Two protective battle platforms orbit the planet, each with a flotilla of destroyers, corvettes, battleships, and fighter carriers nearby to defend the platforms from any assault and offer coverage for the planet's defense. They outnumber us three to one, and any attack would be a suicide mission. But no one has taken the new capabilities of the *Queen Rosalind* into account. We are too thin to strike both platforms simultaneously, so we select the one missing the battleship I destroyed and aim for it.

Fighters stream from our fighter carrier before we fly in range of the platform's defenses and head for the surrounding naval vessels. Moments later, defending fighters rush toward them in defense, and a dogfight starts as they tangle with each other.

Our battleship and destroyers maneuver to a tee formation and approach while I hang back on my yacht, tempting anyone to threaten me. As if reading my mind, two destroyers break from the main fleet and home in on my ship, bringing a smile to my face. *Feeling confident with just two?* Settling into my seat, I prepare for the onslaught. Ishtar has joined me again as my assistant, and she follows my instructions to the letter. The destroyers separate to make themselves harder targets and bombard me from both sides.

Chatter from the rest of our fleet fills the cockpit, notifying us of progress in the conflict. With time to spare, I check the status of the vessels on the second platform. They are staying where they are, believing the existing flotilla enough for the engagement.

"How close will you let them get?" Ishtar asks.

"I'm interested in their intentions. They can make the first move."

"You won't feign running?"

"No." I shrug. "Let them think we're dead in the vacuum." I look at the scanner. "This looks interesting. Two corvettes are joining us."

The corvettes have split from the main defending force and are heading our way too, splitting as they approach. The four vessels advance into position just outside my firing range. Moments later, a message flashes on my screen. I open the channel.

"Unidentified vessel, surrender and prepare for boarding," a naval commander barks.

I grin. "Why would I do that?"

"We have you outnumbered and have invincible superiority in firepower. Any sign of resistance will cause your destruction."

"We will fire on you if you approach our ship."

"Very well. We have warned you." The screen goes blank.

"You're sure we'll win?" Ishtar glances at me.

"I demolished a battleship. What could these ships throw at us to beat that?"

"They'll shoot you from four different directions."

"That's why you'll watch the shields and divert power where it's needed."

Convinced, Ishtar ceases the conversation and concentrates on her task.

The vessels approach the yacht, move into range, and shoot at us, our shields absorbing the energy without even dipping in their power levels. Wanting them well within firing range so they cannot escape once I shoot, I stay stationary and inert, allowing the ships to continue approaching me. The vessels draw nearer and start a coordinated attack of maser fire onto individual regions of the yacht, intending to have multiply sections of my shielding fail at once. Their assault is barely enough to load the shield generators above idling.

Satisfied they're within reach for my demonstration, I open fire on the destroyer in front of me. The maser bursts, destroying the forward shield before blasting into the ship, exposing several sections to the vacuum of space. It turns, which gives me a shot at the primary drives. After shooting it, the destroyer disintegrates in a flash of radiation, the last evidence of it being debris radiating from the site. As if by cause and effect, the surviving three attackers stop firing and turn to escape my onslaught. I blast one corvette, making quick work of its annihilation and then the other, leaving the destroyer. As it powers away from us, I fire my maser at its rear, driving the beam through the thrusters and burrowing into the drive compartment, disintegrating the ship into oblivion moments later.

It's not a pleasure inflicting so much destruction, and I sigh with regret. How many families will weep the loss of loved ones tonight?

"Things are happening on the other platform," Ishtar says.

As I glance at the tactical screen, I see a flotilla of ships headed toward us. Half the naval fleet is assembled at the platform. Our plan is to devastate the ships at one platform only, so I must speed matters up to avoid a simultaneous confrontation with the reinforcements. There is no other way. I steer the *Queen Rosalind* toward the conflict in progress and join the fray.

"Prepare for battle," I say, glancing at Ishtar as I steel myself for the onslaught.

I head for several destroyers encircling our battleship, pounding at its shields. No one's used missiles so far, which surprises me. Maybe they're too near the platform to risk one going astray and exploding into it. Two corvettes steer my way as I approach. They risk firing four rockets each, streaking toward us at enormous velocity. I activate my defensive masers, switch them to automatic, and start shooting. The missiles explode before they cover half the distance, impressing even me despite my knowledge of the crystal's capabilities. Once within firing range, I fire the main masers, destroying the corvettes before they get a shot off at me. After adjusting my course, I make for the closest destroyer and, with a short exchange of shots, that too disintegrates once its shields collapse.

With me joining the battle, our battleship intensifies its attack on two destroyers, firing missiles at them while still bombarding them with masers. The combination gets through their defenses and wipes out both destroyers.

"Well done," I communicate with the battleship.

"Thanks for the help," Argandea replies. "Let's finish this."

We both change vector and head further into the battle zone. There are eight corvettes, two destroyers, and the fighter carrier left. As I gaze at the tactical screen, I notice our fighters have the edge over the empire's, although there have been losses on both sides. Then I notice a squadron of twenty fighters and two corvettes split off and steer for our fighter carrier. On recognizing the danger, I veer my course toward the attack craft. Several of our own fighters give chase. The carrier has defensive capabilities but cannot withstand a sustained assault. That's why it remains behind the battlefront. Normally, corvettes or similar vessels defend it, but with our low numbers, they leave it to its own defense.

At my current velocity, the enemy will attack the carrier before I can fight it. Even if I increase my speed to the supposed limit for a yacht, I'd be at least thirty seconds away before I could fire at it. With no other choice but to expose the improved velocity potential, I hasten toward the impending battle, decreasing the time for my interception. My acceleration is not enough, so I maximize it, straining the inertial compensation for the ship into overload, the fields just holding. The image of Ishtar staring at me in alarm flickers at the corner of my eye. A bead of perspiration drips from my chin.

As if knowing my intentions, the enemy fighters power ahead of the corvettes, intent on damaging the carrier. I now have a choice — chase the fighters or confront the corvettes. We cannot lose the fighter carrier. Without it, we cannot transport fighters into battle. So, I give chase, telling Ishtar to tell our fighters to attack the corvettes. Realization sets in that the opposing fighters will engage the carrier before I arrive, and I must conclude the carrier will sustain damage. Determination drives me to reduce the destruction. I program my maser cannons to auto-target the fighters as I find and lock their identities into the targeting computer. Once I set the squadron for annihilation, I concentrate on flying within range to fire on them.

The fighters stay in a tight pattern, intent on concentrating their attack. This makes it simpler for me, and I home in on them. They stay in formation, disregarding my approach. I'm impressed by their discipline. When in range, they shoot at the carrier. It defends itself as best it can but has damage inflicted by the severity of the assault. At last, I get within distance and start the auto-fire sequence for the masers, destroying half the squadron before I overshoot and decelerate at a frightening rate to turn for another run at them.

Meanwhile, our fighters are badgering the corvettes like flies at a corpse. They inflict minor damage while the shields hold, but at least they have diverted their attention while I annihilate the fighters. On realizing their vulnerability if they stay in tight formation, the enemy fighters split up and decide to chase me before re-engaging the carrier. That is their mistake. My maser cannons destroy them before they even get one shot at me.

With the fighters destroyed, I change course to help our fighters remove the corvettes' threat, as they near the firing range of the carrier. They can inflict far greater damage to the carrier than the fighters can. The two corvettes' shields have weakened but hold enough for them to start their attack.

I set my course and rush toward the corvettes, targeting a maser on each. Before I have time to act, the corvettes fire projectiles at the carrier. I swear when I realize they've tricked me into underestimating the real danger. I veer off to confront the missiles before they contact the carrier, leaving the corvettes to our fighters and my rear open to attack from the corvettes. I can't help that. With hands flashing over the keyboard, I target the rockets and set auto-fire on the masers. Ishtar's face is a mask of horror as she stares at her visual display, which shows the missiles rocketing toward the carrier. The seconds tick by and, with time running out, we come within range, engaging and destroying each missile, except one, which gets through and explodes into the carrier. A gaping hole appears on its side, but the carrier is still operational.

My patience with the corvettes has run out as they pepper me from my rear, so I target my masers and fire at them. One explodes after five seconds. The other lasts two seconds longer before it too succumbs to my firepower.

"Thanks," I hear from the comm.

"You owe me," I tell the speaker.

Not having time for further discussion, I change course for the rest of the enemy vessels still fighting to protect the platform.

"What the ...?"

I turn to Ishtar. Amazement lines her face. "What's wrong?"

"Look at what's happening with the other platform's ships."

Puzzled, I view the tactical display and frown. Instead of streaking toward us, the ships are attacking each other. "Can we get that on visual?"

"We may not be close enough, but I'll try." Ishtar manipulates the vision controls and zooms in on the ships. She types away at the keyboard, and identity markers appear for each vessel.

They're fighting each other — a full-on battle between the ships — the only explanation being some warships are fighting for us.

"Is it possible for an entire ship to mutiny?" I ask as I glance at Ishtar.

She shrugs. "Must be. Enough to control the vessel. One'd think the captain is leading it, though. I can't imagine Security taking orders from anyone else unless they've turned too."

"Well, let's take advantage of our good luck and finish this attack. I'm keen to escape from here."

"I agree with that."

With that out of the way, I concentrate on reaching our own battle. Once I join the fray, it doesn't take long to destroy the remaining defensive force surrounding the platform and take the platform's defenses out of action, too. I break off and wait near our own fighter carrier for the rest to clean up and prepare to leave.

39

RETURN TO ERIDU

O ur ships congregate within the asteroid belt of the Uruk system, including ten defector imperial naval vessels and crews.

Once the battle at Larsa concludes and the surprising skirmish between the imperial ships has played out, the remaining vessels contact the resistance and confirm our suspicion that they have defected to our side. They herd those still loyal to the empire onto one vessel and keep the rest to tag along with us, resulting in our fleet expanding by three destroyers and seven corvettes. Our little renegade navy has the makings of a respectable force. But the newcomers' trustworthiness weighs on the rebel leadership, many questioning their inclusion in our planning. A few leaders debate the wisdom of their accompanying us to Uruk, but we realize we have to trust our newest recruits, albeit cautiously, if we are to overthrow the empire. Otherwise, we will stay a band of renegades pestering the emperor as a distracting splinter instead of a growing migraine.

After transferring to the battleship, Ishtar and I head for the main conference room to discuss our options. Several fresh faces sit at the table, people wearing mutilated imperial military uniforms. I nod as I find a seat. Introductions can wait for the meeting to start. Our other leadership personnel file in after five more minutes, followed by Argandea as the last.

After clearing his throat, Argandea smiles and speaks. "We've inflicted a minor dent in the empire's naval capabilities. Not only did we destroy the defenses surrounding Larsa, but we also gained several vessels thanks to our esteemed colleagues' defection." Argandea nods at the newcomers who return the gesture. Once he glances at me, Ishtar, and the other long-term leaders, Argandea focuses his attention on the strangers again. "Our question remains: why have you defected? It is unusual for you to behave in such a manner. Not only are you traitors who will be executed if you're captured, but your families will suffer, if not killed. Maybe one of you can act as a spokesperson and explain your actions."

The defectors glance at each other, sorting out their order of hierarchy until they settle on one person to speak on their behalf.

"We haven't formally introduced ourselves yet. My name is Hadanish and I captain the destroyer *Contender*. It seems the others have nominated me as the speaker for our little group for now." Hadanish sweeps his view over the other renegades. "You may not be aware of this, but dissatisfaction is growing amongst the armed services with the emperor's current policies — in particular, the wholesale incarceration and execution of suspected rebels and their households. Once these raids became indiscriminate, discontent seeped into the military like a slow-moving cancer in the empire's body. This frustration is no secret, but your aforementioned threats of retribution to dissenters and their families kept most in check — until now. Speaking personally, I'm sorry today has eventuated. I dedicated my life to the upkeep of law and order throughout the empire, and it saddens my heart that I've taken the actions I have today. But I do not regret it. The emperor's despotism must stop for everyone's good. Otherwise, the empire will degenerate into a quagmire of corruption and suffering where he and his cronies luxuriate in their greed and wealth while their citizens scrape out a living." His fellow defectors' eyes are transfixed on Hadanish's every word. I even spot a tear in one of them.

"These are big words," Hadanish continues. "They may or may not impress you, but I hope that our recent actions will've shown the sincerity of our desire for a better way. When news of the resistance overpowering and confiscating imperial vessels and winning engagements with our navy came to our attention, we knew a time would come when we had to decide between our loyalty to the empire and our belief in justice. We've made our decision. Now you must make yours."

I lock eyes with each deserter and see sadness, sincerity, pride, and ... determination. I notice one in particular. "And do you agree with what Hadanish says?" I ask her.

As she straightens her back and her eyes pierce into mine, she says, "Every word."

"And what is your name?"

"Uttu. What is yours?"

"Halwende."

A collective gasp issues from the deserters.

"You're the one?" Uttu asks.

"I don't know what you mean by me being the one, but I am Halwende."

"You escaped from the palace prison. Many people suffered because of it."

The news shocks me. What of Lilith? Has the emperor realized she contributed to my escape? If she isn't dead, she is in grave danger. And if that is the case, I must save her from her father's clutches. Burying the information within me for now, I ask, "And the others in your crews?"

"We removed those still loyal from the ships before we left Larsa. The rest are loyal to us," Hadanish replies.

"Are there others?"

"I can't be sure. Many question the emperor's actions, but whether they would defect because of it, I don't know."

The meeting continues with discussions about integrating the new arrivals into the resistance organization and the tasks needed to set up our base in Uruk. Uruk is a backwater of the empire with few settlers. No permanent imperial presence occupies the system, and the inhabitants detest the current regime. But there are always those willing to sell information for temporary gain given half a chance, so we must stay vigilant.

My thoughts return to Lilith and the danger she placed herself in by engineering my escape, and I realize I'm obliged to rescue her. I must take her away from her father's reach before he realizes her betrayal. The others will hate my decision and try to dissuade me, but I will do it. I glance at Argandea and then Ishtar.

"What?" Ishtar asks. "I know I won't like what you're going to say."

Without subtlety, I spit it out, "I'm returning to Eridu."

"No!" my friends shout in unison.

"You cannot," Argandea says. "It is too dangerous for you. And we need you with us."

"I have unfinished business there."

"You almost died last time," Ishtar yells in anger as she glares at me. "Can't you stop this selfishness and consider the resistance for one second?"

Her passion drives a knife through me. Regardless, I must follow my convictions. Ishtar doesn't realize how much I'm tempted to forget them and fly back to Helheim and Adala. There is a greater drama at play here, and I must persevere to its completion, no matter my personal consequences. With a matching glare I don't mean, I reply, "I must. It is my destiny. It is part of our destiny."

Ishtar rises with a rapidity that tosses her chair away behind her as she throws her hands up in disgust. "Men and their egos."

I grin despite myself. "This is not ego. If I had a choice, it wouldn't involve returning to Eridu."

"Then why do it?"

"I already said. There's unfinished business."

She shakes her head in resignation. "I'm coming with you then."

"Is that wise after last time?"

"Our destinies coincide, so yes."

"I will go with you too," Uttu says.

Both Ishtar and I glance over at her and her unexpected offer. Ishtar shoots a glance at Argandea.

"I'd be of great value to you in circumventing the imperial security systems," Uttu points out.

I can't argue with that, although the thought of Uttu and Ishtar in proximity send a shudder up my spine. I've seen Ishtar's volatility. I pray Uttu doesn't own a similar temperament.

"Count me in too," Lugal says.

Three more people along on my crusade than I wish frustrates me, but I don't believe I have a choice in the matter. "Anyone else want a joyride?"

Ishtar lets out a hearty laugh. "I doubt it's going to be a joyride. Trouble follows you wherever you lead."

"There is no stopping you," Argandea says. "But at least let's celebrate for one night before you leave."

I nod in agreement. "We should welcome our newest recruits."

With that, the meeting ends, and the attendees disband to their respective lives.

THE CELEBRATIONS ARE full of laughter and banter. Warmth for these people fills my heart. If only they knew what lies ahead. I only understand half of what I suspect.

For once, alcohol flows with no restraint. I sit on the sidelines observing people's behavior with interest until Uttu waltzes toward me, unsteady.

"Dance with me," she demands.

"I'm not much of a dancer."

"You will dance all the same."

"I see I can't ignore you."

"How do you think I became a destroyer commander?"

Ishtar's attention catches my eye, and she is glaring at Uttu. I groan inside as it hits me that I must tolerate these two with their competitions and jealousies on the yacht back to Eridu.

Since Uttu won't accept no for an answer, I rise and allow her to usher me to the dance space, where she cavorts to the music, and I follow the best I can. Just as I decide to leave, Uttu throws herself at me, making me throw my arms out to stop her from falling.

"Take me," she whispers.

Why am I cursed with these delicate dilemmas? Uttu, intoxicated, staggers as I lead her from the floor. As I notice Ishtar again, I get her attention, begging her for help.

"I see someone else has fallen for you," she says in a cutting tone.

I sigh. "What am I supposed to do? Refuse her request for a dance?" My eyes plead for understanding.

Ishtar's temper abates. "No. You're a magnet for women, especially when they've had too much to drink. I know from experience." She grabs Uttu under the shoulder and helps support her as we walk her to a chair.

After lowering Uttu into position, I gaze at Ishtar and smile. "You're a great friend."

Ishtar chuckles. "So are you." She lifts her chin at Uttu. "What do we do with her?"

"Get someone to take her to her cabin."

After arranging things for Uttu, Ishtar and I grab a drink and join Argandea, Lugal, and the others and contribute to the banter circulating in the group. The party ends late, and we retire to our cabins for rest.

The next day, I prepare for departure to Eridu with Ishtar, Lugal, and Uttu, although Uttu struggles to function in between moans of self-pity at her hangover.

40

RECAPTURE

After entering the Eridu system, I fly the Lander to the surface while Ishtar contacts a trusted resistance cell. The four of us then move to an underground fortress near Eridu City. It's divided into an accommodation zone, one as a marshaling station for assembling fighters. We're led to the residential section and given rooms. I'm eager to start what I came for, but Ishtar advises me to wait until intelligence arrives on the latest imperial movements and security status. Since they're gathering information, I ask about the surveillance setup inside the emperor's palace.

"What are you planning?" Ishtar asks, puzzled over why I want details about the interior of the palace.

After studying her and the others, I know it's time to reveal my true purpose for coming to Eridu. "I plan to rescue Princess Lilith."

Lugal, who has just taken a gulp of his drink, sprays it over us and splutters afterward to regain his breath. The other two stare at me, incredulous.

"You're *what*?" Uttu asks.

Ishtar's eyebrows crinkle. "What do you mean, *rescue*? Don't you mean kidnap?"

"No, rescue. She is the one who helped me escape last time. I am indebted to her and want to take her away from her father before he finds out she is his enemy."

"So ... how will you contact her?"

"Find someone able to relay a message."

"I can help with that," Uttu says, frowning.

"I don't like it." Lugal shakes his head. "This is too risky. You can't do this and risk capture again. You are too valuable. Why do you always do everything yourself?"

"I am not letting Lilith stay in her father's clutches." My jaw sets in obstinance.

Lugal shrugs his shoulders and waves his arms in the air as he walks away, muttering his disapproval.

"Well, we won't dissuade you from this, so how do we play it?" Ishtar asks.

"You have informants inside the palace, Uttu?"

"Yes. Contacts open to providing a favor."

"Reach out and find out how Lilith wants to meet us."

"Will do."

SEVERAL DAYS ELAPSE before we receive a response.

Uttu rushes into the fortress out of breath. "It's dangerous out there," she says in between deep gasps. Once recovered, she continues her relayed reply. "The princess says to join her at the tunnel's entrance tomorrow at 2 pm."

I frown. "Which entrance?"

"What tunnel?" Ishtar asks.

"That's all she said."

With pursed lips, I glance at Uttu and Ishtar. "There is a concealed passage leading into the palace. But I'm not sure if she means the interior entrance or the outside one. It's a significant walk between the two. So, if I get it wrong, she may give up waiting and leave."

"This is too dangerous," Lugal says. "But since we can't dissuade you, if you aim for the inside entrance and you're mistaken, you'll meet her along the way."

"True."

To prepare for the rescue, we bury ourselves in a conference room and flesh out our plan for our movements the next day.

OUR SCOOTER SKIMS across Eridu's surface, two meters from the ground. Ishtar in the driver's seat concentrates as we fly toward the tunnel entrance at the palace compound. I fret over the possibility Security has discovered how I escaped the last time and has sealed the passage or placed it under tight surveillance. Although if that were the case, Lilith wouldn't have suggested it for the rendezvous. After ninety minutes, the four of us arrive at the entrance, Ishtar landing the scooter with smooth precision.

"You're sure of this?" Lugal asks again.

"Yes, I must do this."

"So be it. Godspeed."

"We'll see you soon," I say to Lugal and Ishtar, who will guard the scooter while Uttu and I venture through the tunnel to fetch Lilith.

I find the outer door's opening mechanism after a prolonged search, and Uttu and I creep into the subterranean realm. The tunnel's confines cry out how vulnerable we are as we can only move forward or return the way we came. There is no other choice. Lights illuminate as we traverse the depths of the passage into the palace and hopefully to the waiting Lilith. Uttu glances ahead and behind as we progress further away from the comparative safety of the outside. We have weapons, but our pistols will be no match for a security guard detail.

We arrive at the interior entrance and sigh in disappointment. There is no Lilith, but we are five minutes early, so I motion Uttu to wait until either Lilith comes or we open the door. Nervously, Uttu paces the shaft, which annoys me.

"Can you stop pacing?"

She halts and stares at me. "I've never taken part in an exercise like this before today."

"The first lesson you need to learn is to stay calm — and staying calm means standing still."

"Yeah, okay." She stops her pacing but fidgets. That's better than pacing, so I say nothing.

Two o'clock ticks over, and Lilith still doesn't come. So, I use the mechanism to open the door, which slides into its recess with ease.

General Barak and three security personnel smile back at us, the guards with masers aimed, ready to shoot.

"We meet again," Barak says. "Don't try running. There is no escape."

To run is pointless, and I can't close the entrance before at least one guard rushes through to us. Besides, they'll stun us, or worse, before we dash for freedom. With no other choice, I step through the doorway toward them, and Uttu follows me. A movement to the side distracts me, and I turn. Lilith is struggling against the guard's restraint, eyes desperate in defeat. Two guards come forward and disarm us.

"You must plan better next time. We've had Princess Lilith under surveillance ever since you escaped. It was a simple deduction when she started sneaking through the corridors," Barak says.

Making no reply, I straighten my shoulders and prepare for my fate.

Barak's stare shifts to Uttu. She, too, attempts to stand tall with less success than I. "I have no time for traitors." He grabs the maser from the guard next to him and shoots Uttu through the chest, leaving a cauterized but weeping hole where her heart was moments ago. Her body wavers for several seconds before collapsing to the floor.

"No!" I glare at Barak with hatred for his barbarity.

After handing the maser back to the guard, Barak returns his attention to me, calm and self-assured. "You should select your recruits better."

"How you've changed from the days we worked together."

"Everyone comes to understand reality during their lifetime."

"And what of Lilith and me? Will we suffer the same consequence?"

"Unfortunately, no. I don't know what fate Emperor Shulgi has in store for you, but he left specific instructions for me to bring both of you to him unharmed. Now, come. The emperor wishes to speak with you." Barak motions for me to walk along the corridor behind him, which I do with Lilith shoved beside me to do likewise. I take a couple of furtive glances at Lilith as they direct us to our destination. Despite her despair, she strides with dignity to meet her future.

Twenty minutes later, we enter Shulgi's throne room with its immense trimmings of grandeur and are told to stand at attention. The guards step back, and Barak stands to the side.

41

HE MUST DIE

Emperor Shulgi strides in moments later and sits. He stares with intensity, first at me, then at Lilith, and lastly, Barak. "You have done well," he says to Barak. "We have the slippery eel back in our clutches."

"Thank you, Your Imperium."

On shifting his attention to Lilith, his temperament softens and becomes pained. "Why, Lilith? Why do you betray me? I had such high expectations for you. I treated you as my pearl ever since your mother died. You were to continue my rule after me, but you paid me back with betrayal."

"You never loved me." Lilith spits her words out in disgust. "There is only room for one person in your life, and that's you. All you care about is accumulating power to satisfy your greed. And to secure your authority, you destroy and execute those who speak against you. Sycophants you reward with favors while your subjects wallow in poverty. It will be an honor to die."

Shulgi bursts into laughter. After struggling to compose himself, he says, "Your self-righteous dignity is amusing. But die? No, I intend a more useful fate for you, much more satisfying."

"Whatever's in store for me won't be worse than having to spend another second in your presence."

A guard steps forward, intending to punish Lilith for her insolence, but Shulgi holds his hand up, causing the guard to freeze.

"You dare assault the daughter of the emperor?"

On realizing his mistake, the guard bows his head. "Forgive me, Your Imperium."

"We shall attend to that later." His attention returns to Lilith. "You misunderstand me, my dear. You will spend ample time in my presence, especially when you marry a person of my choosing, someone deserving of the offspring of the emperor and who will rule the empire at your side."

Lilith's stoic stance breaks, and she stares at her father in dismay.

As soon as Shulgi sees he has broken her, he smiles and turns his attention to me. Any semblance of friendliness and reason disappears. "Halwende, you conniving viper. Kneel before me."

When I refuse, the guard on my side slams a truncheon into my legs just above and behind the knees, forcing me to the floor.

"We don't know how you keep escaping, especially when we gave chase with the troop carrier. Your disappearances are a mystery. We would extract your secret from you, but we learned last time the uselessness of trying. And now you return with a traitor from the Larsa battle?" Shulgi diverts his attention to Barak. "You could have allowed me to question her before you delivered your punishment."

With head bowed, Barak says, "My apologies, Your Imperium."

Bringing his curiosity back to me, Shulgi says, "We may use other means of encouraging you to surrender information. Eyewitness accounts mention a ship with unusual properties, both defensive and offensive. You don't have knowledge of that, do you?"

I stare straight ahead and stay silent.

Shulgi stands and paces the floor in front of me. "You've caused me immense embarrassment. You make me appear weak with your rebellious attacks on my military. I know of this resistance movement and its web's extent. Before you appeared, it was just an irritation. What is it, Halwende, that drives people to follow you with such loyalty? Anyone would think you were the long-lost mythical heir to the royal throne."

A shaft of dread pierces my gut as he says those words, but I disguise my reaction. They must not discover the crystal's secret power, the old man's knowledge, or the crypt on Larsa.

"Was there anybody at the exterior entrance?" Shulgi asks Barak.

"No one was there when we arrived."

"Pity. They may've become useful."

Shulgi stops his pacing and stands before me. I see his upper thighs as I continue looking straight ahead. "Take him away. I shall speak with him later. Do with him what you please, but he must still be able to talk."

A guard kicks me, forcing me to rise, which I do, the remaining sting of the truncheon lingering in my legs.

"And Lilith?" Barak asks.

After a moment's silence, Shulgi says, "Lock her up for now, too. Next to him if you wish. Their conversation may amuse me."

"Yes, Your Imperium."

"Leave. I have much to ponder."

The guards shove Lilith and me into motion, and we end up in prison cells far below the surface in the palace compound.

With ill-treatment or torture hanging like a guillotine over my neck, I cross to the basin in the cell and wash my face. There is nothing I can do but wait for the emperor's next move. As I sit on the bed and rest my back against the wall, I wallow in self-piteous reminisce of my misfortune and naivety. I should've known the emperor suspected Lilith had a part in my freedom, and yet I thought I could extract her from under Shulgi's nose. My heart weeps for Uttu, who risked her life to help me. She must have realized they would kill her if they caught her. Yet still, she volunteered. I must remember to arrange a commemorative service for her when I escape. What am I thinking? I'm not escaping this predicament.

"Halwende?" Lilith's whisper wafts to my ears.

With my line of thought broken, I glance toward the next cell. "Yes?"

"I'm sorry."

"Why are you sorry? I was the one naïve enough to think extracting you from Shulgi's clutches would be easy."

"But now you'll die."

"I'm not dead yet."

Sobs come from Lilith's cage. "The empire will never be free of Father's tyranny."

I fear she's right. "Never is a long time."

The door to the prison block slides open, and four burly guards file in, stopping before my cell. My stomach clenches in dread of what lies ahead. In anticipation, I rise from my bed as one disables the force field keeping me caged. Two sentries march in and place restraints on me. The senior guard steps in front of me. "We're going to have fun with you." Swifter than I can track with my eye, his fist slams into my chest, forcing me to bow, gasping for breath as tears come to my eyes.

The guards behind me shove me to move. I must comply. After a ten-minute walk, we enter a chamber of terror. After thousands of years of civilization, humanity should've outgrown its thirst for inflicting harm on others for fun, but we haven't. And we should have invented updated means of inflicting pain than those used for millennia. With further shoving, they sit me in a chair and strap me into it. After so many times sitting in one torture chair or another, the scenario is becoming monotonous. But the suffering hasn't. With grunts of satisfaction, the guards leave, and I wait.

The interval isn't long. Barak strolls in and studies me. "It's unfortunate I must keep you in a talking state. There is so much enjoyment I could extract from you otherwise."

"My heart bleeds for you."

A backhand slams into my cheek, and the taste of blood fills my mouth.

With a glare, I say, "What happened to you?"

Another slap smashes me. "Now, what shall I do? I know."

Barak steps behind me where my restraints prevent me from observing. The clatter of small objects being sorted infuses my ears as

I wait. I don't have long for my dread to ferment. Footsteps return, and Barak places a skeleton of a cap on my head. He holds a remote control. "Do you recognize this device?"

"I hope it's something to blow your brains away."

After a hearty laugh, Barak says, "Close. But it won't be my brain; it's yours. Have you ever experienced a devastating nightmare of boogeymen hunting you in the night? That is a fairytale compared to this. Here, let me show you." He presses a button on the remote.

For a moment, nothing happens, and I relax, although Barak's unfazed. A thrum builds in my head until I shriek in pain, the agony threatening to split my skull open. Then images of recent memories appear, but the people in them are hysterical as a demonic monster mutilates and slaughters them. I know the image is a distortion, a construction produced by the device on my head, but the knowledge doesn't reduce the horror I experience as the demon enters my dreams. Perspiration bursts from my forehead as I see the monster closing in on me. I squirm and struggle to escape the confines of my restraints, the effort causing them to cut into my skin as the nightmare reaches its climax and the devil lunges at me, and I howl in horror. Again and again, I scream, trying to remove the monster from me, only to hear an evil roar of pleasure as it plays with my emotions without end. Exhausted, my mind tolerates the torture no longer, and I lapse into unconsciousness.

"HALWENDE? HALWENDE?"

The universe reforms again in my brain as consciousness returns. *Did I hear something?*

"Halwende?"

A female voice. My throat parched, I open my eyes and am confused by my surroundings until I remember the recent past — my capture and ... whatever Barak did to me. "Lilith?" I grate from my raw vocal cords.

"You're alive."

"How long ...?"

"Several hours. I've been trying to get your attention since they dragged you back."

Intent on quenching my thirst, I move to rise but scream in pain instead, as every muscle in my body protests in agony. Undaunted, I gasp air into my lungs and pull myself across the floor to the basin. I flex my legs to remove the cramps and regain control over my muscles and try to stand again, using the bowl for support. With great effort, I lean over the bowl, gasping. After gathering my strength, I suck water into my mouth, the cool liquid restoring my spirits as I gulp it down.

Refreshed, I stagger along the walls until I reach the front of my cage, my legs regaining strength and starting to work as they should. I allow my body to slide to the floor in a sitting position. "Lilith."

"Yes?"

"Has anything else happened?"

"No. They've left me alone apart from feeding me."

As if reading my thoughts, the cellblock door slides open, and four guards march through it. I groan as they restrain me and lead me away as before, anticipating another session with Barak. Instead, I'm led to the elevator and rise to the surface to return to the throne room, where the guards push me to a stationary position, and they stand at attention surrounding me.

A few minutes later, Barak and Emperor Shulgi stroll into the room. Shulgi sits on his throne, and Barak stands to the side. Shulgi observes me for several seconds before he speaks. "You've left me with a conundrum. Your true identity is beyond our ability to discover, and yet you hold great repute. A mysterious and powerful ship accompanies you, but we cannot locate it. The resistance is growing in numbers, strength, and daring, and it started with news of you surfacing. Do you understand my difficulty?" He eyes me with a piercing stare.

I have no intention of replying. Whatever I say will incriminate me. What Shulgi intends is obvious, but I refuse to give him any satisfaction with any pleading or groveling. My dignity will stay intact.

"It is a pity we killed your family. We can't execute them twice. When Barak informed me of their whereabouts, I knew I had the backbone of your particular rebellion broken. By misfortune, which I'll never understand, we couldn't locate you. You vanished. Your execution would have crushed your so-called resistance once and for all. Since your death remained a mystery, a fable started to circulate that you had survived. The hope of your resurrection increased the resolve of what survived of your grab for power. And now this — you've become an irritation to me, an itch, a rash. How should I treat this ailment?"

My thoughts are my own, and my eyes stare straight at him with a blank expression.

Shulgi sighs. "I could've used someone of your caliber. You would have complemented Barak's loyalty. But you are too dangerous." Shulgi's attention diverts to Barak for several seconds before it returns to me. "Yes, you are too dangerous. We will execute you at noon tomorrow, with full media coverage, so your fellow collaborators can see what happens to rebels. You must die."

42

THIS IS IT

Back in my cell awaiting execution, I contemplate my life. Once I consider everything I've achieved, I only have two genuine regrets. The first is my cowardice when Shulgi's forces defeated us in Eridu. The loss devastated me. Despite my earlier bravery, I couldn't endure our defeat on top of the murders of my wife and child. Maybe I should've welcomed being reunited with them again, but I feared death. I challenge anyone to confront their demise without fear. Regardless of our beliefs and creeds, that niggling uncertainty enters our hearts when the time comes to face our mortality.

Still, my adventures on other horizons resulted from that bout of weakness, experiences I wouldn't have had if I had faced my responsibilities — which brings me to my second regret. I will never see Adala again. Her cherubic features, as fresh in my memory as when I first set eyes on her, and her charm far exceed anything I deserve. There is one consolation. I can face my death having had the pleasure of knowing her and sharing my life with her, however briefly.

Why do I always foolishly place myself in danger? I needn't have come back to rally the troops. I fear my pride got the better of me. And I didn't have to come this time to extract Lilith from her father's clutches. I must have a death wish. I still hope to return to Adala and crush her in my arms, smelling the sweetness of her scent.

There is one dread that concerns me, though. Whether I live or die, Shulgi will discover Adala, her planet, and the technology still latent in the portal room below the palace. Contemplating what plans Shulgi may intend for Adala if he captures her sends shivers through me. Sentinel will try to protect her to the death. Of that, I am sure. If only there were a way ...

"Halwende."

With a sigh, my contemplation disrupted, I answer. "Yes, Lilith?"

"What are you thinking?"

I chuckle. "Listing my life's regrets."

"I've interacted little with the outside world, apart from entertaining the sycophantic cronies circling Father. He has seen to that. But I am glad I got to meet you. You are the first honest and respectable person I've met."

Her compliment sends a lump to my throat. "You don't know me."

"That may be. I'm unaware of your history. I see what you do now. You won't let circumstances prevent you from doing the right thing. You could've forgotten me, but you came back for me, despite the risk. Few people would do that."

"They advised me against it."

"Exactly. But you did it regardless. I thank you for trying. If only it had ended differently."

"But it didn't."

"Well, I just wanted to thank you."

"You're welcome."

Silence falls between us, and I continue reminiscing.

Secrecy always covered my youth and origins, as if great danger followed me if anyone discovered my true ancestry. I find it uncanny that knowing the truth is an anticlimax as if I already knew or suspected my royal bloodline, which I did not. My adopted parents made a point of advising me of my lineage back to Dumuzid, King Alalgar's son. But they stressed the distant and faded linkage to such a noble heritage. With knowledge from the research data I received,

I've learned that the connection is not tenuous. The truth's suppression was for my protection.

If I ever escape from my current predicament, which I won't, I must adopt my true destiny and accept my real name, Sargon Halwende, heir to the Rigel throne of King Alalgar. I shall wear my heritage with honor, whatever the cost, and use it as a rallying call to everyone in the empire tired of the tyranny of Shulgi's rule.

I chuckle to myself. What are the odds of the two sons of King Alalgar's heirs meeting under such circumstances after centuries of separation, where myths and legends surround them both?

Our evening meals arrive.

"Any last requests?" the guard says to me, sniggering.

"You could show me the gate to the palace."

He guffaws, appreciating my sarcastic humor as he leaves.

Time progresses, and the lights dim for nightfall and slumber, but I'm too hyperactive to sleep. Tears leak from my eyes as I lie on the bed, thinking of Adala. The anguish I've caused her, not knowing my fate. I will never experience her joy and awe as I take her aboard the *Queen Rosalind,* and we rise into space for her first time. She should not have to bear that worry and pain. It's too late now. This is it.

I must've dosed, as the brightening light announces morning's arrival. I raise myself and stretch, stepping over to the basin to wash my face and drink. Only hours separate me from my end.

"Halwende? Are you awake?"

"Yes."

"Can you hear that?"

I frown. *What's she saying?* "Hear what?" But as I concentrate on the silence of the prison, a waft of sound brushes my ears. It sounds like fighting!

43

RESCUE

What could the noise mean? A spark of hope freshens my heart as the possibilities build in my mind.

"What is it?" Lilith asks.

"It sounds like fighting, but who'd fight in the depths of this dungeon? It'd be suicide."

"That can only mean one thing."

"What's that?"

"They're here to rescue you."

The noise increases and I ache to see behind the cellblock door. *Who is fighting? Why? Have the rebels come to liberate me? Or is someone intent on rescuing Lilith?* Whatever is happening, the noise is getting closer. And if people have arrived for me, I won't leave unless Lilith comes with us. My heart pumps harder in anticipation.

Seconds later, the door blasts apart, and fighters dash through, masers held ready for attack. Confusion overcomes me as I see resistance and imperial uniforms in the same company of soldiers. Maser fire shoots past, causing me to duck and edge away from the door. Eyes wide, my mind tries to comprehend the events evolving before me. One uniformed warrior approaches and shuts off the force field for Lilith's cell, and my hopes fade as I believe they have come to rescue her. The soldier then disables mine and waves for me to follow him.

"Quick," he says. "We have little time."

I see Lilith frozen in her cage, fearful and overcome by the danger, so I rush over and wrap an arm around her as I encourage her to stay near me.

A familiar face approaches. "God, you're a pain," Ishtar says as she slaps my back while checking the door for trouble. "Here, you might want this." She hands me a spare maser. I check it and fire it up for use.

"Thanks."

"Move out," a soldier says, and the rescuers encircle Lilith and me for protection. A vanguard nears the door. Their masers blast through as the front makes quick sorties around the corner to fire a couple of shots in retaliation.

"They have us cornered here," I say. "We'll never escape without another exit."

"Patience," Ishtar says.

I raise an eyebrow at her, but I just receive a wry smile in return.

"Cover!" someone shouts.

The fighters at the door withdraw with speed and hug the wall. The others push Lilith and me to the wall, too. A deafening blast flashes through the doorway as the residue of the maser fire flashes past with the odd item of debris and body part.

"Go!" the soldier orders. The warriors move in unison, dragging us both with them.

We rush through and along the corridor. Lilith screams in fright as she sees guards lying on the floor, lifeless, with limbs missing and blood splattered on the walls and flowing on the ground, making our path slippery in places. Our rescuers don't wait for us to comprehend the turn of events or mourn the dead, merely lifting Lilith so that she doesn't hinder us. Smoke burns my eyes, and the stench of burned flesh and death lingers in the stagnant air.

We have free rein without resistance to the elevators, but our rescuers push past them to an emergency stairwell with the door missing, where more fighters wait for us. After a slight pause, we move into the staircase. It's clear at present, and we start our climb to the surface. I spare a glance up and groan as I see no end in sight to our ascent.

My lungs scream for air as we climb at a sprint. One of the imperial soldiers now carries Lilith. After ten flights of stairs, a maser blast shoots past, exploding against the stairs below us. The fighters in front fire back, and a shootout starts. I hug the wall as we continue climbing at a snail's pace until we reach the next exit.

"This way," one soldier says as he opens the door, checking for enemy guards before dashing through.

I don't know how far we must still travel for freedom, and I doubt we'll ever make it. But I prefer dying in this fashion to being executed in front of a gloating Shulgi. I'm pushed through the door with the rest of the team covering the rear as we continue along the corridor we entered. Emergency lights shine a harsh glare from above us.

Another passageway branches off ahead of us. After checking, the vanguard dash across and wait for us. I check the passageway and spot a soldier preparing to fire. In one smooth motion, I roll over to the protective wall on the other side, raising my maser and blasting him dead before he can complete his action. The fighters behind have stopped with the threat, Lilith with them. Maser fire blasts the wall as the enemy continues their attack. She's cornered unless we can fend off the assault. A resistance fighter returns from the front and stands next to the corridor. He pulls a grenade from his pouch, activates it, and bowls it the length of the passage. A blast shoots out from the opening as the grenade detonates, the noise deafening me for several seconds. In the confusion and smoke, the trapped fighters rush across the corridor entrance with Lilith before our adversary can re-group and renew their assault, allowing us to continue our intended escape.

We reach a reinforced metal door, and a guard punches a code in the keypad. A green light illuminates above the door, and he forces it open, ushering us through the gap. Maser shots ring out as the last of us rush in, felling two fighters. Those already through, return, lift the fallen by the collar, and drag them into the chamber. The guard slams the door shut and shoots out the lock.

Everyone heaves for breath as we rest until the leading soldier orders, "Move!" seconds later.

I scan the room and wonder where we must go. We have barricaded ourselves into an enclosed space with no exit other than the entrance we used. On thinking those thoughts, loud booms reverberate against the door as the enemy behind it tries blasting their way through with their masers. It won't be long before they bring heavier artillery to bear and gain entry.

The rescuers move to the back wall. I follow, disheartened that we have trapped ourselves. But as I draw near to the rear wall, I spot another exit from the room, one hidden until opened by the guard.

Lilith has regained her composure and requests her protector to release her. She draws near to me again. "Another one of my secret corridors."

I shake my head. "How do you know these secret passages?"

"Oh, I'm sure others know of them, but few have knowledge."

The soldier helping Lilith prompts us to move, so we follow those in front through the secret door and into a long passageway with pounding echoing behind us. Once everyone enters the corridor and the door closes, we jog along the tunnel, which has a slight upward grade. Several turns change our direction, and we pass branch tunnels, but we continue along the passage. At one stage, I hear a deafening roar from behind us and can only surmise they've discovered the tunnel entrance and blasted it open.

Pounding steps echo from our rear as enemy soldiers sprint toward us. We quicken our pace, and Lilith's guard picks her up again as her step falters from fatigue.

Moments later, we enter a familiar room, only to be confronted by a wall of guards with their masers aimed at us. Without fear, our fighters return fire as they duck for cover. I dive behind a large crate sitting in the room before a maser blast singes my leg as it slams into the wall. The others find shelter, but the first surprise attack hits several of them.

A barrage of maser fire blasts back and forth as the gunfight continues. Apart from the frontal assault, my concern is diverting to the doorway and the enemy still chasing us. If we don't do something soon, they'll pen us in from both directions.

Our leader motions to us to head to another tunnel where the door is open. This one I know well as it leads outside, but we are under heavy attack.

I see the soldier who threw the grenade earlier. "You have another grenade?"

He nods.

"Throw one at them."

He nods again, pulls a grenade from his pouch, and primes it. He asks for cover fire, and I oblige as he dashes into the tunnel, tosses the bomb in, and dashes back. A tremendous roar comes from the passageway as the grenade explodes, forcing rock and debris into the room. By sheer luck, the fallout cascades into the enemy and takes several out of action. It also creates a gigantic cloud for us to hide behind as everyone shakes off the confusion.

"Move!" our leader says again, and we rush to the other tunnel.

Six resistance fighters enter it before Lilith, I, and the others follow. I get a quick sighting of Ishtar behind me. She limps with a large wound in her leg.

I linger until she catches up with me. "Are you OK?"

"I'll live. But remind me to knock you out whenever you get another itch to return to Eridu."

Appreciating her humor, I laugh. "I will."

The soldier with the grenades has fallen back as maser fire blasts us. He sets off an explosive and shouts, "Run!"

We sprint until the roar of the grenade exploding blasts past us and we're knocked over by the resulting pressure wave. The firing stops. As the dust clears, I see the tunnel has collapsed behind us, removing any threat in that direction.

My lungs are ready to explode, and I am almost ready to collapse from exhaustion.

"Keep moving," the leader says. "We must leave this passage before they attack us from the end."

The others move, and I do too, groaning as my muscles protest. Ishtar is struggling with her wound, so I give her support as we increase our pace along the tunnel. We meet no further defiance until we near the tunnel exit, where the noise of battle reverberates to us, our leader motioning us to stop. He sends scouts ahead. They return five minutes later.

I creep closer to hear what they say. There's heavy fighting between the government forces and the resistance, but the rebels are deflecting the attack. They fear the defense won't last long, and we need to hurry and escape on the waiting transporter. With this news, the leaders urge us on, and we moan as we move again. Even the seasoned fighters appear fatigued.

We reach the exit five minutes later. I peer out at the sight of heavy fighting. The resistance is defending the tunnel, and a transporter stands twenty meters from it. They lower the rear hatch for us, and we dash to it, the hatch closing moments later. A judder announces our rise from the ground, and I sense forward movement after that.

"Buckle in," the leader says.

I find a seat and obey, as do the others. An immense wave of relief floods over me as I realize I am flying to safety at last. I glance over at Lilith and give her an encouraging smile. She smiles back, but worry clouds her face, regardless.

A massive jolt rocks the ship, my straps cutting into me from the force. I try peering through to the cockpit but see nothing. Another shudder hits, and then an explosion jolts us as the drive blows apart, shrapnel tearing through the casing as if it's made of paper. Several screams ring out, and the transporter shrieks as the pilot struggles for control. Moments later, it crashes and rolls. People flop in their seats like rag-dolls as the vehicle smashes into the ground in its bid to stop. The force splits the shell in two. The rear, with most of the fighters, takes its own course. A blast cascades through to us, the fuel in that section exploding. I presume they're dead.

The front, with Lilith, her guard, Ishtar, the pilot, and me in it, comes to rest. As the dust settles, I descend into despair, thinking everything was in vain.

44

BACK TO THE CRYPT

There are no words to describe the despair that now threatens to overwhelm me, greater even than when I faced imminent execution. After everything I've endured, everything my rescuers have been through, Barak's soldiers are bound to recapture us, and this time there will be no escape. Despite my mood, I unstrap myself and go to check on the others. Ishtar is moaning; her leg injury requires medical treatment, but she is free of further injuries. I un-belt her and put her in the recovery position.

Next, I check Lilith. She lies unconscious, a nasty bruise developing on her forehead. Otherwise, she looks undamaged by the ordeal. Her guard coughs and splutters, but he recovers. We search each other for wounds, and I get him to tend to Lilith while I go to check on the pilot's condition.

I find wreckage strewn throughout the cockpit and the pilot crushed under an enormous, dislodged stanchion from the transporter's frame. There's little point, but I search for a pulse. Finding none, I close his vacant, staring eyes as much to give me peace as him. So, four of us have survived the crash with the sure knowledge that we will soon be recaptured.

I return to the others. Ishtar has recovered enough for her to take in her surroundings, but Lilith still lies unconscious. "We need to move," I say. "I'll go see if I know where we are." They nod.

As I scramble out from the fuselage, avoiding the wreckage, I emerge beside a riverbed that looks familiar. The ship is a mess of steel and ceramic, half-plowed into the ground where the front section rests. I listen for any sign of chasing imperial forces but hear nothing but the odd twitter of birds in nearby trees. Scrambling over the rocks, I notice we have crashed near a gorge. Its familiarity confirms my suspicion. This is indeed the same ravine I encountered on my last flight. The transporter took the same route. My discovery brings an idea to me, but it depends on finding the door to the subterranean crypt before any troopers find us — and, of course, being able to open it. I see no other means of escape, so I return to the others.

I climb back into the wreckage. "We need to move out. I have a crazy plan, but it'll mean we'll be safe if it works. Can we walk?"

"I'll survive," Ishtar says.

"I'm concerned for Princess Lilith," her guard reports.

That Lilith still lies unconscious concerns me, too. "We can't wait for her to regain consciousness. Can you carry her?"

He nods.

"OK, then. Let's move."

Lilith's guard lifts her inert body, drapes it over his shoulder, and starts moving over the obstacles inside the wreck. Ishtar rises and groans from her bruising. She hobbles as she follows the guard.

Before I leave, I make a quick search of the interior. Lodged in one corner, I find a maser, undamaged and working. A cabinet hangs from the partition between the cockpit and the main section. I scramble over to it and open it. A first-aid kit falls out and multiple survival pouches, strapped to the door, dangle in my face. I take the first-aid kit and four survival pouches and follow Ishtar out.

We assemble by the riverbed. "Here." I give the first-aid kit and one of the survival pouches to Ishtar. "You can use these." I glance at the guard. "I'll keep yours and Lilith's until you're both able to carry them. Follow me."

The guard nods as I make my way into the gorge and the start of my crazy bid for freedom with the others following me. I'm surprised no troopers have appeared yet to investigate the explosion and confirm our demise. Not ungrateful for our current luck, I urge my motley team forward at whatever pace we can manage. To my surprise, it's Ishtar that holds us back. I thought the guard would dictate our speed, given the extra weight of carrying Lilith. But, well trained and fit, he maintains our pace. I pity Ishtar as she struggles with her leg, wishing there was something I could do to relieve her pain, but we need to press on. After telling the guard to continue in the direction I have set, I wait until Ishtar catches up with me, wincing with each step. "Anything I can do?"

She shakes her head. "Not unless you have a magic wand to heal wounds."

"Lean on me for a while."

She nods, and I move in, wrapping my arm around her waist as she drapes hers over my shoulder. We walk faster and catch up to the guard, who had generated a gap.

"You sure I should be so near you?"

I laugh. "You can't hurt too much."

She chuckles. "It has its compensations."

We overtake the others, and I take the lead again with Ishtar beside me. The gorge's entrance is nearby when the first sounds of a troop carrier come toward us. After searching the sky, I detect nothing overhead yet. "Hurry, it's not far now."

"Where are we going?" Ishtar asks in a puzzled tone.

"You'll see soon," I say, adding a silent, 'I hope' in my head.

We round a corner in the gorge, and with a flood of relief, I recognize the old man's fishing spot. I search for the wall I seek and find it ahead.

At that moment, a maser blast fires from a troop carrier above us. It has caught up and is descending. Another blast misses me by centimeters, and I increase my pace to the rock face. The ravine is too narrow for the transporter to land, so it veers to an alternate location to discharge its soldiers.

Taking advantage of the temporary reprieve, I hurry to the wall, desperate to find the concealed door before the troopers return. When we reach the escarpment, I release Ishtar. "We're here."

The guard lowers Lilith to the ground.

"Where is here?" Ishtar asks.

I do not reply as all my attention is now on the rock and the spot the old man showed me. Little differentiates the segmentation in the surface, but the opening mechanism is somewhere within searching distance. Beads of sweat appear on my brow as I focus on the rock, conscious of marching troopers approaching from further up the stream bed. *Where is it?* I wipe my palm along the façade, desperate to find any indentation at all. Time is short. Unless I find the entrance in the next few seconds, they'll recapture or shoot us.

Time is up. A maser shot ricochets off the rock and Lilith's guard fires in retaliation.

Please, where are you? My hand stumbles on the depression I seek, and I press. The door in the wall opens. "Quick! Get inside." I pull my maser out and fire shots in the troopers' direction while the guard carries Lilith through the opening. Ishtar enters too, and I take up the rear. A shot hits my arm as I close the door, sending shards of pain up through it. I collapse in shock, holding my injury.

Ishtar limps over to me. "Halwende!"

Wincing, I open my eyes and blink away the tears. "Feels worse than it looks," I quip.

Ishtar rolls her eyes at my attempt at humor as she inspects the damage.

The troopers pound at the barrier, and their masers fire to break into our tunnel.

"We have to keep moving," Ishtar says, her eyes full of concern for me.

She's right. I am not worried the troopers will break the door down quickly — it is hard to penetrate, probably made of toughened material to withstand maser blasts — but we still need to move. I rise and stagger ahead.

"Where to?" Ishtar asks.

"Just keep going straight ahead."

Lilith's guard lifts her again and starts walking.

"We can support each other," Ishtar says as she grabs hold of me, and we both hobble forward.

It takes us an hour to cover the distance to the subterranean chamber. As we round the last corner, I stop short in my tracks at an unexpected but welcome sight.

The old man is sitting on a lounge chair, gazing at me with a self-satisfied expression. "I had an inkling you might chance this way."

As I break my trance from the relief of seeing him, I glance at the guard. "Take Lilith to the couch." He is happy to comply, gently lowering Lilith and sighing as the dead weight lifts from his shoulders.

A frown marks the old man's brow. "What is wrong with Princess Lilith?" He rises and moves over to her. "She has a nasty bump."

"Our crash knocked her unconscious during our escape," I say. "She hasn't woken up yet. I'm getting worried." I walk over and stand next to him as he bends to examine her.

"Hmm," he says as he prods the spot of her injury. He retreats to a closet, opens it, and retrieves a medical scanner. On returning, he powers it up and waves it over the wound while observing the read-out. "Hmm."

"Is it serious?" the guard asks.

As if exiting a trance, the old man glances at the guard and recognizes him. "Oh, no, no. Just a nasty bump. She needs rest, though, and she'll have a splitting headache when she awakens." Straightening, he looks over at Ishtar and me, becoming alarmed when he sees I am injured, too. "Your arm."

"It's nothing. If you want to treat someone, examine Ishtar's wounds."

Not convinced of the triviality of my injury, he nonetheless goes to Ishtar and inspects her. He goes beyond examining her lacerations, probing and poking her in other spots, and even squeezing her muscles and other areas of flesh. "A fine specimen," he concludes.

Ishtar sniggers, despite her annoyance at his prodding. "And the wound?"

He peers into her eyes, confused. "Oh, oh that. Nothing to concern you. I'll have it mended in no time."

While the old man's attention is on Ishtar, I stride to the food processor and prepare myself an energy drink. Once I have mine, I gesture for the guard to help himself, which he does. As I sip my drink, I move back to Lilith, concerned over her wellbeing and wishing she would awaken. Her face looks peaceful despite her injury. As if in response to my wish, she stirs and flutters her eyelashes. Her arm rises as she winces, and she touches the bump on her head. "Ouch! What happened?"

"You hit your head. You'll be fine after resting."

Her eyes widen as she gazes at the cavern's ceiling and the stalactites spearing from it. "Magnificent. Where are we?"

"Somewhere safe," the old man says as he walks over to her. His gaze appears to chastise me. "This place is supposed to be a secret, you know."

"I had no choice."

"I know. Just clarifying the point. Now, let me look at your arm."

Shrugging off his fussing, I repeat, "It's nothing."

"Nothing, ey?" He glances at Ishtar and the guard. "Half your arm's missing."

Not believing him, I glance at my injury and gasp. He's right. The maser vaporized a large chunk of muscle to the bone of my upper arm. It's amazing it still functions. "Maybe you should tend to it then." After reclining in a chair, I allow the old man to examine me. He packs the wound with a healing bandage and injects an antibiotic. "Those troopers can't break the door down, can they?" I ask.

"No. It is impervious to a normal attack. If they use heavier equipment, they'll just collapse the tunnel. We won't be able to use it anymore if that happens and that would be a pity."

"Why is that?" Ishtar asks.

He glances up at her and grins. "I'll have to go the long way around to my favorite fishing spot."

"Oh." Ishtar smiles, amused at this potential inconvenience.

"Mamagal? Is that you?" Lilith whispers.

Alarmed, the old man rushes to her. "Hush, my princess, and sleep."

"Your name's Mamagal then?" I query.

"You will not mention that name anywhere."

I take that as a yes and wonder why he's fussed but have no energy to ask him.

Mamagal refocuses his attention on Lilith, stroking her cheek as she falls into a doze.

I move off and sit on a couch to consider our next moves. We can't linger where we are, and I need to return to my yacht before it's discovered. The longer we wait, the more troops will arrive and tear the place apart, making any retreat more difficult than it already is. As I focus on each member of the group, I take stock. Lilith's guard and Ishtar are fit to travel, as am I. I don't know if Mamagal is coming with us or staying. My one consideration is Lilith and her ability to walk. Once she is aboard a scooter, she can stay strapped in until we reach my Lander, but my concern remains whether she can tolerate the movement to the scooter and the rough flight we will have to have to avoid the troopers' radar.

On rising from the couch, I approach Mamagal. "Do you think she's fit to travel?"

He turns to me, creases of worry marking his forehead. "It would be better for her not to walk. We will make a litter for her."

I turn to the others with my decision made. "We leave in the hour."

45

ESCAPING ERIDU

Mamagal helps the others make a litter for Lilith while I use the time to explore the crypt again as I consider what lies ahead.

I feel a powerful urge to crack the shell I have enclosed myself in and divulge my true identity to the resistance. Otherwise, we'll just continue fighting with no real focal point.

Ishtar approaches me. "We're ready."

As I turn, I see Lilith lying on the makeshift litter. I look at Mamagal. "And what of you? Will you stay or leave with us?"

Mamagal's gaze turns toward the tunnel from which we came, sorrow clouding his face as he sighs. "I fear I am no further use here, much to my disappointment. I hope I can one day return and fish again in the stream. Can you promise me that?"

I stare into his eyes. "I promise."

"Let's be on our way then."

With the group completed, Ishtar and the guard carry Lilith between them, and we move out through the exit of the crypt. It takes an hour to traverse the distance to the cave containing the scooters. There is no sign of people following or anyone ahead to trap us as we leave. We strap Lilith onto the scooter floor and take seats for the journey, with Mamagal taking the driver's seat. The scooter rises, and we streak from the cavern out into the open air.

My eyes dart outside in every direction, expecting an attack, but the sky is empty of fighters at present. With a sigh, I relax as Mamagal hugs the countryside on the way to my Lander.

As if Barak has caught me napping, a maser shot rocks the scooter, ripping a hole in the side. Mamagal pitches the scooter to reduce the risk of another hit, but it's difficult protecting a vessel devoid of any shielding. I glance at Lilith, concerned. She lies secured and protected from any harmful movement for the time being. As I scan the skies, two imperial attack craft pinpoint our position and speed to close the gap.

I unbuckle my straps and move beside Mamagal. "Any ideas on how to shake them?"

He shakes his head. "None. They must have scanned for us to have located us so fast. I can only weave, but we have no defenses for protection."

As I grit my teeth, my mind speeds up, trying to find options for our survival just a while longer. A maser shot misses us as the scooter weaves, blasting the ground below and destroying a tree. My only choice is to use my maser pistol to attack the ship, even though the impact will be measly. I wish we had more grenades, but we don't. On opening the hatch, I lean out as the wind whips past, careful to have a firm grip on the frame so I won't fall. Any hit I achieve with a maser can do only minor damage against their shielding, but I must try. I target my pistol at one fighter and fire, striking the front, but the shields deflect the beam with no damage. With the spark of an idea, I aim again, this time at the pilot's cockpit window, and shoot. The shot has little effect on the craft, but it temporarily blinds the pilot as the energy dissipates, causing him to lose his concentration for a fraction of a second, and he veers off course.

"Halwende," Mamagal shouts from his seat, "strap in tight. I'm entering a winding ravine, so my maneuvers might get hairy in places."

"I stand warned, but I'll make use of that."

"Suit yourself." Mamagal goes quiet, and seconds later, the light level dips as we enter the gorge. I risk losing my grip as he throws the scooter around the narrowest of openings.

One fighter has followed us into the chasm while the other cruises overhead. The rock face whistles past my head as I lean out, aiming at the ship again. One clip of the canyon wall, and it'll smash me to smithereens. The fighter comes into view, and I fire. The shot fires true, striking the cockpit shielding. With the pilot blinded, the craft veers off course and smashes into the wall, causing it to careen out of control and crash into a ball of flames. I swing back inside and rabbit-punch the air in victory.

"Not bad," Ishtar says.

My triumph is short-lived as the scooter rocks from a maser blast from above us. This one nicks the scooter drive, and smoke billows up, filling the cabin.

"How much further?" I ask Mamagal.

"Ten minutes."

"I hope we have ten minutes."

It's impossible to get a shot at the fighter on top of us. The damaged drive has slowed our scooter, making us an even easier target. Several shots plow into the gorge wall and blast rock through the open hatch. I contemplate closing it but need it retracted for any opportunity to fire back.

The scooter drive screams as Mamagal increases the power to get the last drop of energy into it. I swear it'll explode at any moment.

Darkness surrounds us as we enter a tunnel. Thirty seconds later, we emerge into the light again and to the waiting fighter, who gets a shot off toward us. Mamagal veers hard to the left, and the maser just misses.

The cave containing the Lander is ahead. We'll be there in a minute. Another blast zips past from above, giving us one more reprieve. The entrance increases in size as we approach it, and at last, I have hope we'll make it.

With seconds to go, the fighter fires another shot, and it hits our drive, destroying it and any power we had. Mamagal struggles to control the scooter long enough for us to bridge the distance to the cavern. We are losing altitude fast. With only meters to spare, we shoot into the cave, Mamagal bringing the scooter to a rough stop. When I glance at him, I see he's shaking. But we have no time for debriefing. We must board the Lander and leave before any reinforcements arrive.

"Quick!" I say. "Get Lilith in the Lander." I rush to it and open the hatch. After jumping into the pilot's seat, I prepare for departure, energizing the drive.

Ishtar enters the cockpit minutes later and straps herself into the chair next to me. "Ready?"

Satisfied the hatch is closed and the Lander sealed, I direct power into the drive, and we rise from the ground. "Activate the maser," I instruct Ishtar. "I sense we're going to need it. You're on point."

The Lander rotates as I move it into position for a quick launch from the cave. With power surging, I hold it back. Vibrations reverberate from the restrained energy. "Hold on," I shout as I release the drives. The Lander surges forward. If not for the inertial controls, the acceleration would plaster us to our seats as we shoot from the cavern into the atmosphere. The fighter is on our tail within seconds. It fires a shot, but our shielding absorbs the blast.

As I take a glance at Ishtar, she blasts her own round, directly hitting the fighter. It shows no damage, but I see its shields are drained. "More of those'll help," I say, praising her precision. She glances at me and smiles.

With increasing speed, I power through the atmosphere, entering the first evidence of space a minute later.

"Shit!" Ishtar says under her breath. "Five more fighters closing in on us."

"That'll make life interesting." I bank the Lander, directing it to a vector in the *Queen Rosalind's* direction as I prepare for defensive maneuvers and direct more power into the drive. While keeping one eye on my course, I activate a second maser to support Ishtar as the impending battle intensifies. They must be desperate to capture me to send six fighters after me. Regardless, they are no match for my yacht if we reach it.

Two fighters branch off and join the fighter behind me, leaving the others to power ahead to complete the boxing-in maneuver. I smile at the tactic, as it's what I would choose. With nothing to lose, I veer left and spiral to counteract their move and place us in a better attack position.

Meanwhile, I connect with my yacht. Since modifying the drive with the crystal, I made it possible to remote control its systems from the Lander, thinking that might come in handy. Grateful now for my forethought, I bring up another screen and power up the drive, shields, and weapons, plotting a course in the navigation that intersects with the Lander. It won't give it the ability to dodge maser fire, but it will withstand whatever the fighters can throw at it.

The Lander jolts as a maser strikes our shields with a direct hit, draining their strength. Ishtar fights back with three successive shots at the offending fighter, its shields in danger of failing before it breaks off to recharge them.

"What's your plan?" Ishtar asks.

"We need to get in range of the yacht before any serious firepower arrives. That should take twenty minutes. We must hold these off until then."

"I'll see what I can do."

With things organized with the yacht, I concentrate on the fighters. Locking my maser on an approaching fighter, I fire at it, hitting its shields. The fighter banks away. I review the status of the six fighters, my stomach dropping when I realize they have us boxed. The fighter's incursions were to manipulate us into the right position. A drop of perspiration forms on my brow. *Why are they making me fly in this direction?* If I make a course change, I'll pass within the firing line of a fighter. I suspect they will close in at any second now and pummel us from every angle.

"I don't like this," I say.

"Neither do I. How long till we're within range of the yacht?"

"Fifteen minutes."

"We may not have fifteen minutes."

"I know."

As if on cue, the reason for our particular direction comes onto the radar scan. Five destroyers stand in my way if I persist in flying this course, and the fighters will attack if I veer from it. There is only one choice — take my chances with the fighters.

A communication message flashes at me from the console. I accept it, and Barak's image displays on the screen.

"Hello, Halwende. This is pointless. You cannot wriggle your way out of my hands this time. Surrender and save us the heartbreak of your demise."

"You must be joking. I have no reason to concede. I know what's in store for me if I let you take me, so I may as well make my stand here. It's better that I die fighting than as one of your propaganda stunts."

Barak chuckles. "Is that so? And do the others on board agree? Are you going to decide on forfeiting their lives too?"

"The thing is, I don't intend on dying, nor on being recaptured. Now, if you don't mind, I'm preoccupied at present." I cut the communication and concentrate on my intentions.

As I power the drive to full thrust, I make a tortuous dive away from the threat of the destroyers and toward two fighters. The Lander is not designed for dogfights, but I must take part in one, so I'll cope. I dodge and turn as masers fire past us. Ishtar and I shoot back in kind, sometimes hitting, sometimes missing. Before we destroy any shields on the craft, I pass the two fighters. They bank to chase us. As I glance at my watch, I see I need another minute before the yacht arrives. The other attackers have broken the box formation to pursue me and are closing fast. Shots rock the Lander again as I duck and weave to give myself time. Seconds elapse.

"Can you fly this?" I ask Ishtar.

"I can't fly and shoot."

"That's OK. Just dodge whatever they throw at us."

Ishtar takes over flying, and I concentrate on the yacht's controls.

The yacht comes into radar view. The fighters notice it too as they break their attack to consider the new scenario. A few seconds later, they renew their assault on the Lander, with the yacht approaching at a tremendous speed as I bring it into firing distance of the fighters. The destroyers move, bearing in on me and the yacht.

I get the weapons to lock on the six fighters one at a time and fire at them with full power while throwing them into heavy reverse thrust to slow them to the Lander's velocity and trajectory.

The first fighter disappears in a massive explosion as the shot breaches its reactor and destroys itself. Three more attackers die in quick succession. The other two, seeing their compatriots' destruction, break off the chase and run. They have left it too late, and I destroy them, too.

I now have five destroyers bearing down on me, though, and I prefer not to engage them.

The yacht has pulled up in front of me with the Lander hatch open. Ishtar dives in and crash-stops the Lander.

"You could have been gentler," I say.

"Time is precious."

"Right." I unbuckle and rush to the yacht's cockpit, strapping in and regaining control. On setting the navigation away from the destroyers and Eridu, I pour full power into the thrusters.

A communication flashes on my screen again. It's Barak.

"What do you want?"

"You cannot escape me."

"I beg to disagree."

"I'll chase you and find you and seize you wherever you go."

"Good luck."

"Don't think your friends will help you. By the time you reach them, I'll have either destroyed or captured them."

Ishtar enters the cockpit as Barak talks, and I glance at her as she does me, both of us wondering what he means.

"I doubt you can do that."

"Oh, I know their exact position, and I have a fleet attacking them as we speak. This is useless. Surrender now."

"Never." I cut the communication.

With my systems under control, I set the course for Uruk and enter hyperspace, speculating on whether there's a resistance movement to return to.

46

BATTLE

Chaos surrounds us when we exit hyperspace. A huge imperial fleet is attacking the resistance ships, and, from where I sit, the rebels are taking most of the damage, but not all of it. They have inflicted casualties of their own. Nonetheless, the outcome is inevitable unless something changes the power balance. Ishtar stares in disbelief beside me as resignation and defeat spread across her face.

"Cheer up," I say. "Things could be worse."

"Yeah, right? How?"

"We could have arrived after the battle was over."

Ishtar shook her head. "And what good will arriving now do?"

"Let's see." With that challenge made, I target a nearby corvette and unleash the full power of my maser cannon. Shields and the corvette vanish in a cloud of debris.

"That's just one corvette. You can't defeat the entire fleet."

"We can at least make them bleed while I think of a plan," I say.

My next target is a destroyer. As I approach within firing range, the destroyer turns to face me, discharging its own maser blasts as it moves into position to start its attack on me. Not allowing it to complete its maneuver, I unleash the maser again. The destroyer's shields are stronger than those of the corvettes but last seconds longer before they, too, buckle, the powerful beam punching a hole through the hull and releasing atmosphere into space. I fire several more pulses until I hit the reactor, making the ship explode.

This little sideshow has caught people's attention. A dozen fighters complete their vector changes and race toward the yacht, intent on attack. The battle's intensity has ramped up too, the resistance inflicting more damage on the enemy.

A communication message flashes on my console, and I place it on my screen.

"Is that you, Halwende?" Argandea asks, beads of sweat on his forehead and worry lines crisscrossing his brow.

"Good to see you again. You're in a bind."

"You could say that. Glad you could make it to the party, but I'm not sure you'll help in the end."

"What's the damage so far?"

"I've lost three destroyers and four corvettes. They've destroyed thirty fighters too."

The losses concern me. That's a significant part of our strength. "And what do they have?"

"Three battleships, one fighter carrier, seven destroyers, and ten corvettes."

"Major opposition. I'll even the odds up on the battleships."

"You can't fight a battleship."

"Watch me. Stay safe."

I break the communication and scan my radar for the battleship locations. Once I confirm their positions, I set my course for the nearest one. In the meantime, I get Ishtar handling the fighters' destruction with a second maser cannon.

As I reach firing range, the battleship opens fire on me with multiple masers, the blasts rocking us as the shields absorb the energy. I retaliate with my own blasts of maser cannon, weakening the battleship's shields with each hit. As its shield strength drops, the battleship releases an onslaught of missiles at me.

I count twelve. Bringing up a secondary weapons screen, I

program my smaller gun to mark and destroy the projectiles. They should wipe out the missiles before any can penetrate my defense. Meanwhile, I concentrate on the battleship and continue pounding it with my maser cannon. After several minutes, their shields fail, and my maser carves up the hull, one maser blast after another. Unexpectedly, the battleship explodes into a cloud of debris, making me smile as the last missile sends a shudder through the yacht. My eye darts to the shields' screen, and I sigh in relief when I confirm they have held, but only just. Two missiles may have breached them. With one battleship out of the way, I choose an easier target and chase a corvette, destroying that once I'm within firing range.

The battle's balance of power has leveled. The resistance is holding on without incurring losses for now. I take stock and assess strategies to get the imperial devils to retreat. As I review the screen, I count two battleships, one fighter carrier, three destroyers, and five corvettes left in the enemy fleet. I could target the fighter carrier, but it's too well protected by fighters, destroyers, and corvettes. My best choice is to attack another battleship. The potential fallout from unleashing so many missiles perturbs me, but if we are going to have a chance, one less battleship to fight will increase our odds. So, despite my misgivings, I set a course for the nearest one as I check my shields and weapons. Ishtar has been swatting at any fighters game enough to approach us. As I glance across at her, she smiles as though enjoying herself.

We enter firing range, and my missile warning activates. I study my radar. The battleship has released twenty missiles.

"Ishtar, can you help me with these missiles?"

"Sure."

I set my maser cannons to target the fast-approaching missiles as I watch Ishtar firing at the nearer ones. Within twenty seconds, we have destroyed the projectiles. As I consider relaxing, a second missile alarm sounds, announcing another twenty projectiles heading our way. We're halfway eating through them when a third alarm sounds, and another barrage of twenty missiles streak toward us. Whoever's captain on the battleship doesn't want us anywhere near them.

Out of the corner of my eye, I watch Ishtar as she targets, locks, and fires one missile at a time, like a machine, as I set up my automatic operation to achieve the same result. With so many projectiles bearing down on us, I decide to use my large maser cannon to reduce the numbers en masse. One firing of that takes out ten of the furthest missiles that are still clumped together. I target and fire once more and remove another six, leaving the rest for Ishtar and my automated guns while I concentrate on targeting the battleship that is annoying me. Mercilessly, I aim the cannon and pound the ship's shields, destroying them and smashing through the hull until the maser finds its mark and takes out the ship's reactor, disintegrating the ship.

The resistance has wiped out two enemy destroyers and two corvettes without loss, leaving the balance of power favorable to us for the first time and giving me hope that we can win this battle.

Just as the tide turns in our favor, my jaw drops as another imperial fleet exits hyperspace near us. The size of the armada is monstrous — one battle cruiser, three battleships, two fighter carriers, twenty destroyers, and fifty corvettes. Whoever has entered the fray isn't leaving anything to chance. We have no hope of winning against such odds. Our only choice is to retreat, and that'll be difficult without incurring heavy losses.

A communication message flashes on my screen, and Barak's self-satisfied face beams at me. I should have guessed.

"What do you want?" I ask, anger clenching my jaw.

"Isn't it time for your measly little rebellion to surrender?"

"I suppose I should feel honored that you consider me such a dangerous threat that you bring a monstrous fleet against a few ships."

"I'm leaving nothing to chance. You've escaped through my fingers enough. This time you either surrender or die like the vermin you are. I'll give you five minutes to think through it." He cuts the communication.

Once more, I face defeat but this time, instead of indulging in despair at the inevitability of it, my mind races for a solution. I glance over to Ishtar, whose eyes stare back at me, distressed and defeated. There must be something I can do. *Think!* Desperation burrows deep into my memory as I try to recall something I read, and the kernel of an idea develops from nowhere as the information passes forward into my consciousness. *That could work. It has to work.* I smile, confusing Ishtar entirely.

47

VICTORY

"Argandea, you need to withdraw to protected positions," I say once I connect with his battleship.

Confused, Argandea replies, "We'll just be floating asteroids for them to pick off one at a time."

"Trust me. You will want excellent protection."

"Why, what are you going to do?"

"Cause an explosion like you've never seen before once I get it assembled."

Distraught, Argandea shouts, "You're not blowing up your ship?"

"No, nothing as melodramatic as that. You must do something for me, though."

"What's that? I'll do whatever you say if it saves us from this."

"When I give the word, you are to fire off your entire missile reserves at the enemy. It doesn't matter where you aim but targeting the battle cruiser will distract the other ships, allowing time for my surprise to move into position."

Argandea sighs. "OK. I hope you know what you're doing."

Grinning, I say, "I hope I do, too. Now, I have things to prepare. Wish me luck." I cut the communication.

As I set up to connect with Barak, I glance at Ishtar. There's no time to warn her about what I propose doing.

Barak comes on the screen. "So, you have an answer for me?"

"Yes. I'll yield to you."

"No!" Ishtar shouts, tears threatening to break from her eyes as she looks at me in dismay.

After waving to her to calm down, I continue with Barak. "I will surrender if you let the others go."

"You're not in a position to bargain."

"I'm the one you want, not the rest."

Barak glares at me as he decides. "OK, then. Agreed. I can wipe up the rest of this riff-raff any time."

"I'll come over to you in my Lander. Give me twenty minutes to prepare."

"No tricks. Any backing out on our agreement and every one of you die."

"No tricks."

"I'll expect to see the Lander leaving your yacht in twenty minutes. There'll be consequences if it doesn't."

"It will go." I end the communication.

"What are you doing?" Ishtar cries. "We can't surrender!"

"Nor shall we." I grin at her.

My response has her perplexed.

"I said the Lander would leave. I didn't say I'd be on it."

"What on Eridu are you planning then?"

"Just look after the ship. I must arrange things, and there's little time."

She nods, and I rush from my chair to my cabin. After locking the door, I open the safe and take out a crystal, placing it in my pocket. With the safe locked again, I run to the Lander.

One minor piece of detail I've kept secret is that the Lander possesses one missile on it. With as delicate a touch as I can muster, I remove the warhead cap and search for a space for the crystal to sit. One exists just under the detonator. I use a screwdriver carefully to extract several wires from the circuit and rewire them with the crystal included. Once finished, I place the crystal inside and replace the cap. Wiping perspiration from my forehead, I look at my chronometer. I have five minutes left. With a last check, I seal the Lander and prepare it for departure. Within a minute, I'm back in the yacht cockpit and seated in my chair, bringing up the screen for me to remote control the Lander. On powering up the drives, I open the yacht airlock for the Lander to leave, and I drive it into space, setting a course for Barak's battle cruiser moments later and, to my relief, within the twenty-minute time limit.

"Now the fun begins," I say to Ishtar with a mischievous grin.

The Lander gets within firing distance of several ships in Barak's fleet and cruises closer with each second. A communication message flashes on the Lander screen, which relays back to me. It's Barak. *Shit! I can't let him notice I'm still on my yacht.* Not yet. Knowing I must respond, I open the channel but audio-only.

"What is it, Barak?"

"You shy?"

"No, I'm having trouble with the Lander visuals since you broke them when we departed Eridu. Haven't gotten around to fixing it."

"I confirm you've come to your senses. Now that you're within firing range, I can annihilate the rest of you."

I pretend anger. "That wasn't the agreement."

"Well, I'm breaking it. I'll enjoy watching you look at your rebellion destroyed ... again."

"You'll pay for this."

Devilish laughter echoes through the cockpit as I cut the communication.

"What are you doing?" Ishtar asks, baffled.

"You'll see in a moment."

After reconnecting with Argandea, I say, "OK. Give them everything you've got. Once you've fired them, take cover as quickly as you can."

"Will do," Argandea says, as confused as Ishtar.

Everything's set. The Lander is almost where I want it as I bring up its weapons screen and set the missile onboard to self-destruct at my command.

Moments later, volleys of missiles launch from Argandea's ship and streak toward the imperial fleet. They pose no threat to the armada, but they will keep it occupied while I place the Lander in the position I intend — in amongst the flotilla of ships.

A communication message flashes on my console from Barak. Tempted not to answer the call, I relent and put it on the screen with video, as it's now too late for Barak to change the outcome.

"What are you do– Where are you? That's not the Lander. You're still on your yacht." Barak frowns, his face changing from concern to nervousness.

"Very observant of you. I'd like to stay and chat, but you'll become busy very soon." I cut the call and press the missile's self-destruct button.

If I'd understood the consequences of my actions, I might have had second thoughts about going through with it, but I didn't. With one blinding flash, the universe itself explodes as the missile detonates. The fabric of space-time warps and buckles as gravity waves ripple from the epicenter — like a stone thrown into a pond. The energy unleashed disintegrates the entire imperial fleet but a few. Afterward, when events settle, only Barak's battle cruiser and two destroyers remain. Even those have suffered severe damage, judging by the jets of atmosphere issuing from breaches in their hulls interspersed with smoke and debris.

I hold on to my seat for grim life as the waves toss the *Queen Rosalind* around like a balloon caught in a jet stream. Warning lights flash as systems fail and circuits short. The violence eases, and I regain control of the ship.

Once things settle, I breathe a sigh and glance over at Ishtar, whose clenched knuckles stand whitened across the armrests of her seat as she stares dumbly at me.

"That was exciting," I say.

48

LEAVING

Still staring at me, Ishtar tries to comprehend what's happened and why I'm so nonchalant after almost dying. Her face tells that story as I watch her. Her tension relaxes as she unclasps her hands and flexes them. She continues staring until she can get some words out.

"What ... did ... you ... do?" she asks, pausing between each word.

"I destroyed a missile."

"That's not any missile I've ever seen."

"Well ... I made a slight modification."

"Slight? That wiped out half the universe."

I shrug. "Got the required result. Look for yourself. It demolished Barak's fleet."

As if on cue, a call flashes on my console from Barak and his face, pale and shocked, appears on the screen, all the usual smugness gone. Crew with fire extinguishers rush past behind him, busy putting out fires. Wisps of smoke cross between Barak and the camera.

"What did you unleash?"

With a clenched jaw and hardened eyes, I respond. "I will not tolerate your ruthless emperor's corrupt and decadent regime, nor you as his lapdog. This is just a sample of what'll happen if you continue hounding me. Now that I have your attention, I put you on notice. Surrender the empire to those willing to run it for its citizens."

After several seconds, Barak gives a bitter laugh. "And you're the one to rule? Is that your noble intention? You want to replace the emperor. What claim do you have to rule, you coward?"

Barak's reaction isn't as I expected. "Since we're name-calling, I could call you a turncoat. But that's childish. Return to your master and lick your wounds. I put you on notice, though. Don't chase me, or there'll be consequences. And end your campaign against the resistance. Make peace with them."

"No. Never. You will die for this. You will pay with your miserable life once you watch everyone around you die like the filth they are. Farewell until we meet again." Barak cuts the communication.

His parting threat plagues me as I ponder his spy network's extent.

A noise from behind distracts me, and I turn to see Mamagal enter the cockpit, looking confused and concerned. I raise my eyebrows, wondering what he wants.

"What was that explosion?" he asks.

"Rigged a missile to explode with a minor surprise in it."

Mamagal looks shocked. He glances at Ishtar and back at me. "Can we speak in private?"

"Sure." I rise and lead him to a meeting room abutting the cockpit.

Once the door is closed, Mamagal stares at me. "What was the little surprise?"

"I placed a small crystal in the detonation circuit. It released its power when the missile exploded."

"Are you crazy?" Mamagal is furious.

"Crazy? I thought you wanted me to use the crystals against the empire. Isn't that why you told me about them?"

"Yes, but not like this. You could have ripped space-time itself and pulled us through to another universe. Your tomfoolery is why our ancestors hid the crystal technology in the first place."

I defend myself. "It was not tomfoolery. It was desperation. Barak threatened our last hope, and if I hadn't done it, we'd all now be dead." I pause and add, "To be honest, I didn't expect it to work."

Mamagal paces the room, his anger cooling. "You must forget this incident and never try it again, regardless of your peril."

"I promise."

Puzzled, he stares at me. "Still, I am curious how you even knew it was possible."

"I read it somewhere."

"No. Scribes never recorded that knowledge."

"I'm sure I read it." Confused, I scratch my head. "I think."

"You may have seen information on its power, but not how to use it for destructive purposes. A rumor suggests royal blood has a natural affinity with the energy emanating from the crystal, but that's hearsay."

"It doesn't matter. I won't do that again."

"So, what are your plans now?"

"I'm not sure yet. I need to discuss it with the others."

With a nod, Mamagal gestures the discussion is concluded and leaves the room. I follow him.

"Barak has left," Ishtar says.

"We haven't seen the last of him." I stand with my fists on my hips, wondering what to do next.

A call comes in, and Argandea appears on the screen, looking shaken. "Is it safe to show ourselves?"

"Yes. Were any of our ships damaged by the explosion?"

"It smashed a couple, but we can repair them. I'm glad we weren't any closer, though."

After staring at him for a moment, I decide. "We must talk. I'd come over, but I'm minus a Lander."

"I'll gather the leaders, and we'll join you. Give us an hour."

"That's good. See you then." The call ends.

Seeing Mamagal still in the cockpit, I ask, "How's Lilith?"

"She's regained her health. She didn't need the explosion's trauma, though."

"Good ... good that she's healing, I mean. Is she able to attend a meeting?"

"It should be possible."

I want her there then.

Argandea, Lugal, and Ninsar join Ishtar, Mamagal, Lilith, and me in the larger meeting room on the *Queen Rosalind*. General chatter circulates in the room as they discuss recent events. Once everyone has settled, and under Mamagal's scrutiny, I call the gathering to order and deliver a battle summary, leaving out the cause of the explosion's severity.

"So, what is our next move, then?" Argandea asks.

"I've told you Barak's comments before he left." I glance at each of them. "He won't give up trying to destroy us."

"We can't hope to withstand the strength of the imperial navy with what's at our disposal." Lugal fidgets.

"Not to mention Hadanish seems to have deserted us. So much for his fine speech," Argandea says bitterly.

"And we've compromised our hideout," Ninsar adds.

The suggestion I intend to place on the table makes me nervous. It will endanger more people. But I see it as the only chance to regroup and prepare our defense for Barak's inevitable future onslaught. He'll come at me with all his strength next time. I'm counting on it.

"We must move to a more secure location," I say. Their eyes bore into me with laser intensity.

"Where?" Argandea asks.

"A place I know." I gaze over at Mamagal. He nods in approval. "I'll give you the coordinates once we are underway."

"Will there be more ships there? More weapons? A stronger military?" Lugal asks.

"I ... am unsure. I must investigate stories I've read."

"What is the point of going, then? Our position won't be any better. Worse even since we'll lose our familiarity with our surroundings and our power base."

"Barak, or anyone else, doesn't know of it at present." With a glance at Mamagal, I add, "And it's a place of great significance in our history."

The others whisper amongst themselves, speculating where this planet could be. After their discussion, they agree to accept my proposal, albeit with conditions.

"How long before we can leave?" I ask.

"We must repair several ships," Argandea says. "They should be space-worthy in a week."

"We'll need that time to replace our supplies," Ninsar says.

"And our people on Eridu need rescuing," Lugal adds.

"I'm uncomfortable with delay," I say. "It gives Barak an opportunity to rally. But I trust you knew this when you answered me. A week from today, then. Let's be on our way. There's much to do."

49

LATEST RECRUITS

The time has arrived for our departure, and I'm eager to be underway. But we have last-minute arrangements to make. Argandea has provided me with a shuttle to replace the Lander I blew up, restoring my mobility between ships.

One of the new arrivals from Eridu is Zabada, and it pleases me he's with us. I invite him to stay with me on the *Queen Rosalind*, which he accepts. He, Mamagal, and I pass pleasant evenings discussing history and my adventures since I parted from him last.

Lilith, who has recovered from her ordeal, roams the yacht at her leisure. She has relayed stories of life in the imperial palace with her father, too. Many make me shiver. The wait has provided me recuperation time after my torture from Barak and escape from prison.

I laze in the cockpit's chair, rechecking the status of the ship on our day of departure, when proximity alarms blare, alerting us of incoming ships. My stomach churns as I view the radar screen. Have we waited too long to leave? But I become puzzled when I see the details. One battleship, twenty destroyers, and fifty corvettes appear from hyperspace. A large fleet, but not the navy I expected Barak to bring against me. Myriad civilian spacecraft are intermixed with the military vessels, too.

I contact Argandea. "What's with those ships?"

"I don't know. They're hailing us. Wait a minute. I'll see if I can include you in the discussion."

After several seconds, Hadanish comes on the screen. "I'm glad we're not too late. Sorry for any inconvenience my sudden arrival has caused, but I contacted naval officers who have the same reservations as I do with the emperor's means of keeping his grip on power. This little collection of ships is at your disposal to defend your efforts."

With raised eyebrows, I glance at Argandea. "What do you think?"

"Well, first, I'm reprimanding you, Hadanish, for telling no one when you left. We thought you had deserted. Second, why should we trust these people?"

"I'm sorry for leaving as I did. I suspected you would've stopped me if I'd asked."

Argandea grunts.

"I know these captains and trust them. Besides, they will surrender their lives and those of their families if they return to the empire."

"Won't they lose their families, anyway?"

"They're on those civilian crafts."

"Oh. And who's on the others?"

"People friendly to our cause."

"And what is our cause?" I ask.

Hadanish gives me a blank stare for a moment. "To overthrow the emperor and his cadre of cronies."

"Well, every able body will count in the days ahead. I wish we'd had a warning, though. This makes our travel more complicated. But we'll survive."

"OK," Argandea says. "I'll get these ships assembled into an organized fleet and tell you when we're ready to leave."

"Good. I can't wait to go." I cut the connection and sigh, wishing we had already gone.

50

RETURN TO HELHEIM

O ur motley fleet emerges from hyperspace on the outskirts of Helheim's star, and we cruise toward the planet through normal space. My heart leaps into my throat at the thought of seeing Adala again. I left promising trade deals and a ship to take her into space, and I return with an entire flotilla of ships and the news of an impending space-based war that will dictate the fate of her kingdom.

My shuttle descends through the atmosphere toward Heimstadt and Adala. Nervous tension magnifies my apprehension.

Ishtar notices. "Will you say calm? I thought you'd been here before today. Why are you so tense?"

I blush. "No reason."

Ishtar, Lilith, Zabada, and Mamagal go with me to the planet Helheim, or the orb Mamagal and Zabada know as Ur. As I have lost my ability to communicate with the people of Heimstadt, I have no means of announcing my return. So, I land on the city fringes and wait for someone to notice me.

Ishtar and her colleagues survey the landscape, fascinated by its exotic nature, while I pace the ground, waiting.

An hour after our landing, we hear approaching scooters. Four vehicles come into view. One is a troop carrier. The others glance at me in some alarm, but I assure them not to worry.

These scooters have enclosed cabins, so I can't see who rides inside them. I wait as they land in front of us. No movement or opening of hatches occurs for a while. Then the hatch of the lead scooter opens. But the darkness within makes it impossible to tell who greets us. The tension is killing me as no one disembarks.

Impatience gets the better of me. I walk over to it and shout, "Hello? Is anyone there? Remember me? Halwende?"

"About bloody time you returned," the roaring voice of Sentinel gushes from the hatch just before he emerges.

A gigantic grin covers my face when I see him. He grins too. We stride to each other and hug, slapping each other's backs and staring at each other until our greeting has run its course.

"We had lost hope of your return." Sentinel frowns. "You'd better have a good excuse for Adala. She'll be fuming once she gets over the shock."

"You haven't told her then?"

Sentinel gives an impish smile. "I thought I'd give you that pleasure." He glances around at the others. "Are you going to introduce us?"

"Of course. Everyone, meet Sentinel. His real name is Ranulf, but he becomes grumpy if you call him that." Sentinel punches me in the arm. "Ow!" I rub the center of the pain. "Sentinel, these are from a planet called Eridu. We will become better acquainted with Zabada and Mamagal in the days ahead. Ishtar is one of the key leaders in the resistance movement against the Rigel Emperor. And Lilith is Emperor Shulgi's daughter."

They acknowledge Sentinel as I introduce them, but Sentinel is distracted by Lilith, who is staring at him in a way that shakes his equilibrium. On becoming aware she is staring, she reddens and apologizes.

"Let's take you to the palace so you can refresh yourselves." Sentinel glances at me. "And become reacquainted."

I blush, wanting to punch him but resist the temptation.

Sentinel ushers us into his scooter, and we fly to the palace and the royal conference room, where they offer refreshments, and we wait. I pace the floor, impatient to be reunited with Adala.

The door opens, and Adala enters. She stops when she sees me and spins to Sentinel behind her. "Why didn't you tell me?"

"I wanted to surprise you."

She huffs and becomes flustered, her norms of behavior thrown by my presence. She turns to me again, blushing.

I am transfixed where I stand as I stare into Adala's eyes, wanting to rush to her and hold her but afraid to do so.

After recovering from her trance, Adala strides over to me and slaps me with all her strength. "How could you?" she says before bursting into tears.

Confused and with a stinging face, my mouth opens and closes soundlessly. I glance at her and then Sentinel several times, noticing Sentinel is enjoying every minute of my discomfort. Seeing Adala's distress, I step forward and hug her as she cries on my shoulder.

"I thought you were dead," she says between sobs.

"I'm sorry. Events sidetracked me, and I couldn't return when I wanted to."

With her flow of tears ending, Adala wipes her face and gives me a wan smile. "My behavior is inappropriate for a queen greeting her guests. We will talk later." The others stare, astonished when they hear Adala is the queen.

"We shall, as we have desperate news we need to discuss with urgency," I say.

"We'll consider this — amongst other things." Her composure recovered, her typical suggestive remarks have returned, which sends my heart racing.

I introduce my companions. Adala takes her time eyeing Ishtar and me before she moves on to the others. She notices Lilith's frequent fleeting glances at Sentinel and conceals a slight smirk with difficulty.

"Now, what is this urgent news you have, Halwende?" Adala asks as she looks at me again.

"We must prepare for war."
Adala stares at me in disbelief.

The End

Complete the story with Halwende's Reincarnation
(See next page for details)

You may be interested in reading more from John Wegener with Halwende's Reincarnation. Click Here.

Thanks for reading this book. If you loved the book and have a moment to spare, I would appreciate a quick review on the site that you purchased the book from, as this helps new readers find my books.

Subscribe to my Newsletters and receive three free episodes of The Chronicles of Gatacus Todd.
Type http://subscribepage.io/g4r4f8 in your browser.

ALSO BY JOHN WEGENER

Books

Reach For The Stars Trilogy

FTL

Centauri

Ceti

Reach For The Stars Box Set (Books 1-3)

Loki's Fall

Zodiac Series

Scorpius

Libra

Halwende's Legacy Series

Halwende's Redemption

Halwende's Resurrection

Halwende's Reincarnation

Halwende's Legacy Box Set (Books 1-3)

Solar Dawn Series

Lunar Rift

Other Stories

The Dark Ages

SAGI

Short Stories

The Love Particle

ABOUT THE AUTHOR

John Wegener grew up in the Adelaide Hills of South Australia. He now expresses his imaginative dreams by engaging in writing after a 34-year career as a Chemical Engineer in the steel industry, which has taken him to many countries and allowed him to experience many cultures. John currently lives in Wollongong, Australia with his wife and children.

Click on johnwegener.com to find more of my books or read his blogs. Type subscribepage.io/g4r4f8 to subscribe to my emails for more stories and information.

www.ingramcontent.com/pod-product-compliance
Lightning Source LLC
Chambersburg PA
CBHW071235250626
47163CB00001B/186